BLURBS

This story did not disappoint. It's twisted in all the best ways – Goodreads

J.B. Arnold hit it out of the park with this one! – PSCHOLOGICAL THRILLERS BOOK CLUB

Wow! What an intense story—I was on the edge of my seat the whole time – Goodreads

Utterly riveting and disturbingly brilliant! The Hand of God drags you into the darkness of guilt, obsession, and divine retribution—and doesn't let go – Killers Thrillers Facebook Group

I absolutely loved this book! It kept me on my toes until the very end! – Goodreads

Also by J. B. Arnold

The Streets of Floria

Exit 202

A Shadow's Wraith

Copyright © 2025 by J. B. Arnold

All rights reserved.

No part of this publication may be reproduced, distributed, or transmitted in any form or by any means, including photocopying, recording, or other electronic or mechanical methods, without the prior written permission of the publisher, except as permitted by U.S. copyright law. For permission requests, contact [include publisher/author contact info].

The story, all names, characters, and incidents portrayed in this production are fictitious. No identification with actual persons (living or deceased), places, buildings, and products is intended or should be inferred.

Book Cover by Matt Seff Barnes

Edited by Danielle Yeager, Hack and Slash Editing

First edition 2025

THE HAND OF GOD

A BENNETT JENKINS THRILLER

J. B. ARNOLD

Twisted Tales Press

For my firstborn. Love ya baby.

CONTENTS

The Alley	1
The Warehouse	7
Part One	15
The Woman in the Alley	
Part Two	131
The Detective and the Hand	
Part Three	225
The Woman in the Picture	
Acknowledgements	323
About the author	325

THE ALLEY

Saturday Morning, May 9, 2015

Detective Bennett Jenkins had seen death before. Thirty-two years on the force had carved a gallery of horrors into his memory. But this—this was something else. It was like something straight from the pages of a horror novel. Worse even.

He stood in the alley between a deli and a coffee shop, taking in the macabre scene. Stunned by the sight, a single question knocked around in his mind: *How was it possible for a human being to do this?*

The victim sat with her back against a brick building, her burnt and blistered legs jutting out on the asphalt. Her head drooped to the side, practically resting on her right shoulder. The remains of a dress, tatters of floral print, clung to her like Saran Wrap. Blackened soot sprinkled the surrounding ground, clawing its way up the wall that supported her. It wrapped her in a scorched cocoon.

Although the crime scene haunted his sight, the overwhelming stench that crawled into his nose almost caused him to retch. The woman's charred flesh and hair still smoldered under the morning light, wafting and blanketing the open space. Wisps of steam lifted from the body, the ghostly tendrils swaying with the gentle breeze.

Jenkins fought through the nauseous wave, covering his mouth and nose with a kerchief he pulled from his pocket, and forced it back like a seawall. A barricade that would slowly erode with the rising tide. He inched forward, his gaze drawn to the victim's torso. A golf ball-sized blister pulsed there under the seared fabric like a beating heart. Ooze leaked from its core, spritzing like an overcooked hot dog. Its color reminded him of the bile that rose in the back of his throat.

Unable to stomach the horrifying scent, his partner, Detective Angela Barrientos, lingered back near the alley's opposite wall. Like Jenkins, she protected her breakfast with a hand, trying to avert her stare from the gruesome scene. It wasn't every day that a homicide rocked the city.

Jenkins knelt down, his eyes tracing the lines of the victim's face where flame kissed skin. He could see how her lips had melted away, revealing a set of straight, well-cared-for teeth. A stark contrast to the scorched and blackened flesh. Her left ear was gone, replaced by a gaping hole where the ear canal was. The smoldering flesh and cartilage melted together and dripped down the side of her face like candle wax. This was a sight not meant for the human eye. It was almost incomprehensible.

Despite the many years spent patrolling the streets and confronting some of the most unimaginable and heinous crimes, Jenkins's heart still beat. He wasn't immune to empathy.

Was she alive when this crazy son of a bitch burnt her?

The question sounded more like a prayer. He hoped not. The forensics team would have to help answer that question.

With minimal tangible evidence to work with, his sight lifted to the scorched wall the victim slumped against. A stark message awaited him, clawing for his attention. It was the first thing he had noticed as Barrientos had led him around the dumpster minutes before, but the sickening sight of the poor woman had stolen his focus. The identifying number of a Bible verse was on full display, scratched into the soot-stained brick just above her head.

Leviticus 18:22

An icy dread, familiar and chilling, skulked down his spine and wrapped around his gut as he stared at the cryptic message. It teased him; the stitches of an almost-healed wound ripped open once more. This was the first murder the city had seen in over a year.

"Shit," he mumbled.

Jenkins shielded his eyes from the scene and looked back at his partner. The lean and fit thirty-two-year-old stood there, arms crossed over the leather jacket she wore. A tiny mole graced her right cheek, and her dark brown hair, tightly braided, drew attention to her sharp cheekbones.

"Tell me who this is," Jenkins said, his voice blunt and rough like worn pavement. It cut through the murmurs and mumbles of the awakening city.

Barrientos peeked over at the corpse semi-covered by Jenkins's lean figure. As she spoke, her eyes never averted, although hues of green swam in her complexion. It was unlike her; she normally held her composure. "The victim's a female. Mid-to late twenties. Still waiting on forensics to tell—"

"The scene's a fuckin' nightmare, Jenkins!" The interruption came from the mouth of the alley.

Jenkins's glare swept to the source, taking in the youngest member of the group, Cooper Johnson, and his ghostly pallor. The man's stare was lost; terror and hopelessness squatting there like a vagabond. It was a look Jenkins was familiar with, but hadn't experienced in decades. The job had hardened him, desensitized him to the evils he'd seen.

"The son of a bitch burnt her." Johnson's voice rang out once more, like a dejected child's. "He burnt her!"

"Hey, get a hold of yourself, kid," Jenkins called out. "Take a breather. Get a cup of coffee and get your nerves in line." His voice teetered like a father's at a tee-ball game, firm yet caring. "We're all counting on you."

Jenkins's view moved to the man's partner, Georgio Anzilotti. His day-old shave matched the stubble on his head. "Hey, Anzilotti. Help him out, will you? Help him get his head straight."

With that, Anzilotti, an Army veteran and recipient of the Purple Heart who served two tours in Desert Storm, threw a muscular arm around Johnson's shoulders and ushered him away from the alley and the haunting scene.

Jenkins's attention swept back to the victim and the message that waited, tracing the letters with his sight.

Leviticus 18:22? Why the hell did he write that? He shook off the fog that splintered his thoughts.

Minutes later, he ducked under the web of crime scene tape guarding the alley's entrance. Two police cruisers sat there hugging the street's curb like a pair of sentinels on watch. Across the street, a band of onlookers had surfaced, choking the sidewalk, but he ignored their rubbernecking. Debriefing was needed.

The early morning breeze tousled his silver mane as he sidled up with the others near the deli's front doors, eyeing each with his fiery gray eyes. "Let's get to work."

THE WAREHOUSE

SEVEN HOURS EARLIER

Her eyelids fluttered at the cloying scent—not an earthly loam but something fouler. Decay. Rot. Slowly, the tickling sting that polluted her senses lifted her from the blackness. With heavy blinks, she surveyed the space, trying to adjust to the murky dimness. But the only greeting she found was a cold blanket of darkness staring back at her.

Where the hell am I?

Somewhere in the distance, water dripped with a deafening persistence. *Drip. Drip. Drip.* Each drop echoed like a countdown. The sound burrowed into her skull, amplifying the splitting pain that radiated from her temple in savage waves.

As she tried to reach for her head, cold metal bit into her wrists. Glancing to her left and right, she could see that her hands were bound above her by something cold and rusty and unforgiving. She tugged, feeling the restraints protest her efforts. The blackness that surrounded her picked at her like a scab.

Panic snuck in, accompanying an injection of adrenaline. "Help!" The word crept off her tongue in a raspy croak, forcing a series of coughs. With the fit, a sticky liquid trickled down her forehead. The potent scent of iron was undeniable.

She thrashed, pulling and tugging on the chains. "Help me! Help me!" Stone scraped against her shoulders, each movement tearing at her skin.

But the flailing screeched to a halt seconds after it began. Somewhere in the maze of blackness, the opening of a door, the sound distinct and terrifying, forced an end to the din. With wide, tear-filled eyes, she scanned the space in front of her, listening and watching. Her breath came in rapid pants.

The door closed, the grating of metal on metal. She gasped at the sound. As her heart sprinted, her ears picked up the uncanny sound of footsteps—boot soles. Each step reverberated through the concrete floor and up through her bones. And the source was getting closer.

"Hello!" she whimpered, the words coated in sandpaper. "Who's there? Who is that?"

The footsteps continued, slow and deliberate. Each having the effect of a boxer's jab.

"Who's there?" she demanded, feeling an icy tendril of fear wrap around her throat.

From the corner of her eye, a figure emerged, joining the darkness. It was a faint outline, a silhouette of black on black. It hovered paces away, poisoning the air. Her core trembled with anticipation. Whoever this was, he or she wasn't a savior. She knew that immediately.

2

"Please," she whispered, her voice echoing in the cavernous space. "I don't know what you want, but please let me go."

The figure shrouded in black remained motionless, positioned just beyond her reach. Its face was lost in the shadow of a hood. It tilted its head left and right. A beast examining its entrée. Only its breathing was audible: steady, controlled, calm.

The silence stretched between them like a living thing, broken only by the tenacious drip of water somewhere in the cavernous darkness. Amelie's eyes darted around the space—looking for anything, any detail that might help her understand why she was here, what it wanted.

"What do you want from me?" The question came out as a sharp demand, anger mixing with boiling fear. "Money? I don't have any. Just tell me what you want."

Still nothing. Not even a shift in posture.

The hooded figure finally moved, taking a single step closer. Boots scraped against the concrete, and she could see the edge of dark jeans beneath the hoodie. Still, its face remained hidden, and the silence felt more menacing than any threat it could have spoken aloud.

In that moment, staring at the void where features should be, Amelie realized that whatever was coming next had nothing to do with ransom or robbery. This was something else entirely, something that made her previous pleas for mercy seem fruitless.

3

Her screams, raw with terror, reverberated through the warehouse. She clawed and grasped at the fistful of hair it used to drag her. The jet-black hair everyone loved. Her legs kicked and jerked with each violent yank, striving for leverage, striving for release.

"Let me go!" she wailed, hysteria exploding from her parched throat. "Let me go!"

The figure in black fought against her efforts with little regard, pulling her by the hair along the cold, damp floor. Plodding through puddles of stagnant water. Together, they crossed through a large room and down a claustrophobic hallway. A staircase waited at its end. A rusty fixture hung from the ceiling above; its slivers of welcoming light pierced the gloom and highlighted the ascent.

As they approached the first step, it yanked Amelie to her feet, ignoring the pleas falling from her trembling lips. The black hood it wore shielded its features, but she knew it was a man. Tall, broad shoulders, strong. And then, with the precision of a pugilist, he buried a fist in her gut. The air in her lungs rushed out, and she buckled over, gasping and wincing from the shot. A tick later, he threw her limp body over his shoulder and started up the flight.

4

The moon and its magnificence came into view after he trudged through a steel door. She bounced on his shoulder with each stride. Gravel crunched under the soles of his boots. With confusion and weariness, she glanced around, tears falling from her bloodshot eyes. An empty lot and rust-stricken structures long forgotten, crumbling from time and neglect, peppered the space. None of this looked familiar.

His strides slowed seconds later, and he dropped her to the ground. She struck the surface with a *thud*, a grimace splintering through her body. Sharp fragments of chipped stone sliced and poked her flesh. As she looked up at him, she tried to beg, plead for her life once more, but the words lodged in her throat. "Please." It was the only word she could manage, and it came out in an exasperated whisper.

The lunar light highlighted his profile as she tried to crab-walk away from him, but his face remained hidden. Blood from her fingernails and hands stippled the loose gravel with each claw for freedom. But after backpedaling, she found herself pinned against a vehicle. An old relic from the seventies. Rust ate away at its bumper and back fender.

He matched her retreat, a hovering predator toying with its prey.

She tried again, fending him off with an extended arm. "Please. Don't hurt me." The wound on her temple throbbed like a beating heart; hues of crimson and brown trickled down the side of her face. "Please!"

Without emotion, he reached into his front pocket. His fingers returned a second later with a set of car keys. And then, in silence, he leaned over her and opened the car's trunk.

5

The wails and screams continued as the vehicle lumbered down the gravel road. Total darkness accompanied her on the journey. That and the powerful scent of gasoline. A can of it jostled around her knees. She pounded on the trunk's steel panel, clawed at the fabric lining the space. But there was no response, no acknowledgment of her cries. After some time, her mind slowly picked clean the desire to live, stripping her of hope. She lay there, staring off into the blackness, knowing the inevitable was on its way.

Minutes later, the engine's roar slowed to a purr, and the car crept to a steady crawl. From within the trunk's cavity, she felt the motion slow to a stop. She heard the car door open, and those menacing footfalls that seared into her memory sounded again—the *click-clack* of boot soles on concrete. A haunting reminder of her future. The sound approached, rounding the trunk's corner. And then the moon's light filled her eyes.

She stared up at the faceless monster, its flesh hidden behind a cloak. Incoherent mumbles dribbled from her lips; a beseeching sound that should have elicited empathy, but the beast just leered down at her. An emotionless stare that pushed her into hell's depths.

Her last words were barely audible through sobs and shakes. "Please! Don't hurt me!"

With both hands, he reached down, grasping her by the throat. She wriggled, kicking her legs. She scratched at the thick cotton of the hoodie with chipped and broken fingernails. But he ignored her. He wrenched down on her throat, squeezing away and hearing her larynx *pop*. Darkness swooped in, cloaking her sight with a dense coat of pain and suffering. Her swollen eyes fluttered, weeping tears across the crusted stain of blood coating the side of her head.

Then all went black.

PART ONE

I

Friday Night, May 8, 2015

His gaze pierced the mirror, scrutinizing the reflection staring back at him. Almost a stranger's face. He had turned thirty-four the previous month, and the reality of middle-aged life didn't sit well. Thirty-four? To him, it was simply a number, but subtle changes were baring their teeth, and he didn't like it. The wisps of gray flecking his full head of wavy auburn hair, the faint wrinkles, and crow's feet. Signs of time's unforgiving, slow passage.

What the hell happened to you, David?

As he leaned in for another disapproving glance, a rush of swirling water interrupted his thoughts. Using the mirror, his eyes darted to the row of stalls behind him. As the whirring flush ended, an older man in his late fifties emerged from one of the many olive green doors. His brow was slick with sweat, and his wrinkled forehead gleamed under the harsh fluorescent lighting.

The emerging occupant, his shoes scuffing against the worn linoleum, shuffled forward into the room's long corridor, heading straight for the row of sinks. Ignoring the unspoken boundaries of personal space, the man ended his journey by settling himself right next to David, regardless of the many basins flanking their left and right.

David disregarded the intrusive proximity, pretending to take little notice of the man's presence. He opted to wash his hands, praying a subtle moment of small talk didn't arise. He was wrong, of course.

"Hey, buddy," the older man spoke, his voice a deep, gruff sound, the product of years of smoking. His eyes never left the calloused hands he scrubbed with soap. "Any action tonight?"

Feeling cordiality rise from the pit of his core, David countered, throwing himself into the ring with reluctance, "No, not really, man. Just here to meet someone."

As the older man shut off the water's flow, he cast a side-glance David's way for a split second, a flicker of curiosity in his eyes. "Date, huh?"

David drew a shallow breath, his mind itching for an exit. "Yeah," he muttered, not wanting to remind himself of the precipice he was leaping off tonight. The sting of his divorce last fall still throbbed, and it had forced him into reclusion. He'd barely left his apartment in the past six months, except for a handful of outings with friends (drinks after work), let alone a casual evening with another woman. Sifting through the hesitation, he finished the statement. "Yeah, blind date. She's, uh, fashionably late, of course." He'd seen her picture online, exchanged a few texts, but this first meeting brought forth a flutter in his stomach.

The man wrung his hands, the last traces of moisture clinging to his dry, leathery skin falling into the sink. "Blind date, huh?" His stare shot back to the mirror, cocking an eyebrow as he examined his own appearance. "Well, good luck."

With a nod, he ended the brief exchange and strolled away toward the exit; his footfalls echoing against the floor. As David watched, the man's stride slowed, eventually halting completely as he reached and opened the door halfway. The muffled sound of Journey's "Don't Stop Believin'" leaked through the gap. He turned and faced David once more, a coy grin plastered on his lips. "Hope she's a dime, buddy."

David dipped his chin, a subtle gesture of sociability that dismissed the man without a word.

She's more than a dime, asshole.

The door closed a heartbeat later, erasing the lively music and the boisterous chatter from beyond. Silence and solitude crept in again, allowing him to retreat into his thoughts. Releasing a weary sigh, he turned back to the mirror.

You've got this. You've always had it. Just ask her questions and engage. Be cool and let her talk. That's it, man. Do your part, and everything will be fine. It's not a big deal. You've done this before. It's like riding a bike.

The poignant pep talk offered a temporary reprieve, but beneath the surface, a wellspring of uncertainty threatened to drown him.

2

Minutes later, David reclaimed his stool at the bar, the restroom's stale air still clinging to his clothes like a bad memory. The upbeat guitar riffs and ballads from before had expired, leaving the room's clamorous energy dry and still. Only a few distant murmurs lingered in the air—the crack of billiard balls, snippets of conversations, coins landing in the bartender's tip jar—but his attention was absent.

His gaze shifted to the cell phone resting face down on the bar's counter. It hadn't vibrated in his pocket, but he wondered if he had possibly missed her text while relieving himself. Overcoming the hesitation, he reached for the device, gripping it on the sides and lifting it to face him. The screen bloomed to life, flooding his face with vibrancy under the bar's dim lighting. The time read *8:47 p.m.*, but there were no new messages.

She's almost an hour late. Is she not coming?

His free fall of doubt came to a screeching halt a heartbeat later.

"Fuckin' Dave Miller. Is that really you?"

The voice hit David like a slap. He knew that voice. He had known it for years. The faint Southern charm that painted each word was recognizable. His shoulders tensed as he turned, already knowing who he'd find behind him. Tanner Brown stood there like a conqueror surveying his domain: chest puffed out, that trademark smirk plastered across his face, dirty-blond hair perfectly disheveled in a way that probably took an hour to achieve. The man was brash and presumptuous, and although David always played nice and was cordial, he cared little for him.

"Hey, Tanner," he said, his voice flat and emotionless.

"What the hell are you doing out so late?" Tanner called out again, a grin beaming David's way. "Thought you'd be home grading papers and changing your Depends. Isn't it past your bedtime, Grandpa?"

David shook off the jab with a dry scoff, his hazel eyes hiding the annoyance that now accompanied the uncertainty flowing through his core. "Just unwinding, man. You're hilarious, by the way."

"Yeah, that's what the ladies say." Tanner stepped forward, closing the distance between the two. His shoulder-length, dirty-blond locks bounced with each confident stride as he took a seat to David's right. He leaned over, raising his voice as a new song painted the room. "Seriously, though," he said, the scent of cigarette smoke and scotch heavy on his breath. "Dude, what are you doing out this late? I don't think I've ever seen you here before."

David's stare darted to the phone in his hand for a split second before returning. He couldn't place why, but the idea of dispelling the truth—he was on a blind date—threw kindling on the fire. "Just hanging out, Tanner. You know, unwinding after a demanding week, that's all."

Tanner's light brown eyes drew to the wall of spirits and wines, reading the drink special. He registered David's response hardly at all. "Yeah, I hear you, man. I do. It was a long week. Spring fever is hitting hard."

Silence ensued, an uncomfortable moment that reeked of awkwardness. David knew Tanner, but he wouldn't consider him a friend. More like a longtime acquaintance. They worked for the same school district and had interacted at meetings, but never in a social circle. Not just the two of them.

"Hey, sweetie," Tanner rang out, shattering the void. He waved his hand at the redhead to their left behind the bar, demanding her attention. "Can we get some drinks, love?" That Southern drawl was on full display. Hook, line, and sinker.

David watched the man, listening to the smoothness in his voice. Even under the dim lighting, he could see the tan line on the man's ring finger where his wedding band should have been.

She paused her swirling wipes of the counter and looked his way, delivering a nod. The bartender approached the two, a genuine look of satisfaction gracing her youthful, lightly freckled face. "What are we having, boys?"

Tanner leaned forward, making sure his voice was audible over the music. "An old-fashioned for me, darling." His eyes drifted from the bartender's gaze, sweeping over her chest for far too long before redirecting David's way. "What are you having, man? First round's on me, fucker."

David hesitated. A few drinks were planned for the evening, but he expected a different companion: bright, charismatic, and female, as nerve-racking as that sounded. Not to mention her jaw-droppingly beautiful looks. A stark contrast to the stool's occupant next to him.

He stared at his phone once more, a sense of doubt bubbling from the lifeless black screen. The desolation and emptiness. The coldness. She hadn't responded to either of his messages in the past hour. If she were running late, she would have texted by now, right? The truth slowly pushed its way through the light, suppressing the hope that lied to him.

She's not coming, is she?

"Dave?" Tanner asked, that same brazen tone he always used slathered each syllable. "The lady's waiting, man."

The directness brought David back, and he tried to collect himself with a brief glance the bartender's way. "Oh yeah, sorry. I uh . . ."

Tanner's glare darkened, a layer of annoyance claiming his regular cocksure expression. Without acknowledging the bartender, he called out, waving a hand her way, "Just bring him the same, doll. A second old-fashioned, will ya?"

With that, she strolled away to mix their drinks, leaving Tanner with his thirst and David with his thoughts.

Tanner spun around on the stool, eyes sweeping across the open bar. He took in the couples crowding around the pool table, eyeing a brunette in a halter top. "Slim fuckin' pickings, huh?" he joked, not expecting an answer. A slight head bob resonated with the music's beat.

David didn't respond. He barely heard the man's mock, merely sitting there, staring at the lifeless screen. Ever since they had agreed to meet three days ago through the dating app, he knew this was a bad idea. It festered in his mind, tormenting him, strangling his thoughts. Deep down, he knew he wasn't ready. To start this charade known as dating. However, he was here, suffering from the obvious and reproaching himself for his naivety.

"So, since you're here alone, interested in a wingman?" Tanner asked, breaking the unsufferable silence.

David wasn't. He didn't want a wingman. He didn't even want to be here, but the longer his thoughts settled, allowing the truth to blanket him, the less it stung. This wasn't his fault. He'd put himself out there, taking the risk. The ball was in her court, and the weight of her decision to show up or stand him up would linger on her conscience.

"No." David leaned over, raising his voice a few decibels over the music. "Not really, man. The funny thing is, I was supposed to meet someone."

"Really?" Tanner's eyes never swayed from the brunette leaning over the pool table. "Thought you were just hanging out. Blowing off some steam."

"Yeah, well"—David ran his fingers through his auburn hair, swiveling on the stool to face the open room—"doesn't look like she's coming."

After a few seconds, Tanner cast a side-glance Dave's way and replied, his regular assuredness layered on each word, "Her loss, man."

The words struck hard, and they peeled away a layer of doubt. But they made sense.

You're right, Tanner. It is her loss.

"Here's your poison, boys." The bartender's soft voice cut through the bar's hum from behind them. She set each glass down on the wooden bar top.

In unison, both men swiveled around to meet the flavorful drink sitting before them. Each frosty glass glistened with condensation.

"Let me know if you need anything else, ' kay," she called out, aiming that pleasing smile directly at Tanner.

"Will do, hon," Tanner replied, delivering a playful wink her way. A look that spoke volumes about intent. With that, he reached down, his fingers brushing the cool glass, and lifted it to his counterpart sitting next to him. "Let's make tonight memorable, man. Cheers."

David nodded, feeling the anxiousness and self-doubt that clung to him like talons rinse away. Maybe tonight could be something after all. Like Tanner said, it was her loss.

The two men's glasses met with a cheerful *clink*. "Cheers, Tanner."

3

The world had tilted sideways somewhere around drink number six. David gripped the bar's edge as Tanner unloaded another story packed with crudeness and debauchery—something about a parent-teacher conference gone wrong.

"So there I am," Tanner slurred, cigarette dangling from his lips, "talking to this kid's mom at a parent-teacher conference. She dressed up for the occasion too. Dude, everything was hanging out, and she slowly kept leaning forward across the table, inch by inch. The twins were on full display, if you get my drift."

"Enough! I get it. I get it."

"Ah, you should've been there, man. I'm telling you. If another mother hadn't knocked on the door and interrupted our session, who knows what would have happened."

"I think we both know what would have happened," David said, his words clumsy.

"So it's not just me, right?" Tanner joked, gesturing to himself. "All I'm saying is her eyes said a lot more than 'Thank you for helping my son with his algebra' as we finished up."

"Yeah, I bet they did." David laughed, turning away and taking a sip of the bronze liquid. As he lowered the glass, he felt Tanner nudge his shoulder.

"Hey, man. Check it out. See that brunette by the pool table? The one with the ass that could stop traffic? She's been looking over here for the past hour."

David followed Tanner's gaze to a woman in a halter top who was indeed glancing their way. "She's probably just wondering why that creepy drunk guy keeps staring at her."

"Creepy? I'm as charming as they come, Dave," Tanner countered, dismissing the barb without another thought. "Nah. I think she's wondering which one of us is going to buy her next drink." Tanner stood up unsteadily. "Let's find out."

"Tanner, don't—"

But Tanner was already moving, weaving between tables like a shark through the shallows. David watched him approach the woman and her obviously large boyfriend. The conversation started friendly enough—Tanner's charm was legendary, after all. But then the boyfriend's face darkened, the woman stepped back, and Tanner's voice rose a few bars.

That's when Miguel appeared. Nearly seven feet of pure muscle wrapped in a black T-shirt with *SECURITY* printed across the chest. His voice was quiet but carried the weight of absolute authority.

"Gentlemen. Time to go."

"Hey, listen here, man—" Tanner started.

"No. You listen." Miguel's massive hand settled on Tanner's shoulder. "You've had enough fun for one night. Both of you. Out."

Tanner glanced back at David. "Can you believe this bullshit?"

Seconds later, they were escorted out. With a resounding *thud*, the door slammed shut, leaving David and Tanner to lock eyes on the sidewalk. Before they knew it, both erupted in an avalanche of guffaws, the carefree sounds piercing the night sky. Each hunched over with their palms on their knees for several moments while the drunken laughter dripped from their lips.

"Man, screw that place," Tanner said, ending the clamor and wiping his mouth with the back of his hand. "Hey, there's another place nearby—another Irish pub, but not run by Nazis like this shithole." He gestured to the corner a hundred feet away. "Interested?"

And even though Tanner's offer to find another watering hole sounded tantalizing, David declined. It had been a night of exhilarating fun, his actions wildly out of character, yet the strong liquor coursing through his veins sustained his cravings. He had already eclipsed his quota and then some.

"As awesome as that sounds, man," he slurred, a sway in his stance as he righted himself, "I can't. I need to get home. If I'm lucky, I'll sleep this off before responsibility digs its claws in. Grades were due on Wednesday." A mock look of panic crossed his face.

"Man, fuck that," Tanner countered, lighting a cigarette, the red ember glowing under the moonlight. Billows of smoke exited his nostrils as he exhaled. "Grades can wait, man."

"I wish," David responded. "I've put them off for too long. I still like to believe I'm a reputable teacher after all these years."

Tanner took a long drag, eyeing his drinking buddy. He held his tongue for another breath before finally continuing, his loose features turning familiarly rigid. "All educators are reputable. Don't forget that. Just don't let the admin control you. You're not their puppet, man. A Saturday is a Saturday."

David's glare sharpened. "Yeah, I know. I just need to catch up, get my books updated. I've been so preoccupied with other things, I've let the assignments pile up. Now, I feel like I'm drowning. Know what I mean?"

"I do, Dave Miller. I do." Tanner stood a little taller, a slick grin forming across his lips for a split second before relinquishing to the sloppy intoxication once more. "You've been busy with the ladies, right?"

David scoffed. The outcome of his one and only blind date was a complete failure; the woman never arrived, leaving him waiting in vain, but that was in the rearview now. "It's not like that."

Tanner glanced up at the clouds hiding the moon above their heads. "Sure you don't want to grab one more? A midnight nightcap?"

For a heartbeat, David considered. "Yeah, I'm sure, man." A yellow cab drove past the two, and he flagged it down with a wave and whistle. The vibrancy of its taillights shone on the street's dark asphalt.

"Suit yourself." Tanner snuffed out the cigarette with his heel, releasing the final plume of smoke from his lungs. "More for me, man."

David laughed the self-assured statement away, knowing exactly what the man meant as he stepped toward a parked car. "Hey, aren't you married, man?"

"Technically," Tanner stated. "But it's complicated. We're uh . . . What does that guy Ross always say on *Friends*? We're on a break at the moment." A sinful smile matched his slurred speech.

"On a break," David chuckled, wondering if there was any truth to that, but not really caring. "Sure, man. Sure. Anyway, I have to get going, Tanner. Six hours and some electrolytes are screaming my name, man. Thanks for this, though. I really needed it," he stated, stopping as the taxi pulled over near the curb.

"Yeah, no worries." Tanner offered a weak wave before turning and strolling up the street with a slight, ever-present stagger. "See you around, Dave Miller," he called out, never turning back to acknowledge a response.

David opened the cab's door, watching Tanner briefly before he disappeared around the corner. Unbeknownst to him, he sported a smile on his lips before he climbed inside.

***

Ten minutes later and an Andrew Jackson poorer, David climbed the narrow stairs to his one-bedroom apartment, each step a minor victory over gravity and bourbon. On more than one occasion, his foot missed a step, and he nearly flattened out, but caught his balance before disaster struck. As he staggered over the landing, heading to his locked door, he rummaged through his pants, finding his keys. Home sweet home.

Once inside, he emptied his pockets, placing his keys, wallet, and phone on the turquoise console table on the wall opposite his bed; a conventional routine he was barely aware of any longer. A hot, invigorating shower, followed by four Tylenol, concluded the evening's theatrics. Then he crawled into bed, hoping sleep would take him quickly. He was wrong.

As he lay there, hair still damp, and stared at the shiplap ceiling, his mind wandered, eluding the rest he needed. He thought about his chance encounter with Tanner, how free he felt while they talked. Maybe it was just the booze, but his opinion of the guy had changed some. Regardless of his previous views, Tanner wasn't that bad. He could be a friend. He needed a friend. The only person he really ever spent social time with these days was Jenna.

But as his eyes hovered over the rich wood grains coating the ceiling, noting the deep brown swirls and knots, he also thought about her. Amelie. Her high cheekbones, piercing blue eyes, and straight, jet-black hair. It was her idea to meet at O'Malley's. She picked the spot and the time. Why hadn't she shown up? Why did she stop texting?

The uncertainty and doubt forced his hand, and he sat up in bed. Sitting on the edge of the mattress, his toes sunk into the soft carpet below, he then stood, leaving the comforts of his bed behind. Crossing the room in a few strides, he grabbed his phone off the console table. Before bringing it to his eyes, a glimmer of hope blossomed in his core, wondering if he'd see a missed message from her. But as he raised the phone and its vibrant glow illuminated his face, the crushing truth reintroduced itself. There were no messages, no pleas for forgiveness, no lame, rehearsed excuses. Nothing but a handful of notifications and calendar reminders for the coming days.

When his head met the pillow again, a sense of resentment engulfed him, but he couldn't allow the feeling to take root and linger within his thoughts. He desperately needed some sleep. As he closed his eyes, a single phrase muttered from his lips before he drifted away into slumber: "Your loss, Amelie."

II

Saturday Morning, May 9, 2015

A searing shrill ripped through the dawn, burrowing into his temple. Again and again, the sound echoed through the bedroom, a relentless, eroding tide of annoyance punctuated by brief silences.

Through the haze, a single bloodshot eye eased open, absorbing the faint light invading the space through the shutters. As he gained clarity, he traced a line to the source of the wail sitting atop the nightstand. The alarm clock sat there, mocking him. It read *7:00 a.m.*

After shaking away the fog, he forced a tired hand toward the deafening beast. His fingers reached for it, stretching across the mattress until they silenced the alarm with a tap.

He rolled onto his back, fingers locked behind his head, while he allowed the memories from the previous night to manifest. One by one, the escapades of the evening exploded within his mind like fireworks on the Fourth of July: the cab ride home, O'Malley's, Tanner, and finally the girl. Amelie. The dark-haired, third-generation Puerto Rican-American goddess who stood him up.

What the hell happened to you last night?

Regardless of the painful throb pulsing in his skull, he couldn't allow the sting she caused to derail him. Even on a Saturday, work beckoned. He had shit to do.

As he sat up, untangling his legs from the mess of sheets, his view drifted to the cell phone lying near the alarm clock. He resisted the initial urge to scoop it up, but succumbed after a deep breath. The casing was cool in his hand as he lifted it, watching it spring to life. And his heart skipped a beat at the sight. There in the lower left corner, hovering above the green messages icon, was the number *2*.

"Those have to be from her, right?" he whispered.

But his presumption was only half correct. After his thumb touched down on the green icon, the senders of those messages appeared.

The first showed the initials *TB*, and he instantly knew that meant Tanner Brown. His brazen partner in crime the previous night. Shaking his head, David chose not to open the message, knowing it could wait. Probably just some crude joke or a dick pic. He'd read it later.

Instead, his attention was drawn to the second message. It was from Amelie, and the timestamp read *2:17 a.m.* He bit his lower lip, feeling an injection of anxiety release in his system. What did she have to say? Did she have a valid excuse for no-showing? Or was this something else? Would he find out that she wasn't interested after all, that the date was a mistake? The barrage of questions came in relentless strikes, carrying an escalated pulse with it.

But after a few seconds, he broke through the lingering worry and opened the message. He had to know the truth.

There wasn't a message, though. Just an obscured image he couldn't make out. Bringing the phone closer to his face, he studied the thumbnail, wondering what the hell it could be before clicking on it. Once it filled the phone's screen, the image didn't bring any clarity. Sand? Maybe a face? He couldn't be sure.

"What is this shit?" he mumbled under his breath.

He scrolled up past the picture, finding the series of messages he sent her while waiting in O'Malley's. Two pathetic texts stared back at him:

Hey, just got here.
Should I order you a drink?

But the one that caused his shoulders to slump was just below the previous two. At *8:27 p.m.*, he sent:

Super pumped to meet you, beautiful. Hope you're ready.

Smooth, David. Real fuckin' smooth, Casanova.

His thumbs went to work once more, scrolling back to the image. He studied it, zooming in and out with his thumb and index finger, trying to make sense of its meaning or purpose, yet coming up empty.

"Where's the message?" he whispered.

Impulse led his next action. He started writing her back but stopped mid-phrase:

Hey, what happened to you last—

His eyes hovered over the words, wondering why his gut seemed to twist in knots. She hadn't apologized or even attempted to explain her absence. He was grateful that she finally responded, confirming that nothing terrible had happened to her, but why no message? And what the hell was the picture of?

With hesitation, he deleted the half-written message, setting the phone back down on the nightstand. "If she wants to talk, she can use her big-girl words. I don't have time for these games," he stated, a hint of pettiness pulsing through each word.

2

A long shower followed before he finally plopped down in front of his PC, a steaming coffee nearby. The mug was a gift from his ex-wife, a gag gift from three years back: white ceramic with black writing, it read *Nacho Ordinary Husband* below a cartoonish image of a sombrero. He'd meant to rid the loft of the subtle items that reminded him of her, but hadn't committed to the task. Internally, he wasn't ready. And besides, he liked the mug and found it humorous, regardless of the memories that were attached. Nostalgia isn't always the bearer of warmth. Sometimes it picks at the scabs that will never heal.

With the comfort of some scrambled eggs already digesting in his gut, he powered on the computer. The lingering effects of the night barely registered any longer. After a few moments, the monitor sprang to life, and he typed in his login. The clock read *8:16 a.m.* Time to get to work.

An hour and forty-five minutes later, he logged out of his grading software. A sense of accomplishment resonated within. He sat there for several moments, fingers drumming on the desk. His mind teetered, not really focused on school or his students, but on the events from the previous night. Specifically, the woman who didn't show up. And the odd message she sent him.

Once he stepped away from his desk, a tense vibration purred from his pocket. The pulse stopped him mid-stride. He reached inside and pulled out his phone, wondering if he would finally see an actual message from Amelie. There wasn't a new message waiting for him. It was a call from his friend Jenna.

"Hey, just checking in. I'm dying to know what happened. How'd the date go?"

"Hey, Jenna." He sighed, thoughts of the night spiraling in his mind. "Well, let's just say things didn't go as expected."

"Oh no." He could hear the concern in her words. "What happened? Was she rude? Did she drink too much? Tell me everything."

The barrage of questions hit his ears like a battering ram. "No, no, no. Nothing like that."

"Then what happened, David? Don't leave a girl hanging, man."

Why didn't you show up, Amelie?

He hesitated, a tinge of shame and self-pity bubbling.

"Um, the date never happened," he finally responded. "She uh . . . She never showed up, Jenna."

"Wow." Jenna didn't continue right away, but he could hear her breathing through the speaker. A subtle, yet tense inhale and exhale. "That's *not* what I was expecting to hear, my friend. Did she at least tell you why?"

He bit his lip, thinking about the question. He wished he had an answer. "Hey, why don't I tell you all about it over lunch? Available? Eleven o'clock?"

She responded immediately. "I'm free. Where are you thinking? The usual?"

He knew the answer before she even asked. "Yeah. I'll see you there. Victor's."

He dropped the phone back into his pocket and grabbed his keys and wallet before leaving the loft. Victor's

Restaurant and Sports Bar was a short drive away, but he opted to walk. Fresh air and sunshine were the only remedies he needed to shed the remaining effects of the previous night's booze. And he looked forward to talking to his friend.

3

She sat across from him, nodding as he spoke. Her straight, tawny hair parted down the middle of her scalp. Her green eyes fixed on her best friend. She listened to his story, etching every part into her memory. That was her gift. Able to recite data and facts with authenticity and precision, Jenna must have been a wise, maternal elephant in a previous life. She never needed to write the trivial down. It just seared itself into her mind.

A margarita stood before her, and she traced her index finger around the rim, feeling the condensation and salt on her fingertip while David continued with his recap of the night. Several times, she wanted to interrupt, ask questions or make comments, but she held her tongue. There'd be time for that later.

A server clad in the customary black approached the bistro table, interrupting David mid-tale. She held a circular tray above her head with a single palm. The *sizzle* and smoke from the tray's dish filled the air as she lowered it and placed it onto the mosaic tabletop in front of them.

Jenna, staring fixedly at the food, broke her silence. "This was a good call, David. Victor's famous fajitas. The best in the city." She tucked wisps of her hair behind her ears as she leaned forward, inhaling the smoky pleasure wafting around the table. She smiled his way, a subtle gap in her front teeth on full display. "Just what I needed to get me out of this funk."

David thanked the server, watching the young girl walk away. His attention drew back to Jenna, smiling as he watched her fill a tortilla with steamy slices of peppers, steak, and chicken. Under the dim light, he could barely see the smattering of freckles that adorned her nose. "Funk?" He leaned forward and grabbed his own tortilla, mirroring her actions. "What's going on? Is everything all right?"

With a mouthful, she answered, "It's nothing." She waited a second while she swallowed the bite. Wiping her mouth with a napkin, she repeated the statement, "It's nothing. Don't worry about it. Just stuff with the boys' father, you know?"

He knew to an extent. He was married once. "How are the kids?"

"Good. They're good. Growing like weeds."

"I've heard that's usually the case, Jenna." He grinned at her.

"Anyway, enough about me and my disaster of a life." She continued. "Tell me more about your night. What else happened?"

"Honestly, there's not much more to tell." He watched as she sipped from her margarita. He mirrored the action. Just water for him, though, especially after the escapades of the previous night. "I showed up, waited, had some drinks, and went home alone."

That calming nod flew his way once more. "Well, at least you had some drinks. Hopefully, you blew off some steam. You've seemed so tense lately, so distant," she replied, then a wan grin formed before taking another bite. Her green eyes pierced him as she chewed.

"Yeah, I know." He was keenly aware of what she had hinted at. Life hadn't been ideal lately with the divorce and his failed attempt at dating. Not to mention the demands from the school district. He had been distant. He lifted his tortilla, taking a generous bite.

"But maybe this was a sign, you know," she stated. "Maybe this thing with this mystery girl you met online"—a tinge of sarcasm melded with her subtle eye roll—"isn't in the cards. Maybe you're not ready to get back out there and start over."

His head nodded as he listened to her. She always had a way of saying the right thing at the right time. Maybe that was another one of her gifts? "Yeah, maybe, Jenna.

Maybe." He wiped his mouth after taking a sip of water. "I guess we'll see, huh?" He winked at her.

"I know we'll see, David Miller. You, my friend, are a rock star, and rock stars fuck shit up. Am I wrong?" That hallmark smile he adored followed.

The grin returned. He held her stare for a moment, appreciating the energy she always brought, the strength and support. An advocate like no other in his life. "No, you're not wrong."

"I know. I know." She tucked the strands of hair behind her ears once more. "I *always* know, mister." A playful barb he always found amusing. She waggled her eyebrows before diving back in and ripping off another bite.

He didn't respond. He just beamed her way, taking a bite of his own.

Silence followed for the next few minutes while they enjoyed the savory meal. The only sounds emitted were from the restaurant: the quiet murmur from other patrons and the hustle and bustle of the staff. A television hung on the wall to their left; the sound was inaudible but not quite mute. A news broadcast.

Halfway through their lunch, the server returned with a bowl of freshly made guacamole— David's favorite. Both dove in, scooping up the green treasure with golden chips.

"So what else is happening, David Miller?" Jenna asked before polishing off her margarita. The final slurp ended the act. "Outside of your failed love life, I mean."

"You're hilarious," he replied before pausing. He held up an index finger, signaling a response was coming, while he chewed the morsels in his mouth. He continued after swallowing. "You'll never guess who I ran into last night at the bar."

She shifted in her seat, sitting a little taller. "I'd imagine you're correct. The chances of guessing are a million to one."

"Ha ha, smart-ass," he mocked.

She returned his sarcastic look, raising an eyebrow.

The server brought a fresh margarita seconds later, placing it down in front of Jenna. Her eyes became saucers at the sight of the drink. She immediately took a sip. "Who'd you run into? An old fling?"

"No, no. Nothing like that." He scoffed, reaching for another chip. "While I was waiting at O'Malley's, I ran into an old acquaintance. Remember Tanner Brown. That's who I had a few drinks with. We hung out and talked."

She knew the man. Not well, but they had gone to the same high school. He was two years older, and no matter the setting, she'd always caught his eyes drifting her way, taking in far too much of her.

She held her tongue, thinking about his words before responding. "That guy's... kinda a *creep*, David," she stated, a sour look forming across her face. Her tone implied more about David than the man in question.

"Hey. I just said I ran into him," David replied, feeling her eyes judge him. "I didn't say we were playing golf next weekend or heading to Cancún for spring break."

"Golf? Cancún? Really, David?"

"It could happen." The smile he wore was forced.

"Sure it could, buddy," she mocked, reaching for another chip. She mirrored his smile. "Sure it could. Keep telling yourself that. Great self-therapy."

He blew off her teasing, rolling his eyes. "Anyway, we're not besties. I just saw the guy at a bar, and we had a couple of drinks. That's all."

"Yeah, well, maybe choose better acquaintances to run into." A hint of humor returned to her voice and manner, erasing the sudden rigidity. "That's all I'm saying."

He nodded in her direction, knowing she was just looking out for him. She had always done that, and he appreciated it. "I'll do my best, dear."

Her view glanced at the television before returning his way, a sparkle shining in her green eyes. "You better." She leaned forward, taking another gulp of her drink.

As he searched for something new to talk about, his stare drifted to the television as well. A local news broadcast had interrupted the previous night's sports highlights.

A reporter with chestnut hair pulled tightly back stood in an alleyway, flanked by two police cars. Yellow tape hung between the two brick buildings, barring anyone from entering. The woman shielded her eyes from the midday sun. She spoke as the cameraman panned away and into the alley, but David could barely hear her. His focus was on the video.

As the camera steadied at the alley's entrance, a bold caption emerged on the lower left of the screen:

Local Woman Found Dead

But the morbid words weren't alone. An image appeared as well. And the sight caused David's breath to halt.

It was her. The jet-black hair, piercing blue eyes, and the smile that made him quiver.

Amelie.

III

Saturday Afternoon, May 9, 2015

"The hell do you mean, *her*, David?" Jenna's voice pierced the casual atmosphere as she lifted herself from the chair, eyes dancing between the television and her lunch date. "Her? Meaning the girl from last night?" She wavered at the set, dubiety strangling her words and actions.

David stood as well, straddling his seat. Like a moth to the flame, he couldn't pull his eyes from the television screen. His heart hammered in his chest, a snare drum relentlessly pounding while blotches of black swam in his vision.

"What are you talking about?" The apprehension forced a few other patrons to glance their way, but she ignored the looks. "David!"

The demanding call broke him free from his trance, and his view snapped her way. After a moment of silence, he finally answered, "That . . . that's her, Jenna. My date from last night." His face was stark white, the blood drained, leaving only a ghostly pallor staring back at her.

The news broadcast cut to a commercial, wiping away the truth. But that image, that small rectangular photo of the twenty-nine-year-old woman, seared into his memory. Her smile. The shine that radiated around her like an aura, a warm golden glow that shimmered and pulsed with gentle light. It was haunting.

"She's fuckin' dead?" Jenna fumbled with the words, struggling to discern the scene as her piercing gaze held on to him. "The girl who stood you up last night is dead?"

He collapsed back into the chair, jaw hanging open, voidness swimming in his eyes. Eternity seemed to pass before he finally responded, "Her name's Amelie."

2

Local Woman Found Dead

The caption had burned into David's thoughts, striking him over and over like a battering wave. The oceanic blue banner, the foamy white lettering of the words. Like a set of ethereal tentacles, they dragged him down into the depths, drowning him. He couldn't breathe. But minutes later, Jenna pulled him to the surface with her gentle voice.

He sat there slack-jawed, trying to process the truth.

How was this possible? How was Amelie dead?

"David. This is fuckin' crazy, man." Jenna sat across from him, trying to make sense of it herself. Wisps of tawny hair that had fallen into her eyes, she tucked behind her ears. "What do you think happened?"

His blank stare shifted, landing on his longtime friend. With a subtle shake of his head, he answered, but the empty words mirrored his look, "I . . . I don't know. Maybe it was an accident or something."

From the moment the newscast aired, Jenna could see the shock slowly devouring him, and it crushed her. This was David Miller, her best friend. She held no one higher within her circle. She needed to help him.

"Yeah, David. Maybe it was just an accident. I think it would be smart to find out for sure, though." Jenna's words were soft, yet layered with a thin coat of confidence and support. "Maybe it'll bring some clarity to the situation. Know what I mean? I think it'll help to find out what happened to her."

He found a sliver of comfort in the soothing purr of her voice, and it helped him wade through the icy waters. "All right, all right." A nod followed. "I'll do that."

"Good. And I'll come with you. We can find out what happened to her *together*."

"Thank you, Jenna. I appreciate that. I appreciate you."

"I know you do, but hey, it's nothing." Her warmth filled the space. "You'd do the same for me. And anyway, like you said, it was probably just an accident. I'm sure we'll find that out soon enough."

Fueled by the confidence and compassion in her voice, he felt a surge of hope, but a persistent, gnawing ache remained hidden. "I still can't believe she's gone," he stated, voice shaky. "I mean, we never actually met, not in person, but . . ." he trailed off, dropping his eyes to his lap.

"But what, David?" Her green eyes sparkled under the dim lighting above, urging him to share his thoughts. "But what?"

He shoved away the hesitation with a sigh. "For the past four or five days, we'd exchanged texts, like hundreds of them. Nothing serious, just casual flirting, you know?"

"Yeah, okay. I can see that. Go on."

His view drifted to her once more. "Well, even though we'd never actually met, I felt like I knew her. Like we'd known each other for years. It's crazy."

She waited a few moments, cogs and pistons pumping in her mind. "This whole shitshow is crazy, man. All of it. But I really think we should get out of here and try to find some answers."

He held her thoughtful stare, feeling the weight bear down on him. She was right. The only way to shed the illness clinging to him like a parasite was to find out what really happened. Jenna had a way of patching the leaks when they sprang.

"Okay," he answered. "We should probably stop by that alley. Maybe someone can shed some light on the truth."

"The alley sounds like the ideal place to start, my friend, and I'll drive, okay?" That little grin reappeared on her lips, showcasing the gap between her front teeth that he adored. The warmth from the view touched the chill in his bones.

"Yeah, you'll need to drive. I walked down here, Jenna."

"Walked?" Sarcasm leaked from the word. "You just continue to surprise me, David Miller. It's like I don't even know who you are anymore. First, you're dating, as fuckin' crazy as that sounds, and now you're out strolling through town like some carefree lunatic. Who the hell are you, man?"

He chuckled at her playful tugs, feeling the final tendrils of shock loosen their grip and wither away. She always made him feel better. "I guess it's the new me, Jenna. That's who."

"Well, I think it's time to say, 'Au revoir' to this joint and get moving, my friend. Ready?"

He was ready.

3

The familial scent of Newports clung to the silver Volvo's upholstery, mingling with the lingering odor of stale coffee. The glossy cover of the latest *People* magazine shone from the footwell, among a collection of crumpled fast food receipts, their edges dog-eared and faded. Empty Starbucks cups littered the back seat, accompanying a stack of forgotten junk mail and a gym bag. Most would balk at the sight, but David never flinched. This was Jenna, and he accepted her in all her messiness.

He peered out the passenger side window, the streets outside a dizzying blur racing past him. Upon embarking, Jenna had turned on the radio and the newest song from Dave Matthews played in the background, but he wasn't listening. He was so absorbed in his thoughts that the world seemed to fade away, leaving only the silent weight of his own mind.

As the Volvo made its last turn of the drive, the scene from the television loomed before them. Two brick buildings stood tall against the sun's backdrop. But what the newscast had displayed was a mere morsel of the overwhelming reality. Four black-and-white cruisers lined one side of the street, and a band of unmarked black SUVs lined the other. News vans and reporters choked the sidewalk, held back from the property by a web of crime scene tape. Frenzied chaos reigned in the sight as Jenna drove past the bedlam. She whipped the car around at the nearest four-way intersection and parked it.

In uncanny unison, both opened their doors and exited the vehicle. The air buzzed with the voices of reporters and cameras whirring.

David's breath hitched as he circled the car, the tumultuous sounds amplifying the frantic thumping of his heart. He met Jenna, and together their burning glares took in the scene.

What in the world is happening? he asked himself.

Without a word, they crossed the street and approached a small group of onlookers huddled against the barricading streams of yellow, staying clear of the reporters and their cameras. Faint murmurs and snippets of chatter hung in the air. Through the confusion, they stood shoulder to shoulder under a canopy of maple trees and listened.

"That poor woman," a middle-aged woman wearing a jogging suit whispered to herself. Saturation hung in her eyes.

A man a few years older, hefty and sporting a fresh layer of sweat from their run, leaned into her and wrapped a beefy arm around her waist. "I can't believe something like this would happen so close to home." His tank top clung to his slick flesh.

David thought, *This wasn't an accident, was it?*

A slight breeze picked up, shuddering the fresh shoots of leaves above their heads. The flurry of air carried the scent of a woman's perfume, a mix of vanilla and something spicier. Not overpowering, but pleasant. David wondered if Amelie wore a similar scent. He glanced to his right, seeing the owner. A petite, twenty-something brunette stood next to him. Her eyes were wide and distant, a layer of fear strangling her face.

David scanned the rest of the cluster, hearing other quips of somberness and confusion. A breath later, he felt a gentle touch. His stare darted to his forearm, seeing Jenna's fingers resting there. He looked at her, noticing the worry lines deepening around her eyes, her usually bright face clouded with concern.

Near the alley's entrance, an uproar of shouts erupted, capturing his attention. "Detective Jenkins! Detective Jenkins!"

The reporters huddled on the sidewalk sprang to life, trying to gain the man's attention. David stepped off the curb, staring past the calamity and craning his neck toward the source.

"Detective, Detective! What happened to that young woman? We need answers!"

The man in the spotlight, a few holes into the back nine of his life and proudly sporting the silver mane it gifted, strolled down the alley's fairway toward the pack of cameras and microphones. The warm afternoon breeze caused his jet-black sports coat, left unbuttoned, to dance and flutter with each step. His height and lean frame were strikingly apparent with each effortless stride.

A weighty solemnity hung in the air as he halted before the throng of reporters, hushing their calls with his mere presence. The silence pulsed with anticipation, a vibrant hum that exploded into relief as he addressed the horde.

"Ladies and gentlemen," he called out, his voice gruff and demanding. "I understand you're searching for answers, and I'll share what I can, given the circumstances."

David stepped forward and approached the group of reporters, his stare locked on the detective. He could hear Jenna's light footsteps right behind him.

"Between eight and nine p.m. last evening, an assailant abducted a young woman in her parking lot. That young woman's body was found in this alley early this morning." He paused, letting the news marinate while a light breeze ruffled through his neatly groomed silver hair.

Someone killed her?!!

The news shook the ground David occupied; the blow delivered a dizzying left hook. A hollow ache, cold as winter's breath, settled in his chest, mirroring the icy chill that snaked down his spine.

"As of now, we have no leads, no suspects," the detective stated. "But homicide is diligently combing her apartment, the parking lot where she was taken, and this surrounding area. We're collecting as much information as we can. This is a crime scene, everyone."

"Who was the victim, Detective Jenkins?" Dressed in a navy pantsuit, a reporter near the front posed the question, shattering the one-sided affair, her eyes reflecting a profound weariness. "Can you give us her name?"

"Yes, yes. Who was she, Detective?" other members of the horde echoed, the tension and hysteria of the scene winding up.

"Who was this young woman?"

"Why was she murdered, Detective?"

"Are you aware of a motive?"

Her name is Amelie, David thought.

The detective waved off the onslaught of questions, gesturing for control. "Hey, I need order here. Settle down, everyone," he countered, silencing the uproar. "Further discussion of the crime is impossible at this time. Out of respect for the deceased and her family, her identity will remain anonymous for the foreseeable future. Once we gather more information, the department will organize a formal press conference to provide you with all the details. Until then, hold the young woman's family in your thoughts and prayers and know that we will find the culprit behind this heinous crime. That's all for now."

The crowd's desperate pleas and nervous shouts faded behind him as Detective Bennett Jenkins, a veteran of thirty-two years, turned and walked away, dismissing the masses without another word.

David stood among the group of reporters, Jenna at his side, watching as the detective's towering frame strolled off. The man joined two others dressed just like him and a woman in a leather jacket. He watched as the four exchanged inaudible, terse words, their hard glances at one another intensifying the already frigid atmosphere.

The news that Amelie was murdered hammered away at him like a vengeful wraith. How could this be real? His mind raced, searching for purchase, trying to process the overwhelming truth. It staggered him. But somehow, hidden deep in the bowels of the cavern collapsing around him, an urge manifested, a need. He had to talk to the detective.

4

One by one, the news vans slowly peeled away from the scene, carrying the reporters with them. The last of the onlookers had dispersed, too, leaving behind an eerie silence broken only by the distant sounds of the city. And the hushed voices of two friends.

David and Jenna waited near a parked police cruiser, watching a series of department personnel come and go:

lab techs, patrol officers, and others. A beautifully orchestrated waltz. The stream of yellow tape held them back from the dance floor.

"This is insane, David." Jenna held his cell phone in her hand, staring at the screen. "How is this possible? Didn't he say she was abducted between eight and nine?"

"Yeah," he said, but he wasn't looking at her. His stare remained on the alley, watching and waiting to talk to someone, anyone.

"How did she text *you* at 2:17?" She looked up from the phone, wide-eyed, with a grimness hanging on her face.

He didn't answer right away. His view and attention remained on the scene before him. Photographers documented every intricate detail of the alley, etching and logging potential evidence into their database. A technician set up a makeshift office on the trunk of a car, hammering away at the laptop's keyboard.

"I'm not sure, to be honest," he finally said, breaking the silence. "I'm guessing there's a time delay or glitch in the network. There's no other logical explanation, Jenna."

"And what's with the grainy-ass pic?" Jenna held the phone up facing him, the afternoon sun gleaming off the screen. "What the hell does it mean?"

David looked back at her. "I've been asking myself that all morning." His eyes dropped to the sidewalk.

All morning, Jenna.

As his attention redirected to the crime scene, he watched a caravan of detectives exit the entrance; Detective Jenkins in the rear, walking alongside the woman wearing a leather jacket. The group stopped near one of the black SUVs.

Jenkins, standing a head taller than the others, reached into his jacket pocket. His hand returned to the light of day holding a pack of Marlboros. He pulled a cigarette out, lighting it with a chrome Zippo. Smoke danced from his lips, swirling around the small group.

David watched, following the mannerisms of the four huddled in a semicircle. He could hear nothing from that distance.

A heartbeat later, two members of the group walked away, disappearing from view as they slid into an unmarked black vehicle. The sound of their doors shutting reverberated along the asphalt, creating a metallic echo in the air. After snubbing out the cigarette with his heel, Jenkins and the only woman of the quartet followed suit, entering another car.

The soft roar of engines filled the air as the two SUVs inched away from the curb, making their way toward the remaining few looky-loos. Jenna and David included.

The first rolled past them, turning right and meandering up the avenue. Jenkins wasn't in that vehicle. As the second approached, David overcame his hesitation and gestured at the driver. He stepped off the sidewalk, invading the street.

The car stopped, and David rounded the vehicle, amping up the moment's tension. He peered inside the cab, vaguely seeing a silhouette through the window's dark tint. Slowly, the glass lowered, the mechanical sound dampened by the powerful V8 engine. Detective Bennett Jenkins sat there, his tired and weathered face distraught and wearing a look of annoyance.

"Listen," he started with his husky voice. "I've already told the reporters everything we know. Just let us do our jobs and we'll solve this case, okay?"

"Sir." David's voice cracked as he responded, "Sir, I just need a second of your time." He could feel beads of perspiration gathering on his forehead. "I . . . I knew the girl, Detective. I mean . . . I sort of knew her."

Jenkins's eyes narrowed, taking in all five foot ten of David. The wavy auburn hair, the T-shirt, the cargo shorts, the flip-flops, and the bold dragon tattoo on his forearm. A scrutinizing look that bordered on judgment. The indicting eyes of a man used to sizing people up: criminals, suspects, and civilians alike.

"I'm sorry to hear that, son. But there's nothing I can discuss further about what happened. We have to go now."

David stepped forward, resting his fingers on the window frame. He leaned in, demanding the detective's attention. "There's something I need to tell you, Detective. We—she and I—were supposed to go on a date last night, but she never showed up." He could feel Jenna hovering behind him.

A quiet stillness overtook the car as Jenkins listened, chewing on the words. "I'm sorry to hear that." A glimmer of empathy bathed his gray eyes. "Listen, if you need some support with grief, the department has a hotline that—"

David cut the man off, his voice heightened. "I don't need grief counseling, Detective. I'm shaken up by this, of course, but what I need is for you to listen to me for a second. Please."

The detective's stare flipped to Jenna upon seeing her deliver a meek wave and mouth the word "Please." As he redirected his haughty look, he nodded in David's direction. "All right. Go on. You have thirty seconds, son."

David delivered a nod of his own, rapping his fingers on the door's cool steel. "I don't know what this means, but I received a text from her late last night. Like really late. Like after"—his eyes drifted up to the nearby building's third floor before coming back just as quickly—"you know."

"What time?" Detective Jenkins asked without a hint of emotion.

"After two a.m. At 2:17, sir."

The detective broke his hard gaze, glancing at his passenger. He leaned to his right and whispered the woman's way before returning to David. "She texted you at 2:17? Are you certain about that? It was from her number?"

"I'm one hundred percent sure. Look, I'll show you." David turned around, gesturing for his phone from Jenna. After he retrieved it, he turned and displayed the cryptic image the detective's way. "Look, right here, 2:17 a.m."

The detective gazed at the screen. To David, the silence stretched on, each second feeling like an eternity.

With a sharp and intense gaze, Jenkins methodically examined the image, allowing his eyes to linger on every corner as each detail imprinted itself on his mind. "What is it?"

"Honestly, I don't know. I woke up this morning and found it waiting for me."

Taut seconds passed before another sound resonated. "What's your name?" the detective asked, his tone layered in a concoction of concern and muddiness.

"David. David Miller."

"Well, David Miller, I have a meeting with the chief in five minutes. He needs a debriefing pronto, but I should be free shortly. Can you meet me at the station in an hour? I'd like to discuss this matter in more detail. Something seems *amiss* about this message."

The way the detective said the word bothered David. The tone, the buried contempt, hidden below the surface. "Yeah, that's not a problem. We'll see you there in an hour."

With that, David watched as the window rolled up, sealing the two detectives in a sarcophagus of pitch black. Then, like the vehicle before, the SUV turned and disappeared around a bend.

David turned to Jenna, his mind a pile of mush and rot. "Think you can take me to the police station?"

She forced an uncomfortable smile. "I'll not only take you, I'll hold your hand the whole fuckin' time we're in there, buddy. This shit is crazy, man."

He forced a smile of his own. "Thanks, Jenna. Thanks."

IV

As the silver Volvo descended into downtown, leaving the rolling hills of the East Side behind, David and Jenna found themselves in the center of what the locals called "Second Saturday." Artists, hobbyists, food vendors, and shoppers littered the streets and sidewalks for the once-a-month event, straining access to street parking. The two friends circled the area three times before finding a spot a few blocks away from the police station.

The air beamed with energy as they exited the car to laughter and friendly murmurs of fascination and delight. David led the way, cutting a path through the mass of bodies, the scents of sunscreen and sweat thick in the crowd. As they worked their way through the throng, he had to ignore the hawking calls from those peddling goods. Live music and chatter filled the air, mixing with the aromas of sizzling food while the midday sun warmed their backs from above. The hordes of visitors and sellers alike doubled the five-minute walk.

As the precinct came into view (a cold and weathered, three-story brick building from the fifties), the event's fun and carefree atmosphere vanished. The smiles and laughter were gone, replaced by a sense of lost hope and misery. Two officers manhandled and shoved a man wearing handcuffs forward, moving him through the set of double glass doors. Shouts and expletives rang out from inside, filling the air with tension.

David paused a few feet from the station's entrance, keeping Jenna squarely behind him. The abrupt halt resulted from a group of homeless people crouched in an alcove to the left of the doors. Rigid stares and scowls fell his way from the threesome, but he ignored the looks. It was the smell that almost forced him to lose his lunch. A wave of nausea rolled over him as the acrid stench, thick and suffocating, clawed its way into his lungs. Holding his breath, he maneuvered around a man clad in a three-piece suit standing in the doorway and entered the building, Jenna at his heels.

Inside was just as disorderly. Detainees, both men and women, formed a line against the left side. And there was no discrimination among them. A myriad of races and cultures. A modern-day Village People on full display. They leaned against the bleak, colorless interior wall, contrasting with the shiny chrome they wore around their wrists. An oppressive hum mingled with the aggressive silence of the officers standing guard.

This area of the first floor, known collectively as "The Intake," emanated despair. The sight of the waist-high, heavily scuffed wall that ran the length of the room created a sense of isolation, cutting off this section from the desks, cubicles, and labs beyond. A transparent pane of bulletproof glass adorned the wall, reflecting the dim light of the room. Two secretaries sat behind the divide, hammering away at keyboards, answering phones, and failing to hold back the galled tones in their voices as they processed the detainees one by one.

What a shithole, David thought, glancing back Jenna's way. She mirrored the look, a trace of revulsion taking over her typically placid features.

As David's gaze swept back to the secretaries behind the glass, a cold sweat slicked his skin, triggering his primal internal warning system. In his peripheral vision, a set of dark, emotionless eyes bored into him from across the room.

A short, rail-thin man, hands securely bound behind his back and flanked by two officers, glared his way. The man's greasy, long hair parted down the middle of his thinning scalp obscured the sides of his face, yet did little to hide the piercing, black daggers aimed at the schoolteacher.

David avoided the automatic impulse to acknowledge the stare, endeavoring to overlook the uneasy sensation it brought. But anxiety forced his hand. His eyes slowly drifted from the glass to the man leaning against the wall across the room. With confirmation made, he quickly abandoned the look and redirected his sight to the secretaries behind the pane of glass. But now, the tense feeling of being watched and tracked magnified. Were every man and woman wearing cuffs and sporting that hallmark look of hopelessness staring his way? The officers and presumed lawyers in their three-piece suits too? He was like a caged animal at a zoo.

Without another option and suppressing the urge to hightail it out of there, David stepped forward and filed into the queue on his right. A dingy sign that read *CIVILIANS AND VISITORS* was at the front of the line. It was the shorter of the two by a head, but still daunting; a gauntlet he'd have to run in order to share his information with Detective Jenkins.

2

Thirty grueling minutes later, David stood before the barrier segregating The Intake from the rest of the precinct. The middle-aged secretary, plump in the cheeks and wearing too much blush and eyeshadow, stamped a series of papers and mumbled under her breath. Even through the circular vent fixed into the glass, the words were incoherent. But he could sense annoyance lying under the surface of her moving lips. She didn't seem like a woman who enjoyed her profession. Let alone interactions with others.

A manila folder snapped shut after she placed the stack of papers inside, and the weight of them sent a dull *thud* into the wire basket sitting on her right. Another criminal processed and ready for their lengthy stay. Her gaze finally left the desk and fixed on the man standing on the other side of the glass.

David forced a smile, hoping for one in return. He didn't receive it. Her vacant expression sent a wave of worry in his direction.

"What can I do for you, sir?" The words were accompanied by a long-suffering sigh, which revealed her discontent.

"Hi there . . . I'm um . . ." David stammered, feeling her fierce glare slice through him. His eyes drifted to the small chalkboard nameplate with curly hot pink lettering proudly displayed on her desk. His stare fell back on her, unable to break away from the thick emerald eyeshadow she boldly wore. "Hi, Daisy. I'm here to see Detective Jenkins. He's expecting me."

She held his stare for an uncomfortable moment, silent as the dawn, before her attention swung to the monitor to his left. Without a word, she tapped away on the keyboard and maneuvered the mouse. And then, "Identification, please."

David leaned forward, resting his forearm on the short counter. "Identification?"

"I need to process your ID, sir. All civilian personnel must pass clearance before entering the precinct." Her tone hadn't changed, still weighted with annoyance and lacking patience.

"My ID?" David reached into his back pocket, sensing Jenna's hovering. "Yeah, yeah. Okay." He pulled his license out from the worn leather wallet, ignoring the faded and creased photo of his ex-wife hidden underneath. Without hesitation, he dropped the card into the opening between the glass and the counter. "Here it is, miss."

The plump secretary known as Daisy promptly scooped up the driver's license and started typing once again on the keyboard. Seconds later, the whirring sound of a printer replaced the *click-clack* of the keyboard.

Daisy reached across her desk and lifted a rectangular item from the printer, dropping it along with David's license into the opening. The adhesive paper, a few inches wide and long, held David's name along with the photo from his license.

"Make sure you wear this at all times while inside the precinct," Daisy called out, barely making eye contact. "Forensics and the detectives' offices are just past the door there to your right, and have some patience in case Detective Jenkins is on the phone or with someone. Understand, Mr. Miller?"

David's stare drifted to his right, seeing the scuffed and bland reinforced steel door Daisy referenced. With the dull paint and dim fluorescent lighting from above, it was hard to spot unless one was actually looking for it.

"Yeah, I understand. I can do that, miss," David stated, locking onto the secretary once more. "But, um, I'm not alone, though. My friend is with me." He glanced over his shoulder, seeing Jenna's toothy grin aimed Daisy's way. The slight gap between her front teeth always made him feel at ease. "Does she need a sticker too?" he asked, peeling the back away from the paper and affixing the visitor pass to his shirt.

Daisy's eyes narrowed as her view slid past David, seeing the petite blonde behind him. Jenna stood there and gave an uneasy wave aimed the secretary's way. Daisy held the look for a few breaths before she called out in her monotone voice, "Identification, please."

3

The desperation and tension didn't end as they stepped through the steel door a minute later. No, the hopelessness from The Intake wafted along with them, a constant reminder of life on the other side of the tracks. A life neither David nor Jenna was familiar with.

As the door closed behind them, its pins securely locking in place, a quiet tension radiated through the long hall they now occupied. The canned lighting purred above their heads, mixing with the distant sounds of chatter and a far-off ringing telephone.

The two friends stepped forward, seeing many doors lining the halls, each labeled with a blue plaque bearing a department or an individual's name. They proceeded down the long corridor, reading each door: *PATROL DIVISION, FORENSICS, COMMUNITY RELATIONS*. During the walk, two beat cops passed by, their footsteps echoing against the floor, yet neither glanced their way. They vanished through the steel door David and Jenna had entered moments before.

With every step forward, David's heart raced, anticipation rising, until he found the name he was looking for. *INVESTIGATION SERVICES*. The white lettering popped off the blue background, gripping his attention like a vise. This door, unlike the others they had passed, was slightly ajar, a host of gruff voices mingling within.

With Jenna on his heels, David peered into the opening.

Inside was a large room, wide and long, and like everything else in the depressing building, bathed in a sickening coat of dim fluorescent lighting. It lacked character or color—a stark beige from head to toe. Cubicles hugged the interior walls, each claimed by a familiar-looking blue and white nameplate. In the center of the room was a long conference table, littered with papers and used ashtrays, and surrounded by cheap folding chairs. Several men huddled together, staring at a large map of the city. One spoke, his voice an undertone, as the others listened, heads nodding his way while taking notes in palm-sized journals. Others nursed coffee from their desks, attending to phone calls or mindlessly staring at their computer monitors. The lone woman with the tight braid and leather jacket eyed the pair with suspicion.

David slipped through the opening, knowing his best friend would be right behind him.

4

After entering, the questioning eyes of detectives shot their way. But they diverted just as quickly once David found the man he was looking for. From his desk, Detective Jenkins beckoned the two forward with a subtle gesture. He was deep in conversation with someone on the telephone.

Overcoming the hesitation, David and Jenna sat down across from the detective, not wanting to interrupt the man or eavesdrop on his call. But that was inescapable.

Jenkins sat there, receiver to his ear, not taking notes, just doodling spirals in a journal as he listened. Words and phrases accompanied the nods he delivered, each slowly adding to the suffocating apprehension in the air. But there were some words etched on the pad: *strangulation*, *crushed larynx*, *contusions*, *bruising*.

The words struck David, painting a macabre, vivid image that seared into his thoughts. No matter how hard he tried to suppress the picture, his consciousness drifted to the scene, giving him a front-row seat. That poor woman's pain, her fear.

Why did this happen?

The sound of the receiver returning to its cradle brought him back.

"Forensics," Jenkins said in his deep, gruff voice. He reached into his jacket pocket. The hand returned with a pack of cigarettes, deftly removing one and placing it between his lips. "Just getting back to me with some data."

David glanced Jenna's way, a nervous tic he had no explanation for. As he redirected his attention to the tall, slender man seated across from him, he spoke for the first time, "Did they find out anything? Anything about what happened to her?"

"No, nothing inclusive, or indicative, for that matter. It's too early." Jenkins lit the cigarette, its red ember glowing under the oppressive lighting. "The autopsy is happening as we speak, and the lab techs are searching for hair samples, fibers for trace evidence, fingerprints, you name it. If something is there, they'll find it. They always do." He knew it was a long shot. The fire destroyed any hopes of finding a thread of evidence, but he wasn't about to disclose this. Not to a civilian.

"I'm sorry, son. Please forgive me," the detective said, taking another drag from his cigarette. "But what was your name again?"

He doesn't remember my name? We just talked an hour ago.

"It's David Miller, sir."

"That's right. That's right. It was on the tip of my tongue." Jenkins drank in the pair sitting across from him, taking in every intricate detail. His gray eyes narrowed, their dullness replaced by a burning heat that seemed to emanate from deep within. "Well, Mr. Miller, can I look at the message again? The one you claim is from the victim."

Claim? What's this guy's deal?

David's posture stiffened. "She has a name, Detective. It's Amelie." Jenkins's stare and words induced the same effect that Alice experienced after drinking the potion; he felt like he was shrinking in the chair. "And I'm not claiming anything."

Jenkins nodded David's way, and the power behind his leer slowly lifted. After a few breaths, he responded, "Yes, yes. We know." The detective paused, riffling through the notepad in front of him. "Amelie Castro Rodriguez of 419 Chester Avenue, apartment 223. Physical therapist by occupation, right?"

"Yeah. How did you—"

"We've got more than just lab rats working this case," the detective stated, cutting David off. "Our friends over in IT filled us in on what they've uncovered."

"What more did they uncover?" David asked. They already knew her full name, her address, her occupation. What else did they know about her?

Jenkins stubbed out his cigarette. "Let me see the message once more, and then we can talk."

David hesitated a moment, glancing Jenna's way. There was something unsettling about the situation, a disquieting feeling stemming from the detective's intense gaze and the nature of his words seconds before. But he needed answers.

His hand crept into his pocket and pulled out the cell phone. Life bloomed from the device as he stared at the screen. Tanner Brown's unread text still waited to be opened, but he ignored the green square with the initials *TB—How'd that asshole get my number anyway?*—and opened Amelie's text from late last night at 2:17 a.m.

The image taunted him, its grainy nature, its cryptic meaning. What was this?

A second later, the phone was in the detective's hand. The man's stare tightened, and he rocked the device from side to side, taking in every angle.

"It's from her, Detective. I promise you that. If you scroll up, you'll—"

"I can see that, Mr. Miller," Jenkins interrupted. His thumb moved rhythmically across the cool face of the glass, and his lips had a subtle motion to them.

David could see the man's eyes tracking from left to right.

He's reading our texts.

"So what do you think, Detective?" Jenna chimed in for the first time.

Jenkins paused, his attention drifting toward the woman sitting on David's left. Warmth was lacking in the stare.

"Hi there. I'm Jenna. David's friend," she said, wilting under the intensity of the detective's gray eyes. She attempted her hallmark smile, but it faltered. The gap in her teeth seemed more pronounced, vulnerable. "Uh . . . just here to help, sir. This shit is—This situation is really intense."

Jenkins's stare continued for a prolonged period before he finally broke the unease, dismissing Jenna without a word. His attention flipped back to David. "Why haven't you texted back?"

"I thought about it," David started. "But now that I know she's . . . gone, it's kind of creepy."

"That's completely understandable. It is." Jenkins paused, surveying the man sitting across from him. "If you don't mind, I'd like to run an analysis on your SIM card. If we can trace the text's authenticity and pinpoint the cell tower it pinged, it will help us determine its location. We can attempt to match it with the texts she sent you earlier in the day. See if there are any differences."

"Is that possible?" David asked.

"Oh yeah," the detective answered, his gruff voice full of certainty. "Surprisingly, it's not that difficult. Every phone has a fingerprint."

"Do you think that's necessary?"

"I do, and I think it's wise to understand all possibilities here. Even ones"—he paused, allowing his next words to strike like a sledgehammer—"as bleak as this is. Forensics will back me here, Mr. Miller. She wasn't alive to send you that text at 2:17 a.m."

David's sight drifted to the floor while the detective's words washed over him. They battered him relentlessly, and he felt like he was free-falling off a cliff. His heart leapt within his chest, galloping like a stallion. Seconds later, he lifted his chin, locking onto Jenkins once more. "If she was already dead, who the fuck sent me that picture?"

Jenkins's response was immediate. "We're going to find out. I just need to run that analysis. It's a good primer, a starting point."

David confirmed agreement with a nod.

"Good. That's good." Detective Jenkins stood, cell phone in hand. "It'll just be a few moments. I'll be right back." Rounding the desk, he strolled away through the room and exited the Investigation Services wing.

***

For the next ten minutes, David and Jenna sat there, minds reeling, hearts pounding. They waited in silence, the clamor from the room washing over them: the hushed conversations that seemed to be about the pair, the piercing rings of telephones that made them jump, the distinct sound of shuffling papers that sounded like case files being prepared.

When Jenkins returned, he reclaimed his chair opposite the two, handing back the cell phone. He leaned forward. "The boys over in IT are running the analysis as we speak. As soon as they know something, I'll know something. But it could be a few hours."

"What do you think we should do in the meantime, Detective?" David asked, though his voice came out small and defeated. He glanced at Jenna. "Should we just . . . wait?"

"No, no, that's unnecessary. I'd suggest you go home and get some rest. Clearly, all of this has been taxing." His signature intensity still lived in his speech, but another layer melded with the grit. "I've got your number, Mr. Miller. When I learn something, I'll make contact and maybe we can get to the bottom of this."

David needed more; a deeper understanding gnawed at him. The intent of this visit was to find answers, but now, as he sat there thinking about Amelie, additional concerns and questions arose. Matters demanded to be heard, but he held his tongue, simply nodding in the detective's direction as he rose from the chair. He could feel Jenna matching his actions.

"Thank you for coming in. When I know more, you'll know more, Mr. Miller." With that said, Jenkins reached for his phone, dialing an extension and burying his eyes back in the notebook lying open on the desk.

The two friends excused themselves, leaving the room without another word.

V

David and Jenna exited the precinct minutes later, shielding their eyes from the intense midday sun, its brightness almost blinding. Their minds reeling, a veil of apprehension weighing them down. They came here willingly, hoping to find some clarity, but the news and information they received produced a torrent of additional concerns.

As they strolled down the sidewalk, leaving the precinct's stank and misery behind, the energy of Second Saturday pulsed once more. With each passing step, the drab, dominant hues of slate that smothered the landscape made way for a tapestry of color. Vibrance slowly injected itself, portrayed in a myriad of signs, advertisements, and murals that covered both external walls and parts of the sidewalk. It was uplifting.

But the beauty of the event appealed not only to one's vision. The sounds and scents that wafted throughout the open square also infused a sense of warmth and belonging. Food vendors, hot dogs and street tacos alike, flooded the air with delectables while local bands subjected the hundreds in attendance to covers of eighties ballads. Any other day, this event would have brought some excitement David's way, but the what-ifs that spiraled within kept him from the satisfaction.

David pushed through the throng, a chaotic symphony of shouts and music assaulting his ears, until he found a bench at the edge of the square offering a much-needed respite. He needed to sit, to think.

Jenna joined him, taking a seat on the bench's wooden planks, her stare aimed at the flock of visitors passing by. The atmosphere here lacked demand, and they could finally talk.

After a few moments of silence, she broke the lull, her slender neck craning his way. But the easygoing persona that always lived on her face was absent. "David, I'm worried."

He released a sigh that confirmed the same feeling. "Yeah, I know. I'm worried too."

She shifted closer to him, swiveling her knees his way. "What if the detective calls you later and tells you that text came from an unknown number?"

"What if he tells me it was from her number, Jenna?" he countered, a shakiness slathering each syllable. "Either way, something isn't right about this shit."

"This is wrong," she stated, a wave of unease washing over her as she watched the mass of people moving through the sun-drenched square. "It's all wrong. The woman, the text, and that damn detective with his looks."

David's hazel eyes froze over, a coldness crystallizing. "It felt like we were on trial, huh? Every word scrutinized, every glance charged with suspicion."

"Yeah, I sensed that too." She tucked a loose end of sandy blonde hair behind her ear. "What do you think his MO was? Does he think you had something to do with her murder?"

A second sigh escaped from his lips as he turned and took in the patrons: the oblivious horde nodding their heads, laughing, and ingesting flavor by the mouthful. Ignorance is bliss. "I really don't know, Jenna, " was all he could muster.

He leaned forward, eyes pinned on the conveyor belt of people coming and going. For an instant, the distant sounds of the event muted. Laughter stopped; instruments paused. The deafening silence shrouded him in a state of tranquility. His mind continued to spin, a cog in perpetual motion, but time seemed nonexistent. And a moment of peace almost revealed itself. But . . .

During that moment, his primal warning system triggered on, the feeling of déjà vu sweeping over him. Back at the precinct, he could feel the detainees' predatory eyes boring into him. The same feeling washed over him now, causing alarms to blare. As the sea of people parted and opened up for a fraction of a second, David locked onto something across the square. On the other side, a man cloaked in a black hoodie and sunglasses sat on a bench, much like he and Jenna occupied. The man's stare was fixed David's way. He could feel it.

He leaned forward, eyes glued on the figure. He held the look for several heartbeats, praying he was wrong. But deep within his core, he knew he wasn't.

Why's that guy staring at us?

The gap of bodies closed once more, obstructing the sight. "Hey, Jenna. Did you see that?" He didn't divert his glare her way.

"See what?" She could sense a newly found nervousness in his speech. "What are you looking at?" She leaned forward, tracing his line of sight.

As the words escaped her lips, a narrow passage through the crowd was revealed. The man sat there, face aimed their way. The sun's glare reflected off the Ray-Bans he wore.

"There. Right there, Jenna." David lifted himself from the bench, pointing at the mystery shrouded in unseasonal attire. "A guy's over there, staring our way."

"Where?" Jenna asked, mirroring David's stance and searching through the throng of people. Her gaze narrowed, and the inviting opening suddenly collapsed into a dense mass of sweaty flesh. "I see nothing. Where?"

"He was right . . ." David's voice trailed off as he stepped forward, attention focused on the window that no longer existed. His index finger led the advance. "He was right there, Jenna! Right there. A guy dressed in black. I could tell he was staring right at us."

The opening did not return, and the two of them stared at the wall of humans, coming and going without a care in the world.

2

Moments later, David led Jenna through the labyrinth of sweat-slackened bodies, pulling her along by one hand. Weaving through the boisterous square, their journey finally ended where the man in black once sat. But the bench was now empty.

"He was right here, Jenna." A need wept from David's words like an open wound. He released her hand, gesturing at the vacant bench. "A guy dressed in all black, hoodie pulled up, with dark sunglasses. Right here. He was staring at us. I could feel it in my bones."

Jenna peered around her friend, taking in the ornamental wrought iron and scuffed wood. "How do you know he was watching us?" Her view drifted back across the square where they had sat minutes before watching the horde of human cattle come and go. "I mean, from that distance, he could have been looking at anything."

David chewed on his bottom lip. His sight volleyed between the empty bench and across the square before landing on his friend. "No. He was watching us, Jenna. I could feel it. I could feel his eyes on me. There's no denying it."

Jenna looked up, feeling the scorching heat from the overhead sun. "Well, whoever he was, he's gone—"

"Son of a bitch!"

Jenna's eyes shot to her right. David had darted in that direction, taking swift strides. She followed, calling out after him, "What is it? What's happening?"

David didn't glance back. His pace quickened. "He's there. Right over there," he stated, pointing through the crowd.

Jenna scurried along, closing the distance between the two. She sidled up against her friend as they walked, weaving around a group of sweaty teens, trying to take in what he was staring at. As the scene opened up, her eyes didn't betray her. It was true. About twenty-five feet away, back turned to them, was a figure clad in black. Tall, broad shoulders, imposing even from this vantage point. The man stood motionless near a vendor's booth, an ebony statue guarding the many trinkets and novelties.

As David slowed to a stop, his apprehension chilled the air. He glanced Jenna's way, the look of someone who had just seen a ghost strangling his features.

Who is this guy?

With haste, he continued, the frantic pounding of his heart echoing the tremor in his ears. He could sense Jenna right behind him now, a blonde-haired shadow matching each cautious stride.

The stranger remained, his back facing their way. A dark target pulling them closer and closer like a beacon.

Inches away now, David reached out, fingers drifting toward the man's right arm. As he gripped and yanked, a shout rang out, "Hey!"

With the forceful tug and the sudden yell, the shrouded figure swiveled at the waist and faced them. He towered over David by a head, a menacing juggernaut staring down. But the sinister face they both expected to see was absent. It was a man. They could see that even with the hoodie and sunglasses. Then the mystery behind those aviator lenses shattered like a mirror.

David watched the man remove his sunglasses. Eyes tired, bloodshot. Heavy dark circles peppered the flesh under those battered orbs. He looked like a freight train had plowed into him. More than once.

Tanner Brown.

3

"Dave Miller." With a swipe, Tanner pulled the hoodie from his head, his shoulder-length, dirty-blond hair falling around his face, a few strands sticking to his forehead with sweat. "What's up, man?"

David stepped back, wide-eyed. "Tanner? What are you doing here? Why were you watching us earlier?"

That signature, cocksure grin the man always boasted vanished. A mask of incredulity replaced it. "Watching you? What the hell are you talking about, man?" His stare shot to Jenna, tailing behind David like a timid caboose. "I just got here."

"Cut the shit, Tanner." David's voice elevated, and a few patrons turned and stared in their direction. "I saw you across the square a minute ago. You were sitting on that bench, staring at us." He cocked a thumb in the seat's direction.

"Dude," Tanner started, "I don't know what the hell you're talking about, man. Seriously. I don't. I just pulled up. I thought I'd check out the local entrepreneurs and their handiwork." His eyes narrowed, seeing the heat simmering in David. "What's this about, Dave?"

David eased on the brakes. "Why are you wearing that hoodie? Dressed all in black? Hiding behind the shades?"

The words possessed a need for the truth, but the tone from moments before had cooled to a simmer.

"What's with the twenty questions?" Tanner scoffed. His view drifted to Jenna again, eyes loitering on her and her tank top for a second longer than necessary. "Can you believe this fuckin' guy?"

David shielded his friend. "Tanner. What's with the dark clothes, man? It's ninety degrees out here."

"If it's not fuckin' obvious, Sherlock, I'm sweating out the hangover. The one you spoon-fed me last night, if I recall." That sly grin poked its nose out of the hole it had climbed in.

"Spoon-fed?" David countered, a smirk growing on his lips too. For a second, the memories of the previous night came crashing in like a tidal wave. The laughter, the jokes. He had a good time last night. There was something about Tanner. Something that brought out a carefree nature David thought had died since his divorce. "Self-inflicted is more like it. You did that to yourself."

"Like hell. I was minding my own business, enjoying my Friday night, when suddenly, Dave the Tank fuckin' Miller shows up and funnels my weight in booze down my throat."

"That is not how it went down," David replied. Any trace of accusation fizzled away with each word. "And you know it. Truth be told, it's you who got me drunk."

Tanner rolled his bloodshot eyes. "You can tell yourself whatever you need to, pal. Whatever you need to. Hopefully, it makes you all warm and fuzzy inside. But I was there. I know the truth, Dave."

"Anyway..." David continued, mimicking the playful eye gesture. He still needed some answers. "You sure you weren't staring at us? Sitting over on that bench, watching?"

"I don't know what the hell you're talking about, man." Tanner wiped the slick layer of sweat from his brow. "Like I said, I just got here a few minutes ago. I woke to a jackhammer pounding in my skull. And after downing a gallon of water and swallowing a handful of Tylenol, I pulled on this hoodie and jogged down here, hoping to sweat this shit out of my system."

David watched him as he spoke, wondering how much truth lived in the man's words. But he had no choice but to believe him.

If it wasn't Tanner, then who was it?

4

"Did you get my text?" Tanner asked, pulling his cell phone from his pocket. The man started swiping and searching through the device.

David remembered the text, but hadn't opened it yet. The other late-night message's unknown source commandeered his thoughts, a persistent itch he couldn't ignore. It was all he could focus on.

"Yeah, sorry about that, Tanner," David replied, feeling a tablespoon of guilt surface in his gut. He had bigger things to worry about, but now that he was standing in front of Tanner, that feeling wouldn't go away. "I have it here." David rummaged through his own pocket, awakening the sleeping beast from its cavern of cotton and polyester with a simple touch. He pulled the phone out and mirrored Tanner's actions.

That coy grin resurfaced on Tanner's face as he eyed David, his prominent dimples reappearing under the afternoon sun. "I didn't hear back, but I handled it. Sealed the deal, if you know what I mean." A wink followed the statement.

David found Tanner's text, the green square with rounded corners. The one with the white initials *TB* in the center. His thumb moved toward it, but his sight drifted to the message below. The one from Amelie. The cryptic one that haunted his thoughts. A defiant, hemorrhaging wound that won't stop bleeding. He tried his best to ignore the thought, burying it in a layer of desperation. But deep down, he knew it would return; sutures bursting open and saturating his mind in a pool of crimson.

As he thumbed the icon, expecting a crude joke to strike him, he found this message was a picture as well. It was a selfie. But Tanner wasn't alone. Two women squeezed into the frame, their cleavages demanding the center of attention. Their glossy eyes carried the longing look of inebriation, and one had her tongue on full display, ready to lick the side of Tanner's face. Below the picture, along with a timestamp of *1:19 a.m.*, was the statement:

Room for two.

"What the hell, Tanner? Two?"

Tanner Brown, David's longtime acquaintance in the school district, short-time booze buddy, answered with a *tsk-tsk*, his hands held out at his sides, palms up. "What can I say, Dave? When opportunity presents itself, you need to plunge in with intent."

David shook off the response, smiling at the man. "You're a pig, dude."

"Hey," Tanner started, a mock-hurt expression shrouding the word. He held a limp hand to his chest. "You wound me, sir. And I thought we were friends."

David thought about the word (friends). Was Tanner Brown a friend? Honestly, he didn't know.

"Well, I hope you had a good time, man," David said. He could feel Jenna hovering close behind him. He glanced over his shoulder, seeing her stiffened posture, her thin arms crossed over her chest, the intensity of her leer.

"Anyway, Dave, what's with all the questions about me staring at you guys? What's this shit all about?"

David's thoughts leapt to the detainee from the precinct that held him in his crosshairs, that primal feeling of being watched, hunted by a parasitical set of eyes. He knew the man sitting on the bench moments ago held that same look. He couldn't shake it, but his intuition steered him in a different direction.

"Never mind, man. It was nothing." A white lie, but who would know the difference? "I just got confused about something. That's all. Forget about it."

"No worries, Dave the Tank." Tanner's trademark sarcasm invaded the space. "You guys want to walk around, grab something to eat?"

David glanced back at Jenna once more, noticing the aura of agitation simmering off her. She wanted nothing to do with this guy. "Hey, it was great seeing you again, Tanner," he called out, turning to face the man wearing the unseasonable black attire. "But we have to get going. I need to get home. I'm expecting a phone call."

Tanner's expression changed. That mouth full of pearly teeth and the dimples in his cheeks faded to a stone-cold sober look. His sight volleyed to Jenna, witnessing the detestable leer aimed his way. "Yeah, that's cool, David. I'll see you around."

David?

"I had fun last night. We'll do it again." David stepped back, pivoting in the opposite direction.

Tanner delivered a nod, fitting the sunglasses back on his face—a masked facade hiding his thoughts. "See you around, mi amigo. You too, *Jenny*."

Neither turned around to correct him. They didn't need to. Their only focus was on getting home and waiting for an explanation from the detective.

VI

After a short drive back to the East Side, Jenna dropped David off at his apartment. She offered to stay and wait with him, to be an emotional support blanket, per se, but he told her it wasn't necessary. She needed to get home. Her children's needs superseded his.

Saying goodbye, he turned and watched the silver Volvo's taillights recede down the hill. Two faint crimson sparks swallowed by the dipping daylight.

Alone, he waited. Hour after hour passed without a word, the time gnawing at his patience. The once-prominent sunny blue sky had transitioned to hues of orange and lavender. Streaks of paint highlighted the darkening horizon.

He sat on the couch, the one he had picked up at the flea market after moving in. The battered and stained beast was a constant reminder of his divorce. But almost everything in this sparsely furnished place had the same effect. He wished he could go back, do things over. Different.

Erase the one decision that fucked everything up. Starting over at thirty-seven isn't for the faint of heart.

He stared at the cellphone lying on the coffee table. Its sleek black face wielded an arsenal of weapons. Arms that might diminish his intellect or ease his suffering, depending on the information presented.

But as suffocating as the wait was, at 7:23 p.m., the phone that lay there like a wounded, dying animal chirped to life.

Startled by the sudden clamor, his reflexes fired. He immediately reached for the device, his fingertips grasping the smooth, metallic edges. That black, lifeless face now held a heartbeat, and *Detective Bennett Jenkins* awaited.

With a swipe, David accepted the incoming call, but reservations held his tongue. Static filled his ears for a breath before the man on the other end spoke, his brusque voice ushering David back in time to the press conference—the first time he laid eyes on the detective and heard the man speak.

"Mr. Miller? Are you there?"

David's eyes darted to the screen, reading the caller's name again.

"Can you hear me, Mr. Miller? Are you there?"

David fought through the reserve, clearing his throat. "Yeah, yeah. I'm . . . I'm here, Detective." The shuffling of papers sounded through the earpiece.

"Excellent. Thought maybe we had a poor connection for a second." A labored breath followed. "Hey, I wanted to thank you for your patience with this matter. Sometimes, we need further research and analysis to find certainty in situations. The IT boys dug a little deeper, is all I'm saying."

Patience is not how I'd describe it, Detective.

"It's not a problem. Did you find out anything? About the text?"

"Well, that's the reason behind this call, son. But I'd rather meet in person, if you don't mind. I have some interesting details to share with you, and I think it would be beneficial if we talked face-to-face."

Interesting details? What was of such interest and importance that he couldn't share it over the phone?

"Is there something I need to worry about, Detective?" David heard his voice break. "Is something wrong?"

"Honestly"—Jenkins paused, his heavy breathing thundering through the phone—"I don't know for sure."

The power of the statement struck him like a bullet. He could feel the chill inching up his spine, ready to grasp hold of his jugular and squeeze. "What. Does. That. Mean. Detective?"

Silence ensued for an indeterminable amount of time before Jenkins responded, "24th Street Cafe. You know it?"

"Yeah, I know it."

"Good. Meet me there in thirty minutes. I'll tell you everything." The detective ended the call without a rebuttal.

After a few seconds, David lowered the phone onto the plaid cushion he sat on. He felt his heart thrumming in his ears, and a wave of sickness came with his reeling mind. What unspoken dread awaited him?

2

The 24th Street Cafe was your standard bustling mom-and-pop diner. Grit, grime, and greasy menus included. The rectangular cinder block structure perfectly captured the spirit of the fifties, with a jukebox and all the bells and whistles one would expect. Red polyester cushions and backrests adorned the family-sized booths collectively lining the restaurant's perimeter, while a collection of square tables sporting red-and-white checkered tablecloths sat in the room's center. Posters and metal signs plastered the marrow-colored walls, depicting the legends of the era: Dean, Monroe, Sinatra, Presley, etc. Stepping through these doors was like stepping into a time machine.

But that's exactly what David did. He drove down the ribbon of asphalt, leaving the North Side behind. By the time he parked the car and stepped through those glass doors, the sun was a dying ember of pink and orange swallowed by the mountains to the west.

The voice of Buddy Holly greeted him as he entered, followed by the savory aromas of prime rib and fried chicken. He wasn't hungry. Not knowing what news the detective would bring had crippled his mind to that extent.

Interesting details.

As he scanned the diner and all its props, he noted the few occupants: a family of four sat in a booth, and a solitary man with silver hair sat on a red stool at the bar. He ignored the family and the snotty wailing of the infant throwing her tantrum, and approached the man.

Either it was his light footfalls echoing across the linoleum, or the man's uncanny spidey sense springing to life that gave him away. He wasn't sure, but halfway through the stroll, Detective Bennett Jenkins turned around and greeted him.

"Mr. Miller." The silver-haired man patted the plump red seat next to him. "Come sit."

"Thanks for meeting with me, Detective." David finished his approach, claiming the stool to the detective's left. He fell silent, not sure how to proceed. His stare fell on the lone cook behind the service counter, watching the man's expertise with a spatula.

"Hungry?" Jenkins asked, opening the menu in front of him. "Best pot roast in town. I frequent this dive a night or two each week."

David cast a side-glance in the detective's direction. "No. No thanks." He paused, feeling his gut twist in a knot. He wasn't sure he could get a mouthful of water down, let alone a hearty meal. "I'm not that—"

"Not hungry, huh?" Jenkins finished the sentence for him, still staring at the menu. "Yeah, I get it. I'd feel that way, too, if a *ghost* texted me." He let the words settle in before continuing. "Suit yourself, son."

The quilt of unease that blanketed him was dark, heavy, foreboding. He could feel the increased pressure weighing him down.

What the hell does that mean? A ghost?

His neck slowly craned toward Jenkins. "What . . . what was that, Detective?" he asked, voice crackling like a piece of bacon on a hot skillet. "What did you say?"

Jenkins took David in, all of him. His sagging shoulders. Glassy, saturated eyes. Twitchy, nervous mannerisms. The drumming of his fingers on the bar top. Over the years in law enforcement, he'd grown accustomed to sizing people up, citizens and criminals alike. Knowing how to crack the most tight-lipped perp, labeling them, pinning them. Sometimes, and he knew this was a character flaw, he could no longer differentiate between the two (citizens and criminals). But as he sat there on the stool staring at David Miller—the middle school English teacher with the messy auburn hair, the same man who just learned his blind date from last evening had been murdered—he realized the truth. This wasn't a man hiding something or obstructing justice. Nor was it some punk kid lying to the cops. This was a man dripping with need and worry.

"Hey, settle down, son. Settle down. Let's get something in you. Calm those nerves." Jenkins called the waitress over, grabbing her attention with his brash voice. "Doll, can we get two coffees? Black."

Minutes later, David cupped a mug with both hands, the heat radiating into his palms. Steam sifted from the opening, filling his nose with the sweet memories of Sundays when he was married. Those mornings they had lain on the couch, loving every moment with one another. The laughs, the playful tickles under the afghan.

"Hey, I know I spooked you earlier," Jenkins said, pulling David from his thoughts. "But I need to know what's really going on here."

"What do you mean? You said you wanted to meet. Said you had some *interesting details* for me regarding the text message."

"I do. I do. That's for sure." Jenkins sipped from his own mug, the scalding tar sliding down his throat. "They phoned me about an hour ago, IT. That text message you received last night at 2:17 a.m. is one hundred percent from her phone."

David's stare tightened, his reddened eyes desperate for answers. "What does that mean, Detective? If she was already dead, who texted me from her phone?"

"Honestly," Jenkins started, "we don't know. The victim's cell—"

Her name was Amelie.

"—hasn't been located, but we know the message you received last night was from that phone. We've installed a tracker in the network that will alert us when it is next powered on or used. Unfortunately, the device has been offline since 2:18 a.m. Last ping was the same area where we found the victim." He shook his head at the thought. "If someone uses it again, we'll know where and when, and then we can catch the son of a bitch."

David couldn't respond. He sat there zombie-like, eyes glued to the man with the silver mane.

"So the bigger question now, Mr. Miller, is who sent you the text and why?" His detective mode flipped back on, yet this version lacked the intensity. It carried more weight in understanding than indictment. "First, let's focus on the who."

"Who?" David asked, voice barely audible.

"We may be dealing with the murderer here, Mr. Miller. I need you to understand the seriousness of this matter. Do you or the victim have any enemies? Anyone in the city who has ill feelings toward either of you?"

"No. Not that I'm aware of. I can't really speak for Amelie, but my peers, they respect me. My students and parents too."

"An old grudge from the past. Someone you haven't thought about in a while? Years possibly."

David's gaze dropped to his lap. His fingers drummed on his thigh while he thought about the question.

"Anyone who might want to get inside your head? Mess with you?" Jenkins asked.

David locked eyes with the man. "I've always had friends, and others have always liked me. I was never the most popular, but I never felt the sting of someone disliking me. Except..."

"Except what, Mr. Miller?"

David chewed on his cheek. "I'm recently divorced. It's kind of messy."

Jenkins delivered a nod. "Is your ex-wife the kind to hold grudges, son? The type that might take a screwdriver or blade to a set of tires? Hurt someone?"

"No, no," David replied, shaking his head. "Maggie would never do something like that. She's a kind soul. Heart of gold."

Jenkins offered a meek smile. "My mother was much like that, son. A shiny, golden pedestal rising above the rest." The detective's eyes brightened, a flash of warmth swimming in the lake of gray. "But you brought up your ex-wife for a reason."

David released a sigh. "She's the only person I've ever hurt, Detective."

"I understand. Do you think she could be behind this? Any of it?"

"No, no. Not at all. It can't be her. She'd never stoop so low. Too much morality runs through her veins. She's a firm believer in speaking up and hashing out issues."

"I see. I see. If you don't mind me asking, what grounds fueled the divorce?"

A blanket of somberness and shame covered David, cradling him up to his nape. Despite the privacy it deserved, someone had leaked their divorce to social media. Broadcasting it to the masses. If the detective wanted to find out what happened, it was out there for the plucking.

"I'd rather not say. I'm not very proud of it, and speaking about it reopens the wound, sir."

Jenkins left it alone, seeing how it affected him. "I understand. You said her name was Maggie, right? Maggie Miller?"

"Yeah," David confirmed. "You probably would know her by face. She's a local celebrity. She's on your television nightly at six o'clock."

The connection flipped on like a light switch. "Maggie Miller. Channel 23?"

David answered the question with a simple nod.

Jenkins sipped his coffee, a network of thoughts and ideas railroading through his mind. He sat there, the sudden break in conversation throwing coal in the engine.

"Hey," David called out seconds later, breaking the moment of peace. "Are you by any chance going to communicate with her in any way? I promise you, Detective, she has nothing to do with this."

Jenkins listened to the plea, could see the concern in David's eyes, but due diligence was required here. He couldn't leave any stone unturned. "This is an open investigation, Mr. Miller, and as of now, we know bupkes. I'm sure your ex-wife has nothing to do with this, but we need to follow up on every lead. Even ones that will ultimately lead nowhere. Which I'm sure this will."

"Okay," David agreed. "I get it. I understand. But . . . where do we go from here?"

"What do you mean?"

David shifted on the stool. "What happens next? Is there anything I can do, or should do?"

"As of now, Mr. Miller, you need to go home, try to rest, and take your mind off this. I know that won't be easy, I do, but nothing will benefit from you fretting about this. We're only ankle-deep in the investigation, so we'll find out what's going on. We'll make the connection between the victim—"

Amelie.

"—and the text, if there is one. And honestly, son, I doubt these two events are related. I think someone is just having a laugh."

The words should have brought some relief, but David deflected each like a soldier's shield on the battlefield. "Should . . . should I be worried, Detective? Am I in danger?"

Jenkin's face cooled to ice, the warmth of assurance crystallizing into a layer of frost. He didn't want to spook David, usher in any ill thoughts that would feed the dread, but he couldn't lie to the man either. "I don't know for sure, son, but my gut feeling says there is nothing to worry about. But, it also suggests the use of caution. Until we know for sure, keep your head on a swivel. Be aware of your surroundings. Know what I mean?"

He did, but it brought little comfort his way. Was there someone out there, someone with a grudge, someone toying with him? Was it Amelie's killer? The latter shook him to his core.

"I have to run, Mr. Miller," Jenkins said. "But we'll be in contact." The detective stood and reached into his billfold, tossing a five-dollar bill on the counter.

"Are you sure there's nothing I can do? Anything?"

"Just go home, son. Try to take your mind off this. Read a book, play a game. Something to exorcise the stress and worry from your thoughts. Occupy your mind."

David watched as the detective sauntered away, his lean silhouette vanishing through the diner's glass doors. He sat there for another thirty minutes, watching those doors, wondering what was waiting for him on the other side. Was there anything to worry about? Was this just a sick game of someone intent on screwing with him? He couldn't decide. But eventually, he left the 24th Street Cafe, making a beeline to his car after thanking the waitress. He didn't know why, but he felt like someone or something was following him as he drove back to his apartment.

VII

2015

Darkness consumed the warehouse, breathing and pulsing with malevolent intent. It swallowed the faint slivers of warmth that dared penetrate the boarded windows, leaving only a blackness in its wake. Like a virus, it spread to every corner, every crevice, every forgotten space. The gloom infected each room, each corridor, poisoning the structure's very foundation like a modern-day epidemic.

The building groaned under the weight of its own decay, settling deeper into the earth with each passing hour. Somewhere in the walls, pipes leaked their metallic tears, creating a symphony of drips. The air itself felt thick, contaminated with years of neglect.

But deep within the structure's bowels, down the groaning rusted industrial staircase, through the waterlogged hall where black mold meandered in intricate patterns, and past the basement's padlocked steel door, something stirred in the suffocating darkness.

From inside this concrete tomb, a faint glow illuminated the basement, shining through the cloud of dust that floated in the stagnant air. The dim radiance highlighted the abandoned bookshelves, filled not with literature but with scribbled notebooks. Printouts of profile pictures littered the desktop, the subjects' smiles frozen and damning. But the light also highlighted something else. Someone, actually.

He sat hunched in a chair that had molded itself to his form through countless hours of searching. His pale skin taking on the sickly blue pallor of screen light. His dull eyes, bloodshot and rimmed with exhaustion, swept over the glowing rectangle like a predator searching for prey. A rhythmic *click-click-click* punctuated the silence as his forefinger scrolled, sifting through the endless Facebook feed like a digital rosary of judgment.

His breathing was shallow, controlled, almost meditative. Each exhale carried with it a whispered fragment of Scripture, verses about punishment and purification that he'd memorized in childhood. The words escaped his cracked lips like incantations, blessing his unholy work.

He made mental notes of the names, the profiles that triggered something deep in his brain, something that had been cultivated by years of isolation. Before him lay the digital menu of human frailty, and he could almost taste the fear, almost smell the tears as he searched for her.

From somewhere within the darkness above, a woman's scream rang out, raw and primal, its echo striking plaster and drywall before dying. The sound was followed by muffled pleading, words that might have been prayers. Yet, he was unmoved by the disruption, his focus unwavering. Her time would come soon enough. But first, he had another to find.

The endless scrolling suddenly stopped, the wheel's hypnotic clicking ceasing like the dead. A heavy silence filled the room, broken only by the distant sound of chains rattling somewhere in the darkness above. His tongue darted out to his thin lips, an unconscious tic that surfaced whenever the hunger surfaced.

Is this her?

He sat there, hunched forward, transfixed by the profile he'd found. The treasure he'd unearthed. His eyes—pale blue and shot through with yellow veins—danced along the screen, moving past the profile image with reverent slowness, ingesting every detail of the biography below it: thirty-three, single, mother of two.

His bottom lip trembled, not with emotion but with anticipation. The thick, suffocating void of the basement expired as his stare shot back to the photo, and for a moment, he could already see it. The blood, the flames.

Single mother. The words rolled around in his mind. A *tsk-tsk* followed the thought, but the judgment rode alongside an electric thrill. It justified his plan, his purpose. She had chosen this path, and now she would face the consequences.

Heavy breathing replaced the silence, slicing through the still air. The newfound excitement fled to his extremities, making his fingers twitch and his toes curl inside his oversized boots. His pulse raced with a rapid beat that pounded in his chest. The endorphins flooding his veins pulsed and quaked, awakening the dormant monster from its restless slumber.

Weeks had passed since his last act of divine intervention, the memory fading like old photographs but never truly out of reach. The urge had festered deep within during the quiet times, stirring about like a blind crab scuttling across the ocean floor of his consciousness, a constant reminder of his holy responsibility.

But now, the insistent need to cleanse and rectify surged back with force, a tidal wave of divine urgency that threatened to drown him in its righteousness. It was overpowering, magnificent in its clarity, and he was helpless to suppress it any longer. Nor did he want to.

His finger went back to work with renewed purpose, scrolling through her photos. The images she had carelessly scattered across cyberspace for anyone to find, anyone to judge. Twenty-five to thirty pictures were there, teasing him, pulling him along like a puppet master: a shaggy-haired dog in a Halloween costume (vanity in all its forms), countless selfies posing with Starbucks cups (gluttony and pride), her two sons (bastards born in sin), and the truly damning vacation collection titled *Spring Break, Pismo Beach, 2013*.

She was wearing a red bikini that might as well have been woven from the fires of hell itself.

It's her. The certainty settled over him like a shroud.

After clicking on the first vacation photo, the image expanded and filled the screen. He cocked his head, studying it with intensity, devouring every pixel, every shadow, every curve that proved her guilt. "The single mother of two," as he had christened her in his mind, lay on her stomach, elbows dug into the warm sand, her hands supporting her chin in a pose that screamed seduction.

A flirtatious grin beamed his way through the monitor, reaching across cyberspace to mock him with its shameless confidence. The angle, innocent as she probably thought it was, revealed just enough flesh to confirm his initial thoughts. *Impure and soiled.*

Scrolling to the right, a new image appeared. The pose added another charge to her indictment. The single mother of two waded through the tide, her reddened flesh sprinkled with the dying sunlight. Two young boys flanked her sides, their souls stained by association. The youngest, clutching his mother's hand with the trust that only children possess, stared wide-eyed at the camera.

From his vantage point behind the screen, he could see how the left side of her bikini bottoms had shifted, revealing a subtle tan line that might as well have been a map. The sight made his breathing shallow, made his vision narrow to focused rage.

He sat there for minutes, staring at her, memorizing her carefree smile, her nonchalant laugh that he could almost hear echoing through the monitor. It was a sickening display, nauseating in its casual dismissal of moral law. Children born out of wedlock were abominations according to the Scriptures. And repercussions were just around the bend: pain, misery, and hellfire after she drew her final breath.

Mumbles leaked from his mouth, incoherent syllables that gradually formed into fragments of biblical verse. The sounds echoed through the concrete chamber, pitch heightening with each recitation as his excitement grew. A repetitious chant jumbled together like a looping, run-on sentence, a mantra of justification that had guided him through his previous act of salvation.

The words gained strength, became a prayer, became a promise. Again and again, the litany broke the silence of his underground cathedral, building to a crescendo that made the very walls seem to vibrate with anticipation.

And then, with sudden finality, the chanting ceased.

His eyes, wide and gifted with new life, darted to the pad of paper lying on the desk beside a collection of newspaper clippings. With the careful penmanship of a monk, he wrote:

Deuteronomy 23:2.

She must burn.

The words seemed to glow on the page in the screen's pale light, a death sentence crafted with biblical authority. Above, another scream pierced the darkness, weaker now, more resigned. He ignored it as well.

Soon, it would be her time.

VIII

Tuesday Morning, May 12, 2015

After a grueling weekend that bled into Monday, Detective Jenkins and the others sat around the conference table sharing evidence and theories on the Amelie Rodriguez murder. The regular perps in the city were each mentioned, but nothing seemed to stick. Their largest leap came when the victim's apartment complex delivered the CCTV footage from the parking lot.

Detective Angela Barrientos ripped open the envelope it was mailed in, holding the disc out for all to see. "This is it, boys." As she moved toward the television cart, she presented it dramatically, much like a model from a game show would. "Grab your popcorn and get ready to solve this case."

With the playful display, Anzilotti flung a few catcalls her way, but Jenkins quickly put an end to it with a stare; his fiery gray eyes turned up to broil.

"Just play the damn video, Barrientos," he demanded, irritation sticking to every syllable. "We don't have time for this shit."

She locked eyes with him, feeling the heat from his stare. "Yeah, you got it, boss." A tinge of sarcasm stuck to each word as she placed the disc in the DVD player tray. She claimed a seat a few chairs away from Johnson, squeezing the remote in a death grip.

The screen bloomed to life seconds later, showcasing a recorded shot of the victim's parking lot. A timestamp hung in the lower right-hand corner that read *8:23 p.m.*

The four detectives leaned forward in their chairs, focused on the video. There wasn't much to see, though. The video displayed a parking lot light buzzing with frenzied moths. It cast a dim illumination on the space below. The back ends of three vehicles were there. To the left of the cars was a motorcycle, parked diagonally in the fourth stall.

"Is this it?" Anzilotti asked, his hands held out at his sides, palms up.

Barrientos glared at him. "*Shhh*. Keep watching, man."

Seventeen seconds in, motion appeared from the right. A woman came into the frame, walking across the asphalt. She had a tall, slender build with jet-black hair cascading down her back. Her form-fitting floral dress revealed a peek of bronze skin with each stride.

As she reached the third vehicle, she rummaged through the purse she carried, removing what must have been car keys. A tick of the clock later, the vehicle's trunk was open, and more motion appeared from the right. A figure clad in black from head to toe emerged from the shadows. Something long and metallic was in the perp's hand. The tip sparkled under the lighting. The assailant advanced quickly, closing the distance between the two before striking the woman in the head with the weapon it gripped. She never saw it coming. Her limp body crumpled to the ground twenty-three seconds into the clip.

"Pause it, pause it," Jenkins called out.

Barrientos did just that, extending the remote toward the cart. The screen paused, capturing a lurking figure hovering over a body lying on the ground. A black hoodie hid its face in a veil of darkness.

"Rewind it. Back to the beginning," Jenkins said, authority strangling his syntax.

They all watched as the screen reversed before it stopped on its own. Barrientos pressed play again, and they all consumed a second helping of the violent feast.

During which, Anzilotti broke the silence. "Crowbar?"

"Nah, my money's on a lead pipe," Barrientos countered before they watched the victim's body fall to the ground again.

This time, as the perp stood over the lifeless victim lying on the ground, Jenkins didn't call out to stop the action. The video continued. Grueling seconds passed, anticipation permeating the room while the assailant hovered there, possibly admiring their handiwork. But as the timestamp changed to *8:24 p.m.*, the figure dressed in black fled in the direction from which it had appeared, out of the frame to the right.

Disturbed looks shot through the room as the video continued, each member not knowing what was to come, but less than a minute later, the pulse of red taillights filled the area the perp had fled. Following the crimson glow came the back end of a vehicle, maybe a foot of it in frame. The car had a vintage look to it. Square fenders and chrome accents. Rusted out and oxidized too. A classic in its day, but a junker by any means now.

Seconds later, the perp's black silhouette reappeared in the footage and opened the car's trunk. He then strolled to the left, heaved the victim up off the unforgiving ground, and carried her on one shoulder. It was an effortless act done with precision and strength. Her limp body ended its journey in the claustrophobic confines of the trunk. After closing the lid, the perp rounded the vehicle. That's when the taillights reengaged, and the car drove out of sight. The video ended a breath later.

"That's it, right?" Anzilotti asked, his stare moving from detective to detective. "That's all we've got?"

Barrientos sighed. "Yup, that's all we have to work with."

"It's a start!" Jenkins exclaimed, leaving the comfort of his seat. He stood in front of them, hands perched on the tabletop. He looked at each person, holding their attention with his intense gray eyes. "It might not be much, but it's what we have to go on. So put on your fuckin' detective hats and let's get to work."

The intense demand blanketed the room.

Being the man's partner, Barrientos had felt Jenkins's wrath a handful of times and wasn't a fan. She looked up to him as a mentor, but his fiery side always left a bitter taste in her mouth. "All right. I'm guessing the perp is male," she stated, choosing to stand as well. Better to follow suit than ripple the pond. "Medium build."

"Good. That's good. What else do we have? What about the car?" Jenkins asked.

"I'm thinking of the late seventies Cadillac my old man had growing up." The group's attention turned to Anzilotti. He rubbed his shaved head as he spoke, "You know, square fenders and large, rectangular taillights."

"Yeah, but what we just viewed wasn't a single, solid taillight." The new voice came from Johnson, the youngest member of the investigation department.

They all turned and gave him their full attention, surprise and interest evident on their faces.

Usually passive and reserved, the twenty-six-year-old returned their stares.

"Go on, Johnson." Jenkins's voice cut through the tension, encouraging the young man.

Johnson blew out a breath, feeling the sets of eyes boring into him. He knew it came with the profession, but being the center of attention always made his skin crawl. "Um, you may have overlooked it, but the car's taillights are separated into five distinct pieces."

"What are you saying, Johnson?" Barrientos asked.

"I'm saying those taillights . . . they're unique. Different." He swallowed, pushing down the fluttering butterflies in his gut. "What I'm trying to say is, the red plastic shield isn't a solid piece. It's five parallel pieces stacked on top of one another. And to my knowledge, only one car ever had that look."

"And what car is that?" Jenkins asked.

"I think it's a Plymouth Grand Prix, sir. My grandmother had one."

2

Three hours later, Jenkins slammed the phone down hard enough to rattle the coffee mug perched on the edge of his desk. The DMV records yielded exactly what

Johnson had predicted: three late-seventies-era Plymouth Grand Prix vehicles registered within the city limits, each one a potential key to unlocking Amelie's murder.

"Barrientos!" he barked across the room. "Come over here for a minute."

She approached with cautious steps, recognizing the storm brewing behind his gray eyes. "What do we have?"

"Three cars. Three owners." Jenkins grabbed a manila folder and flipped it open, revealing the DMV printouts. "Margarette Kowalski, forty-seven, lives at 512 Height Street on the East Side. A recluse by nature, according to neighbors. She never leaves the house, keeps the drapes pulled. Rarely seen at all. Weighs in at about three-hundred-plus pounds according to her license renewal eight years ago."

Barrientos raised an eyebrow. "Hard to picture her hauling a body around. The perp in the video was tall but not wide."

"I had a unit drive by the address." Jenkins continued. "The car wasn't there. The property looked abandoned. Eviction notices covered the front door. It appears the housing authority has condemned the home. The car and Margarette Kowalski are nowhere to be found.

"I think we can rule that one out, Jenkins. We're not looking for a three-hundred-pound killer."

"My thoughts exactly." Jenkins turned to the second page. "Then we've got Harold Finch, fifty-six, postal worker. The vehicle's been sitting in his garage for the past eleven years, according to the neighbor I spoke with. Doesn't run. A lifelong project that's stalled for years because of finances."

"All right, and the third?"

Jenkins's jaw tightened as he read the final entry. "River 'Rio' Ramirez, thirty-five, just got out of Lerdo Correctional three months ago. Did a nickel for possession with intent." He looked up, meeting her eyes. "And get this, his last known address puts him six blocks from the victim's apartment complex."

Barrientos felt her pulse quicken. "That's a hell of a coincidence."

"Indeed it is." He beamed, knowing exactly what she was thinking.

"Field trip time?" she asked, mirroring his look.

"You're driving."

IX

Monday Evening, May 18, 2015

The past nine days were a blur. David eased back into his regular life, trying to put the events of that dreadful Saturday behind him. After taking a few days off from work, he returned to the classroom. The steady demands of teaching, grading, and lesson planning preoccupied his mind. Routine, routine, routine. And it was a good thing.

On two occasions, he tried to contact Detective Bennett Jenkins to get some insight, but his calls always went straight to voicemail. The man never returned his call, a silence that David interpreted as a stall of progress in the investigation. But which investigation? Amelie's murder or the phantom text message? He considered the lack of news to be a good omen. He had nothing to worry about.

During this period, his mind still looped to the woman in the alley—Amelie, his date on that Friday night—but the sting that bored into him like a javelin slowly faded.

His mind wasn't perfect, but it was healing, mending back true to form.

Jenna came around, checking on him, delivering groceries and everyday necessities. Her presence, whether she knew it or not, pulled him from the pit he had climbed into.

A semblance of normalcy had resurfaced.

Until...

Late on this Monday night, David sat alone on his plaid couch, watching reruns of *Friends*. He and his ex-wife loved that sitcom. Every week, as soon as the new episode aired, they would gather to watch their favorite characters: Joey, Chandler, Monica, Rachel, Ross, and Phoebe.

A collection of empty beer bottles and a pizza box littered the coffee table in front of him. Laughter filled the space with each classic one-liner.

Nostalgia. Carefree nostalgia.

During a commercial break, he felt a sudden vibration from deep within his pocket. Expecting a call from Jenna, he reached in and pulled out the phone. The screen illuminated his face in pastel light. His eyes, droopy from the beers and dim lighting, widened at the sight, and an avalanche of fear collapsed on him. He felt like he couldn't breathe.

Amelie's number appeared. But it wasn't a phone call. Another text awaited his panicked eyes.

The phone slipped from his grasp. Time seemed to slow as he watched it free-fall, a tumbling hunk of metal and glass. It landed in his lap, face up, staring at him with a message from the dead.

Instinctively, he swatted the device away, and it fell onto the matted carpet under his feet. He could no longer see it. Yet, like a marionette controlled by a puppet master, he felt his torso lean forward, peering over the couch's edge. Slowly, the phone came into view, and he could feel it calling his name. A chant that pounded with intent, forcing his will.

Against his better judgment, and despite every synapse firing and ordering him to stop, he picked it up.

With his pulse racing like a Thoroughbred, his thumb pressed down on the green messages icon. It was another picture. Or was it the same? He didn't know it, but stark differences were present. The first image he received nine days ago was a tapestry of pixels, indecipherable by even the local forensics technicians. This new picture, however, had some of the same qualities—the jumbled squares, the distinct color patterns—but this image's resolution was clearer. His eyes didn't deceive him. The figure was blurry, but the outline of a face was unmistakable. A face with blonde hair. His breath hitched in his chest at the sight, and the icy fingers of death slid up his spine.

Blackness encroached, an invading tether inching closer from every direction. Before he succumbed to the dark, his eyes took in something that wasn't possible. The world knew about his marital problems thanks to the internet and Facebook, but outside of his wife and Jenna, few knew the other woman's name. The woman he had cheated on his wife with. A single act of infidelity shattered his marriage and his life. But there, plain as day, was the woman's name right above the picture.

Heather Stoneheuer.

Part Two

X

Monday Night, May 18, 2015

A sliver of moonlight filtered into the bedroom through the sheer curtains. It crept along the windowsill and the wooden floorboards, casting a faint beam that ended at the bed. The bed where Jenkins lay.

With the weight of a twelve-hour shift heavy on his shoulders, he left the precinct and drove home. Exhaustion had hijacked his body, aching bones and joints protesting for rest, yet sleep evaded him. He lay there on his mattress, staring at the smoke-stained ceiling, his mind running a marathon.

Why did he burn her? Why leave her in the alley? The verse? How are they all connected?

As the night deepened and the sleep he needed neared, a sound, shrill and invasive, shattered the silence that cradled him.

Ring ring.

The deafening peal came from the front room.

Sweeping his legs from the tangle of sheets, he sat on the bed's edge, staring through the bedroom door, slightly ajar. The floor was cool on his bare feet. After a third sequence, the ringing ceased.

A hush fell, and in the quiet, he felt a sense of peace settle over him.

"Wrong number, I guess?" he mumbled. No one ever called this line. Few even had the number.

As the last word fell from his lips, the beast sitting on a desk in the front room screamed once more.

Ring ring.

With his heart hammering like a drum, he exited the bedroom. Staggering down the dark hallway, he used the wall as a crutch. The soft moonlight that pierced his bedroom was absent, leaving only shadowy silhouettes signaling familiarity. After he crossed the threshold, he approached the corner where the desk sat. On top of it was a telephone. A pulsing red light accompanied each wail.

"Jenkins here," he said into the handset, his voice hoarse.

"Detective Jenkins!" The voice was distraught, agitation melding with relief. "Detective, can you hear me?"

"Who the hell is this?" Jenkins asked.

"Detective. It's David Miller."

Jenkins pulled the handset away from his ear, staring at the caller ID. A local number met his glare, 661 area code. "Miller, how'd you get this number? This is my home."

"I'm really sorry," David answered, his voice racing. "But I have to speak to you, Detective. I've left voicemails on your cell and your office phone, but you've returned none of them."

"Ah, shit," Jenkins said, his old friend guilt resurfacing. He'd heard David's voicemails, but he had nothing to report. "If you're looking for updates on the case, I have nothing to share. When we know more, the press will know, and you'll know, Mr. Miller."

"Detective, I'm not looking for an update," David said, barely letting the man finish. "I have something to tell you." A pause lingered, the only sound being faint breathing through the earpiece. "No, that's not right. I have something to show you, sir."

"What is it, Miller? What do you have to show me?" Jenkins asked.

"It . . . it happened again."

"What happened, son? What?"

"I received another text."

2

Within the hour, both men sat in a booth at the 24th Street Cafe. The hustle and bustle from the dinner rush died long ago, leaving only a sparse few to trickle in and out of the front doors. The usual lively energy was absent, replaced by a calm that was a stark contrast to David. He sat there, dilated eyes, fidgety, while the detective looked at the new image.

"Did you text back?" Jenkins asked.

"Hell no. I was too spooked," David answered.

"Good. Let's keep it that way."

"Think I should delete the messages?" David scratched his chin. Ever since this message came through with Heather's name on it, he had wanted to delete it, erase all of it from his thoughts. If it wasn't there to torment him, maybe it couldn't ignite the bonfire raging within his skull. "Should I block the number?"

"No, I wouldn't do that," Jenkins answered. "We still don't know what's happening here, son."

"Okay. Do you think it's the same picture?" David asked.

The detective's eyes pierced the screen, turning the phone sideways and zooming in on the pixelated image, scrutinizing every detail. He didn't answer the question.

"There's a face there, right?" David continued. "A nose, two eyes, blonde hair."

"It is possible," the detective stated, never averting his gaze. He couldn't leave the man dangling for too long. He zoomed out using his thumb and index finger. "Yeah, I think you're right."

David came here hoping for solace, but the detective's assurance slammed into him like a speeding semi. "Whose face is it?" he asked, his voice quavering.

Jenkins lowered the phone, taking in the man sitting across from him, then put it down on the table. "That's what we need to figure out. There's an underlying reason these messages keep invading your life. Somewhere hidden within this picture is the answer. The person sending these texts may be in the picture, or, on a darker note, the person shown may be a target. If it's the latter, I think we should start with the name attached to it." Jenkins paused, the dying embers in his glare stoked to a blaze. "Who is Heather Stoneheuer?"

Hearing that name was like a kick to the groin. It was a painful reminder of the "mistake"—his infidelity. "She's, uh—" David hesitated, knowing what he was about to say could discredit him. But he had to relive the shame if they were going to find out what the hell was happening. "I slept with her about nine months ago, Detective. One night that I'm not proud of, but it happened. It shattered my marriage, turning my life upside down. I'm still recovering."

Jenkins listened, collecting the fragments and piecing them together. He held his tongue, only delivering a subtle nod.

"We met at my school." David continued. "She was an intern, shadowing the site's psychologist. Young, smart, charismatic. Pretty."

"How'd it happen, Mr. Miller?" Jenkins asked, his gravelly voice smooth around the edges.

Shame wrapped its paws around David, twisting and squeezing his core. "On the occasional Friday afternoon, a group of us goes for drinks after school lets out. We call it 'Spanish lessons.' Just a stupid code name so the kids don't know what we're talking about. A way to celebrate surviving another week in the pits. Know what I mean?" He felt nauseous sharing the details.

"Yeah, yeah. I do," Jenkins agreed. "The other detectives and I do that sometimes after we solve a case."

"Anyway," David started, "she was there, and I suppose we both had had too many drinks. Allowing the liquor to influence our decisions. It started as innocent flirting. It was a stupid choice, and I'll never get over it, Detective. It's really hard to look in the mirror sometimes because I hate myself for the choice I made that night."

"I understand. I do," Jenkins responded. "That pain will sit with you and rot. It'll eat at you. Pick you clean down to your skin and bones, son. I know from experience."

David didn't want to pry; he could sense unease in the detective's words and gestures.

"So where is this woman now?" Jenkins asked.

"After the infidelity went public, thanks to some assholes on the internet and Facebook, she left town," David stated, his mind leaping back to that night and back to the day his wife discovered the truth. "She's up north somewhere. I think she has family in Fresno."

"She ran from the scandal, huh?" Jenkins thought about it for a second. "Can't really blame her there. I'm sure some negativity poured her away from your wife, her family."

"She bore the brunt of it. She did. But she was out of the picture before too many discovered who she was. And I've kept her name out of this for almost a year, Detective. Almost a year. My wife—" David paused and cleared his throat. "Sorry. My ex, Maggie, has done the same. It's too embarrassing and a blemish on her career."

"I see." Jenkins nodded. "So why is Heather's name attached to that image on your phone?"

David's eyes glazed over. "That's where I need your help. I don't know. I really don't."

"Think she's back in town?" Jenkins raised an eyebrow. "Maybe she fled, pulled the stinger out, and now she's ready for revenge because of the embarrassment."

David sat there, trying to form the words. Once the one-night stand had been leaked, he barely spoke to Heather. Their few conversations were terse and emotional, marked by accusation. She blamed him, just like the city blamed her. The situation crushed her. Her wails still rang out when he closed his eyes at night. *I'm ruined. I'm ruined. My career is over. My life is over, David.*

"Highly unlikely."

"How so?" Jenkins asked.

"When she left town, she was a mess," David stated, running a hand through his hair. "Everyone went after her. It was terrible." He paused and shook his head. "They went after me, too, but the few who knew her name dragged her through the mud. She was so humiliated. She left town, and she's never coming back."

"I've worked on these cases for thirty-plus years, son. Nearly as long as you've been alive." Jenkins leaned across the table, the fire in his eyes igniting. "I've learned a thing or two along the way. Here's a bit of wisdom: never doubt vengeance. The most innocent citizen can surprise you. When shame, guilt, embarrassment, and hatred percolate then boil over, anything's possible."

David delivered a meek nod. "I'm sure you're right, but I honestly don't think Heather has anything to do with this. I really don't."

"I hope your intuition is correct, Mr. Miller," Jenkins countered. "I do. But it's a lead. We're going to look into her just in case. Can't leave a stone unturned."

David released a sigh, the air blowing out the *O* of his mouth. "I understand, Detective."

Jenkins shifted on the booth seat. "I appreciate you sharing the details of that story. That can't be easy to revisit."

David didn't respond, holding his tongue as the memories flashed through his mind.

"Now that we've discussed the other woman, let's dive back into the deep end, shall we?" Jenkins's stare drew to David's cell phone lying on the table. "If this new picture is a face, a face with blonde hair, who in your life could it be? Does Heather's hair match the color?"

"No, Detective. She's not a blonde." David shook his head from side to side as he answered. "Not as I remember her anyway. She had red hair that stopped just below her nape. Most would describe her as a ginger."

A dye job? Jenkins wondered.

"Okay, so who else in your life has blonde hair?" Jenkins asked, his tone deepening. "I need to look into anyone close to you. Anyone at all. We don't know what game is being played here."

David bit his cheek. His stare locked on the phone. After a few heartbeats, he answered, "My wife, sir. Excuse me. My ex-wife. Maggie has blonde hair."

Jenkins's eyes narrowed. His thoughts drifted to the news broadcast he watched occasionally. *Maggie Miller. She has blonde hair? Could that be a picture of her? Did she send it? Can she pull something like this off?*

"Would she want to hurt you, Mr. Miller?" Jenkins asked, flushing away his thoughts. "I know you said the divorce was messy, and the ordeal was humiliating. Think she's looking for revenge, for vengeance?"

"I broke her heart, Detective. I know that. My actions humiliated and betrayed her. But she's not one to go after others. She's kind, considerate, and thoughtful. She couldn't hurt a fly. It's just not in her DNA. I think deep down, she still loves me."

"Like I said, wronged people are capable of anything. And I mean anything."

3

Both men left the diner at a quarter to midnight, yet neither could turn off the machines whirring within their skulls. They had answered nothing, hashed out nothing, and even more discrepancies remained. Who was the person in the picture? And more importantly, who is the person working in the shadows sending the cryptic messages? Is it the same person? Maggie Miller? Heather Stoneheuer? Or someone else?

Jenkins returned to his two-bedroom home on the West Side, knowing that trying to sleep was fruitless. The wheels in his tired mind spun, greased and gleaming, pumping steam into the dark sky; a relentless rhythm that would keep him awake. Hours leaked into the new day while he slumped in his desk chair, excavating the internet and scouring details, collecting every shred of intel he could about the two women.

Maggie Miller was local, still living in the two-story home she and David had moved into after they were married. He couldn't find an ounce of dirt on the woman.

The young intern, however, would require some additional services to finish the investigation. She wasn't in Fresno, like David had guessed. Turlock was the city she resided in now. In late August of last year, after the scandal, she moved back into her childhood home with her widowed father. She landed a position at a local elementary school as a counselor, and as far as Jenkins could tell, she had moved on.

He'd still reach out to local authorities in the region. Have them poke their noses around a bit, stir up the dust. He had to know for sure, but it would have to wait until the sun rose.

Before the four o'clock hour presented itself, he was asleep in his chair, face-planted on the desktop's wood grain.

XI

512 Height Street
2004

A staleness clung to the air, the marination of urine and body sweat that stung the senses. It seeped into the floors, the ceiling, the guts of the home. Its pervasiveness multiplied, seemingly viral, showering all in a tight embrace. There was no escape.

The bedroom was dark. A single unshaded lamp in the corner cast the only light. Stagnant water trickled from the roof. Like a babbling brook, it dripped down the room's wall in a lazy stream. The flow pooled in a corner, swelling and rotting the baseboards. Blackened grime ate away at the wood. After years of neglect, a hole slowly formed at the joint. This is where it slept.

The eight-year-old watched with bright eyes, praying and hoping it would appear again. And disappointment rarely gnashed its teeth. With the dying sun, it finally emerged from its den, curious and hungry. Not right away, though.

The sounds were faint, so he pinned his ear to the wall, listening for it to wake. Clawing and scratching from within always signaled its return. Shaking off sleep, it scurried through the labyrinth of wires, insulation, and milled wood.

He backpedaled once the squeaks sounded. A droopy grin creased his face. A stream of saliva fell from his lips. He sat down in the room, legs crossed. Anticipation fattened with each passing moment, knowing it was coming.

From the shadows, it emerged. A pink nose penetrated the darkness. It sniffed the air, searching left and right. Rows of whiskers followed, bathed in the room's gloom. With hesitation, the head broke through the opening, carrying two black eyes and a set of rounded ears. The boy giggled at the sight.

A trail of crumbs marked a path across the soiled carpet. It was a welcoming invitation to his nightly guest. As it tasted the air, the tiny mouse crept forward, nimble paws collecting the morsels. Its elastic cheeks filled with each advance, bulging to capacity. A feast for the king within the walls.

He lived for this moment: the innocence, the imagination it brought. It was his only opportunity to be a child now that he lived here. Lived with her.

From birth, he was bounced around, a ward of the system. Foster families took him in, only to send him packing weeks or months later. A cycle of constant upheaval. But those days of uncertainty and the sleepless nights wondering who the strangers in the next room were—whether they were bad people—came to a crashing halt when Mother opened her doors. He didn't know how he had ended up there, but he was thankful.

His visitor continued along the path of crumbs, gobbling up every speck. It paused with each mouthful, chewing and scanning the room, its tiny whiskers twitching. Giddiness poured from him as he watched it inch close enough to touch. Tawny fur, a long pink tail, sparkling onyx eyes. All inches away. He hadn't selected a name for his little friend yet, but there were a few he was leaning toward. The name Frank, if the mouse was a male, made its rounds within his thoughts. Maybe that would be it.

The trail's end held the real bounty—a mound of crumbs the size of a penny. He spent a fraction of the afternoon collecting the bits. While Mother napped, he snuck out of his room, knowing how dangerous the act was. He knew he should have been reading, as she demanded. Tiptoeing alongside the warped baseboards, he crept past the snoring beast on the couch. He looked under the refrigerator and under the stove, scraping off dried pieces of food with his blackened fingernails.

The mouse (Penny, if it was a female) approached the pile with caution. Beady eyes danced between the treasure and the boy with the droopy grin. After an elongated pause, she discarded concern and started her feast.

A *creak* from the floorboard outside his room pulled him out of the moment. He jerked at the sound, whipping his head in that direction. The mouse fled the scene, retreating into its cavern. The boy's flesh crawled with goose bumps as he slowly raised himself off the floor, unable to look away from the door. He knew what was on the other side.

A blink later, the knob turned with a faint *click*, and the door opened, its hinges screaming with protest. A sliver of cold, dense blackness stole his attention as the door inched ajar. From the void, a voice echoed. One that brought forth an avalanche of fear, but somehow love as well.

"Kenny." The sound scraped the inside of his skull.

XII

Tuesday Afternoon, May 12, 2015

Barrientos guided the cruiser over to the curb and brought it to a halt. The engine ticked as it cooled, a metallic heartbeat in the stifling afternoon heat. "This is it: 605 Woodrow. Welcome to Oildale."

Detective Jenkins sat in the passenger seat, staring out the window at the residence they'd pulled up to. The rusted chain-link fence leaned at angles. His gray eyes swept over the knee-high brown grass that had died weeks ago and the trash strewn about the yard. "You sure this is it? Looks like a crack den."

"Charming, huh?" Barrientos mirrored his gaze, taking in the home's shabby exterior: the sagging siding that looked ready to collapse with the next strong wind and the chipped, peeling paint that revealed rotted wood underneath like exposed bone. A file folder rested in her lap, warm from the California sun streaming through the windshield. "Last known address according to parole. A neighbor across the street confirmed he still lives here. Said she sees that piece of shit Grand Prix coming and going at all hours."

"Think this is our guy? Or are we chasing a ghost?"

She lowered her sunglasses, revealing her determined dark eyes. "He fits the bill perfectly, Jenkins. And I mean perfectly. A laundry list of priors that reads like a criminal's greatest hits album."

"Refresh my memory," he said, cracking his knuckles. The sound was sharp in the confined space of the cruiser.

"River 'Rio' Ramirez is a real piece of work." She handed him the file. "His record started in his youth with petty theft and B and E. You know, the usual gateway crimes for future felons. But once he hit that magical number eighteen, his true skills started to shine, and he graduated to the major league." She took a sip from her water bottle, her throat dry from the heat. "Battery, multiple counts. Solicitation. Drug charges. Assault with a deadly weapon. Armed robbery. You name it, this piece of shit has done it. Been in and out of county and state facilities since he turned that age."

Jenkins thumbed through the folder, skimming the details and memorizing every aspect of the man's face. Specifically, the decades-old scar that ran from his left eyebrow down to his cheek like a lightning bolt carved in flesh. It was an unmistakable trademark he'd earned in a bar fight. According to the report, the other guy had needed forty-seven stitches and reconstructive surgery.

Are you our guy, Rio Ramirez? he wondered, studying the most recent mugshot. The man's dead eyes stared back at him with the flat, emotionless gaze of a career criminal.

"Hey, I don't see the car, though," Barrientos said, her stare drifting around the street. Beaters and jalopies peppered the curbside, but the distinctive rusty '78 Grand Prix was nowhere to be found. "Think he's home? Maybe lying low?"

Jenkins scanned the street again, noting the lack of activity. Too quiet for a Friday afternoon in Oildale. "Could be sleeping off a high. Could be long gone. Who knows." He closed the file with a *snap* that echoed in the car. "Only one way to find out. Let's go ruin this motherfucker's day."

"Right behind you, partner," she stated as she opened the door. A predatory smile appeared on her lips—the kind that said she lived for times like this.

***

Moments later, Jenkins rapped on the security screen; the distinct metal-on-metal sound traveled through the front yard. Almost immediately, a dog's bark rang out from inside the home—deep, agitated, and territorial. The sound was so fierce it forced him back a step, his hand instinctively moving closer to his service weapon.

He glanced behind him with a hint of apprehension swirling in his weathered features. Barrientos stood a few feet back on the concrete walkway, her posture alert and ready. Her eyes were scanning the windows for the telltale twitch of curtains or the glint of watching eyes. She saw neither.

"Rio Ramirez!" Jenkins called out, his voice cutting through the afternoon air and elevating over the dog's violent clamor. "Bakersfield Police Department! Open up! We need to have a conversation with you, and we're not going anywhere until we do!"

He delivered a second, more aggressive series of knocks that rattled the entire doorframe. The sound only intensified the animal's hostility; scratching now joined the guttural growls and barks.

No response.

"Rio! We know you're in there!" Jenkins shouted again, his patience wearing thin. "We can do this the easy way, or we can do this the hard way! Your choice!"

Still nothing.

As he turned and retreated a step, wiping sweat from his forehead, he noticed his partner's eyes flickering with alertness. Her stare was locked on the right window, her body language shifting into another gear.

He caught her eye and nodded in her direction. She reciprocated the gesture in silence, then held up one finger and pointed toward the window. The message was clear: someone was definitely home, moving around inside, and it wasn't just the four-legged beast.

He lifted his forefinger in the air and whirled it in a circular motion—their practiced signal for a flanking maneuver. Behind him, he could hear her footsteps as she made her way toward the side yard, her boots crunching on dead grass and broken glass. She knew the drill by heart: cover the back.

Stepping forward again, Jenkins approached the door with renewed purpose, ready to deliver another series of knocks. But he paused mid-stride when a voice suddenly sounded from inside the home, raspy and clearly agitated.

"Shut up, ya mangy fuckin' mutt! Quit your goddamn barkin'!"

Yelps from the animal followed. Then came the metallic sliding of a dead bolt being disengaged.

A second later, Jenkins watched the harsh afternoon light pierce through the gap in the security screen and land on the sullen, hollow-cheeked face of a short, disheveled woman. His right hand moved instinctively to hover near his sidearm.

"You da police?" the woman asked, peering through the narrow opening. Her throaty voice reminded him of boot soles dragging across gravel mixed with years of cigarettes. "Whatcha want?"

Never pulling his eyes away from her twitchy, paranoid gaze, Jenkins flashed his badge with practiced authority. "Detective Bennett Jenkins, Bakersfield PD. I'm looking for River 'Rio' Ramirez, miss. Is he home?"

Hearing the name sparked an immediate reaction. Her bloodshot eyes went wide with unmistakable concern, then quickly narrowed. She opened the screen door just enough to allow herself to look out into the yard and get a better read on Jenkins. "Ya lookin' for Rio? What for? He don't live here."

With the screen door slightly ajar, a nauseating cocktail of smells drifted in Jenkins's direction like a toxic cloud. Stale urine mixed with the acrid chemical stench of crack cocaine and methamphetamine. He had to fight not to gag as he observed her more clearly, noting the fresh track marks that dotted her arms and the purplish bruises that painted her paper-thin skin.

"He doesn't live here?" Jenkins pressed, his tone becoming more aggressive. "Are you sure? And before you think about lying to me, miss, I should mention that lying to a police officer during an active investigation is a felony. So carefully consider your next words."

The woman's beady, darting eyes skittered across the yard, taking in every detail. "No . . . no, he don't live here no more," she finally answered, clearing her throat. "Haven't seen him in weeks. Maybe a month. He moved out a while back."

Jenkins studied her face, reading the tells: the way her left eye twitched, how her voice went up half an octave, the way she couldn't maintain eye contact. Classic junkie behavior. "You know where I can find him? Because it's urgent that I speak to him. Real urgent."

The woman's head tilted forward, extending a few inches beyond the safety of the doorframe. Her paranoid gaze swept the yard again, taking in both the left and right sides. "Whatcha . . . whatcha need to talk to him 'bout?"

"Police business. That's all you need to know." Jenkins glanced to his right, wondering how Barrientos was doing, hoping she'd found a good position to watch the back exit. "Just let him know we're looking for him when you see him next. And trust me, lady, you'll see him."

She pulled back deeper into the safety of the shadowy interior; her stare hardening into a thin, defensive line. Fear and defiance warred in her expression. "Already told ya. He don't live here no more. Don't know where he went either. Maybe LA, maybe Fresno. Could be anywhere."

Jenkins delivered a cold, humorless smirk, backing away from the door slowly. "Thanks for all your help, miss. You've been really cooperative. Really helpful. I'm sure Rio will appreciate your loyalty when I catch up with him."

Without another word, she slammed the screen door hard enough to rattle the entire frame. The last sound Jenkins heard was the dead bolt's pin locking back into place as he walked toward the patrol car.

Barrientos joined him a minute later, jogging back from her reconnaissance mission around the property. Her face was flushed with heat and frustration.

"Anything?" Jenkins asked, lighting a cigarette. He leaned his body against the vehicle, the hot metal burning through his shirt.

"Struck out. The back door's locked up tight, bars on the windows," she said, wiping sweat from her forehead with the back of her hand.

Jenkins took a long drag, the nicotine helping to calm his nerves and clear the itch that festered. "Think he's in there? Playing hide-and-seek?"

"I don't know. Maybe." Barrientos squinted against the sun as she stared at the windows once more, looking for any sign of movement.

Where the fuck is this guy? Jenkins asked himself as he stared up into the cloudless sky.

"Hey," Barrientos said, interrupting his brooding thoughts. "Let's circle the block a few times. If that piece of shit is in this neighborhood, then that rolling disaster of a Grand Prix is somewhere close by too. That fuckin' *cacharro* sticks out like a sore thumb."

Jenkins stubbed out his cigarette in the gutter, the ember hissing as it died. "Let's roll. And if we spot that rust bucket, we box him in fast."

2

The patrol car rolled down a narrow back alley at a crawl, its tires crunching over broken glass and discarded needles. The sound filled the space with a symphony of poverty and crime. Overturned trash cans leaked their contents across the cracked asphalt, and garage doors served as canvases for an abundance of colorful graffiti.

Jenkins's gaze took in the destitution that infected this part of Bakersfield like a cancer. It spread out over a square mile, holding the unfortunate souls trapped here in its impoverished cycle—generation after generation, with no way out and no hope left.

Ahead, an open garage door came into view like a window to another world. As the car crawled along, he could see a group of young males inside—five, maybe six of them, each sporting the same shaved head.

One held a can of gold spray paint, huffing deeply at the fumes with the desperate intensity of someone trying to escape reality. His nostrils flared wide to capture every molecule of the intoxicating chemicals, and traces of metallic paint clung to his fingers. Another kid, who couldn't have been more than sixteen, paused mid-hit as his lips touched a glass pipe. The young man's dilated eyes fixed on the patrol car rolling past with predatory awareness.

The others in the group leered at the passing detectives, hostility and paranoia burning in their features. Their body language was tense, coiled like a viper, ready to strike. Jenkins could practically feel the hatred radiating from them in waves.

With the windows down, both Jenkins and Barrientos clearly heard the group's farewell calls.

"Fuckin' pigs!"

"Get the fuck out of our neighborhood!"

But the detectives ignored the taunts. Finding Rio Ramirez and his rusted-out '78 Grand Prix held their complete attention and priority. Everything else was just noise.

They circled the block a second time, moving like sharks through water, their trained eyes glued to the strangled neighborhood: the iron bars that guarded windows like prison cells, the pairs of sneakers hanging from telephone lines, the broken streetlights that would leave these streets in darkness when night fell.

But still no sign of the distinctive Grand Prix.

"Screw it," Barrientos said after their third pass yielded nothing. "Maybe our intel was wrong. Maybe the bastard really skipped town."

Considering the apparent failure, Barrientos brought the patrol car to a halt down the street from 605 Woodrow, positioning them with a clear view of the house but far enough away to avoid detection.

The two detectives sat there in tense silence for several minutes, each lost in their own thoughts, wondering if they were chasing a ghost. Yet in the next moment, just as defeat and frustration were ready to settle in, everything changed. Both detectives straightened in their seats as an old car lumbered down the road toward them, moving with a sluggish determination.

The vehicle left a trail of dark, oily smoke in its wake, creating a hazy effect under the harsh afternoon sun. The engine sounded like a dying animal. As the car drew nearer, the driver maneuvered it carefully to the side of the road, parking it just a few houses down from the target address.

Jenkins removed the eight-by-ten surveillance photo from the folder with hands that were suddenly steady with anticipation. He held it up beside the windshield, comparing every detail. Same rusted, oxidized orange paint and gray primer. Was it the right car?

"Let's hang tight for a minute," Jenkins stated, his gravelly voice hushed but electric with tension. "If that's our boy, let's give him a chance to settle in, get comfortable. Don't want to spook him before we're in position. The last thing we need is a foot chase through this shithole neighborhood."

Barrientos remained silent, her complete attention focused on the parked car and the silhouette of a man sitting behind the wheel. She lowered her sunglasses to get a better view, watching and waiting like a predator studying its prey.

Through the hazy windshield of the Grand Prix, they could see him shifting in his seat. The movements were nervous, paranoid—constant checks of the mirrors and frequent glances of the surrounding area.

After what felt like an eternity, he opened the driver's side door and spilled out into the sunny day. This was exactly who they were hunting.

Jenkins took in every detail of the man's appearance, methodically identifying and cataloging his features. Most importantly, the unmistakable scar that ran from his left eyebrow down to his cheek—a jagged white line that stood out against his sun-weathered skin.

"Well, hello there, Rio fuckin' Ramirez," Barrientos whispered from the driver's seat, her voice carrying a mixture of satisfaction and anticipation. "The pleasure is all mine, asshole."

Jenkins released a dry, humorless laugh, knowing she meant every single word. They'd been hunting this bastard for three hours, and now he'd walked right into their crosshairs.

They watched as Rio rounded the vehicle with the paranoid gait of a career criminal. He opened the trunk a breath later. A metallic *thud* echoed across the street as he closed it.

He slunk to the sidewalk carrying a black duffel bag that looked heavy and well-worn. Rio's constant, pressing scan of the neighborhood was clear in his body language as he surveyed his surroundings with heightened awareness.

"Wonder what's in the bag?" Jenkins mumbled, though they both had a pretty good idea. Nothing legal, that was certain.

Rio continued his trek toward 605 Woodrow, his strides laced with urgency but still maintaining the paranoid caution. But as he passed through the chain-link gate, his swift steps suddenly came to a complete halt.

He stood there on the cracked concrete walkway, his street-hardened glare fixed on the property's front door. He was clearly listening to someone—undoubtedly the woman they'd spoken to earlier, warning him about their visit through the security screen.

Even from that distance, they could see his body language change. His shoulders tensed, his head swiveled left and right, and his paranoid glances shot out like searchlights, taking in the neighboring yards and every parked car on the street. He grasped the duffel bag's handle tighter, his knuckles going white with tension.

"Shit," Jenkins breathed. "She's tipping him off."

And then, as if someone had fired a starting gun, Rio fled fast toward the street.

"Fuck! Let's go before we lose this piece of shit!" Jenkins exclaimed, his hand already on the door handle. Barrientos was a step ahead of him, bursting out of the driver's seat with the fluid motion of someone who'd done this dance a hundred times before.

"Rio Ramirez!" she shouted, her voice cutting through the afternoon air like a blade. "Bakersfield PD! We need to have a little talk!"

The man with the scar locked onto her immediately, his eyes going wide with the primal fear of a trapped animal. His shifty movements became more frantic as he studied the woman in the leather jacket who was advancing on him with obvious intent.

But Rio Ramirez had spent most of his adult life running from cops, and old habits die hard. In a flash of desperate movement, he darted through the yard, making a beeline toward the back of the house where he hoped to find salvation.

"Jenkins! We've got a runner!" Barrientos shouted, already in full pursuit, her boots pounding against the concrete. "He's heading for the back!"

The chase was on.

XIII

Tuesday Afternoon, May 12, 2015

Amped by the adrenaline coursing through her veins, Barrientos turned the corner of the house. She gripped her firearm in her fist, its barrel pointed diagonally at the ground. She made slow, cautious strides down the side yard, dry grass crunching underfoot. To her right, thorny rose bushes and the rough texture of a clothesline marked the property line. But the man she chased, River "Rio" Ramirez, had vanished.

With her heart thumping, she inched toward the backyard, stealing a look inside the windows she passed, but with each glance, her view redirected to what was in front of her. If a threat were coming, she'd meet it head-on.

As she reached the corner leading to the backyard, she paused, letting out the breath she held. She couldn't hear anything beyond, but that brought no comfort. Was he right on the other side, waiting to empty his clip into her chest or bludgeon her with an axe? The macabre questions waged war with her instinct to pursue him. Not alone at least.

She glanced back toward the front yard. Where was her partner? Where was Jenkins?

Burying the questions, she pushed forward, raising her firearm. She led with its barrel, turning the corner with a hitched breath. As the space opened up, her vision narrowed, searching for hints of motion. Nothing threatening came. Only the subtle jostle of a tree's limbs in the breeze. The backyard was empty.

Rio wasn't waiting in the shadows or ready to pounce like a rabid predator, but she had a good idea where he had fled to. The gate leading to the alley behind the home was ajar, swaying on its rusty hinges.

With deftness and circumspection, she crossed the yellowed patch of lawn, her firearm an extension of her hands. Pausing at the gate to collect herself, she looked back in search of her partner. Still absent.

"Jenkins! I need backup!" Her voice carried through the sunny day.

Silence.

Where are you?

Gritting her teeth, she pushed through the gate, scanning up and down the alley. There was no sign of Rio, just the constant reminder of the misery these people face every waking hour—the poverty and strangling addiction that gripped like a vise.

"Which way? Which way?" she whispered, her stare volleying back and forth. The choice crippled her resolve, but finally a hint presented itself. The stagnant water of a pothole to her left had recently been disturbed, and fresh footprints fled away from her line of sight.

"Gotcha."

Hugging the backside of a picket fence, she edged down the alley, allowing the deadly tool in her hand to lead each heedful step. Trash cans and discarded furniture littered the space, creating a labyrinth of opportune places for the man to hide. Unless she had lost him, and he was already blocks away.

In mid-stride, something massive crashed into the opposite side of the fence. The wooden pickets shuddered from the force. She flinched, whirling the firearm toward the violent display. The outline of a large dog materialized through the pickets, unleashing a flurry of vicious barks and growls.

She shook off the frenzy, turning to follow the path Rio must have taken. But as the alley opened up to her sight again, a dark profile invaded her peripheral vision. And before she could react, she crashed into the fence, losing her grip on the firearm, which clattered to the ground a few feet away.

She hit the ground with a resounding *thud*, feeling her lungs scream from the impact. A shot of pain exploded in her rib cage from the collision. It bled into her legs, her arms, commandeering her senses. But her fight-or-flight instincts kicked into high gear, and she rolled over, bouncing back to her feet.

In front of her was a man wielding a tire iron. A scar raced down the side of his face, eyebrow to cheek. Rio Ramirez. He held the tool above his head, prepared to bring it down on her skull. As he wound up to deliver the blow, she jumped to the side and somersaulted away from him.

The momentum of the swing caused him to stumble, but he used the fence to stabilize his balance. Snarling, his glare snapped her way, watching her complete the roll and regain her stance. She kept her distance.

"You bitch!" he snarled as he lunged forward, swinging the tire iron in a frenzy across his body, slicing through the air. She dodged each wild attempt, dancing away from the manic criminal. In the thick of the chaotic display, her eyes quickly shot to the gun lying on the ground, though she couldn't possibly get to it without taking a hit.

Feeling the confinement of the alley funneling her in and her side wailing and begging for mercy, she dodged another swing. But during the maneuver, she slipped on a piece of newspaper, landing square on her ass. She locked onto the man, seeing the rage swirl within his light brown irises. It was a primal, vexed look, one seeping with fury. The look of a killer.

He barreled forward to deliver the death blow, but his momentum stopped mid-stride as a shout rang out behind him.

"Rio Ramirez! Freeze!"

Barrientos knew that voice better than anyone's.

She watched as Rio whipped around, taking in the party crasher. Jenkins stood mere feet away, his gun aimed directly at the man's face.

"Don't take another step, asshole!" Jenkins shouted. "I've got fifteen friends with me, and each one is drooling to penetrate your fuckin' skull."

Panting and huffing from the wrangle, Rio's stare darted back to Barrientos on the ground, but she had already reclaimed her footing. Before he could react, a right cross connected with his jaw, and he dropped to the ground like a sack of potatoes.

2

Three Hours Later

The interrogation room's fluorescent lights cast shadows across Rio's bruised face. His wrists were cuffed to the metal table. Barrientos sat across from him, a fresh ice pack pressed against her ribs, while Jenkins paced behind her like a caged animal.

"Let's try this again, Rio," Jenkins said, his voice carrying weight and frustration. "Where were you on May 8th between eight p.m. and two a.m. on May 9th?"

Rio's scarred face twisted into a sneer. "I already told you, cop. I wasn't in town that weekend. I was at my cousin's place in Fresno. Playing poker until three in the morning."

"Right." Barrientos leaned forward, wincing slightly. "And your cousin's name is?"

"Miguel Santos. Lives on Maple Street. You want his address, his phone number, what he had for breakfast?" Rio's voice dripped with sarcasm. "I ain't done nothing wrong."

Jenkins stopped pacing. "Nothing wrong? You just tried to cave my partner's skull in with a tire iron."

"She was chasing me with a gun. What'd you expect me to do, invite her in for coffee?" Rio shrugged. "I thought she was some crazy lady trying to rob me, fool."

Barrientos exchanged a glance with Jenkins. The story was thin, but Rio's demeanor had shifted. The feral rage from the alley was gone, replaced by a defiant man used to rooms like this.

"We'll check out your *primo*," Barrientos said, sliding a photograph across the table. "But first, take a look at this. Recognize the car?"

Rio studied the grainy surveillance photo. It was the eight-by-ten photo from the crime scene. No plates, but the unmistakable taillights of a '78 Grand Prix were on full display.

"What kinda shit are you trying to pin on me? That ain't my car."

"Are you sure about that?" Barrientos asked, "bad cop" seeping from every angle she threw at him. "It's not your car? Because it sure looks a hell of a lot like that piece of shit you roll around in. And it just so happens that the car in this photograph . . ."—she pointed at the vehicle in the image—"this one right here, was seen leaving a murder scene earlier this month."

Rio's eyes narrowed. "Murder scene? What murder scene? You gonna tell me what this is about, or are we gonna keep playing twenty questions?"

Barrientos slid a second eight-by-ten photo across the table. The image depicted the remains of a woman propped against a brick wall, her body crisp and blackened from fire. Above her head was writing etched in the soot left by the flames. "This murder, asshole." She sneered his way, feeling a fresh wave of pain sear through her rib cage.

Rio's defiant stare landed on the image, then shot back to Barrientos within a heartbeat. "What the fuck is this? I don't know anything about that shit."

Jenkins slammed his palm on the table. "Don't play dumb with us, Rio. Amelie Castro Rodriguez. Twenty-nine years old. Found dead in an alley on May 9th. Burned beyond recognition. Your car, that rust bucket, was there that night. It's the car in the photo, asshole. You know it, I know it, and she knows it."

The room fell silent except for the hum of the fluorescent lights. Rio's stare fled to his lap as he shook his head from side to side. As the pendulum swung a fifth time, he finally lifted his chin, locking onto the woman sitting across from him. The same woman he had tried to bludgeon and murder hours before in that alley. "Amelie Rodriguez?"

His stare deepened with the gaze, eyes narrowing to a dark line. "That woman in the picture is Amelie Rodriguez?"

Barrientos shot Jenkins a surprised look, but she quickly abandoned the glance. "That's right. But you already knew that, huh?"

For the first time since they'd dragged him in, Rio's cocky facade cracked. His eyes widened, and he leaned back in his chair as far as the cuffs would allow.

"Amelie Rodriguez? The girl from PT?" His voice was barely above a whisper. "She's dead?"

Barrientos felt a chill run down her spine. This wasn't the reaction of a killer. This was genuine shock. "Yeah. You knew her, right?"

"She . . . Yeah, she worked at the physical therapy office. Sweet girl. Always remembered my name when I came in last year after taking two in the back. She helped me regain my strength and walk again." Rio's hands trembled; the handcuffs links clattered. "Who would want to hurt her? Amelie?"

Jenkins and Barrientos had worked enough cases to recognize genuine grief when they saw it. This wasn't their guy.

Two hours later, they watched through the one-way glass as a uniformed officer uncuffed Rio from the metal table. The man's cousin, Miguel Santos, had corroborated the alibi down to the last detail, even providing security footage from his apartment building in Fresno showing Rio arriving at 9:04 p.m. and leaving at 3:31 a.m. The timeline was airtight.

"What about the car?" Barrientos asked, though she already knew the answer.

Jenkins consulted his notes. "Looks similar, '78 Grand Prix with oxidized orange paint and gray primer with rust spots. But there are too many differences. Just like he said, it's not the car, Barrientos."

"Shit." She pressed the ice pack harder against her ribs. "So we're back to square one."

Jenkins rubbed his temples. "We just blew our best lead. But at least that piece of shit is going away for a while. Battery of an officer isn't something that is swept under the rug, Barrientos."

"That doesn't make me feel better, you know." She winced as her hand clutched her side. "Not one bit."

They stood in the observation room watching the officer lead Rio out of the interrogation room door. He moved slowly, his shoulders slumped with the weight of learning about Amelie's death. Whatever crimes he might be guilty of, murder wasn't one of them.

Jenkins muttered, "Three weeks into the investigation, and we've made pitiful progress in catching this bastard."

Barrientos thought about Amelie's file spread across the desk. Twenty-nine-year-old physical therapist. No enemies, no debts, no reason for anyone to want her dead. Just another young life snuffed out in a dark alley, and they were no closer to finding her killer than they were that morning in the alley.

"Maybe we missed something," she said, though the words felt hollow. "Maybe we need to go back to the beginning, reexamine the evidence."

"Maybe." Jenkins didn't sound convinced.

The investigation was getting colder by the hour, and the two detectives who'd sworn to bring this monster to justice were running out of leads.

XIV

512 HEIGHT STREET
2005

He retreated a step as she squeezed into his bedroom, her meaty, obese frame pouring through the doorway. The moo-moo dress she wore reeked of cigarettes and days of sweat. She stood there under the jamb, breath haggard as she eyed him. "Why?.. why aren't you reading, Kenny?" She wheezed.

The Bible lay on the collection of dirty clothes and rags he used as a bed, but he couldn't steal a look. He froze in place, watching her face sour.

"Boy," she started, her gravelly voice like nails on a chalkboard. "Mother asked you a question. You know what happens when you keep your mother waiting. Have not you learned by now?" She advanced toward him, filling the room with her mass. The rolls clinging to her bones throbbed and jiggled with each thunderous step. Stopping inches away, she leaned down, her vacant stare face-to-face with the ten-year-old. She watched the worry swell in his eyes while her acrid breath painted him.

"I'm gonna ask you one last time, Kenny. Why aren't you reading?"

As he stood there, trembling like a branch in a storm, a dark stain spread across the crotch of his jeans. Her stare drew to it, watching it bloom and flow down his pant leg.

"Kenny!" she boomed, yet the boy remained stoic and mute. "You pissed yourself. Right here in your bedroom, young man. What the hell is wrong with you?"

His eyes welled with tears, and the shame he always felt when she was near took root.

"Filthy boy. Filthy, filthy boy," she snarled, bits of spittle raining on his face.

Through the fear, he choked out a few words. "I'm sowwy, Momma. I'm sowwy."

She pulled back, her eyes darkening under the nest of tangled and sweat-slicked mop she called hair. Her scowl barked his way. "And you're not practicing either, are you?"

He knew she was referring to his homework. The speech therapy; she demanded he do it for an hour each day.

"No, no, you're not, are you? Just like you're not reading."

Shakes quaked through his core as he watched the disgust ooze from her pores. "I'm sowwy."

"Sorry for what, Kenny." She shook her head, tobacco-stained teeth grinding together. "For pissing yourself like a dirty, rotten heathen? Huh? Are you sorry about that? Are you sorry for soiling your jeans, forcing your mother to clean up after you? Wash the piss out of your undies. When are you going to grow up and learn how to be responsible? Fulfill your obligations to this household?"

He flinched at each jab while a solitary tear rolled down his freckled cheek. "I'm s- s- sowwy."

"Stop! Just stop saying that, Kenny!" She took him in, her dull gaze scouring him from head to toe: his blackened, bare feet, the holes in his jeans, the snot-stained wife-beater he wore, his greasy, unkempt hair. "If you were sorry, you'd do as your mother asked, boy. Now, get your ass in the bathroom. It's bath time."

2

An hour later, he remained in the tub. The once scalding tap water had slowly cooled to room temperature, but he ignored the tepid change. It comforted him. He sat there, his eyes dancing across his bare flesh, admiring the angry, red welts cascading up and down his arms and legs, his chest. He knew it meant he was clean. Clean at last.

She remained as well; Mother. She sat on a stool next to the tub, which wailed under her weight. Her voice was calm and soothing as she whispered sweet lullabies into the air. The words pulled him out of the hole he had crawled into. A mother's loving voice.

"Kenny, my love," she continued, stroking her fingers through his hair. "You need to promise me you'll read the Good Book every waking hour, son. I need you to memorize every word, every verse. You need to learn the Lord's word. Okay?"

His neck craned, taking in the angel that brought him into her home. The only person in this world that cared for him.

She blinked at his expression; her one lazy eye stared off into the distance. A smile appeared under the thin black hairs above her lips. "Can you promise me that, Kenny? That you'll read his words every day, every chance you have?"

He returned the look, his own grin spreading. "Yeah, Momma. I pwomise."

"That's good to hear, son. I love you."

"I wuv you too, Momma."

XV

Monday Afternoon, May 25, 2015

The precinct's investigation quarters teemed with frustration and boiling tempers. After three grueling weeks of tracking down leads, interviewing, and sifting through the evidence, they were at a standstill. The four detectives, Bakersfield's finest, failed to put a dent in the Amelie Castro Rodriguez murder. It didn't matter the size of the stone they threw.

They stood around the conference table, hashing out the facts they had already gone over day after day after day. For every inch they gained, the slippery slope dragged them back a foot. It was numbing, and fatigue and defeat slowly surfaced.

Jenkins lit a cigarette, his third this hour. The smoky tendrils reached for the tiled ceiling. He exhaled a plume of gray exhaust, rejuvenated by the instant rush of nicotine. "Anzilotti, walk me through the surveillance footage from the victim's parking lot. There has to be something we're missing."

"We've gone over this, Jenkins!" Detective Georgio Anzilotti exclaimed. A television set sat on a rolling cart near the conference table. He wiped beads of sweat from his forehead as he stepped toward it. "There's nothing new. Nothing we haven't already tossed. We've all watched it, analyzed it. Hell, Johnson and I reenacted it last week."

Jenkins stood there, arms crossed over his chest, hovering like a ravenous wolf ready to spring on a newborn fawn. "Just play the fuckin' tape. There has to be something we're missing."

"Fine" was all Anzilotti could muster. He released a sigh and pushed the power button on the DVD player. "But I'm telling you, there's nothing else to examine."

The other two detectives in the room, Johnson and Barrientos, dropped their discussion and approached the rolling cart. Silence swallowed the room, except for the whir of the player awakening.

A heartbeat later, the television screen flickered to life, and a still frame filled the black rectangle. It was the victim's parking lot. The same footage they had labored over for two weeks. Three sedans and a motorcycle slept, nestled in their corrals of white paint. A timestamp snoozed in the lower right-hand corner that read *8:23 p.m.*

"We know what's going to happen, Jenkins. We've watched it a thousand times," Anzilotti groaned.

"Push play, and shut up!" The command lacked debate.

Anzilotti pushed play. A subtle animation began in the still image. A patch of asphalt illuminated by a streetlight, moths dancing around it while a sycamore's branches swayed above the parked vehicles. After a grueling seventeen seconds, a woman appeared on the screen. She walked toward the third car while rummaging in her purse. The picture was grainy, but they could still make out her features in the night's gloom. Floral dress, bronze skin, and long, jet-black hair. It was the victim, Amelie Castro Rodriguez. After she popped her trunk, another figure advanced from the shadows, dark as the night. She never saw him. He came up from behind and struck her on the head with a blunt metallic object. Tire iron? Crowbar? They couldn't tell. She dropped to the cold black surface twenty-seven seconds in.

Anzilotti paused the clip. "Victim. Perp. Car, which is or isn't a '78 Grand Prix. After that, he picks her up and carries her away, then he tosses her in the trunk. That's it. There's nothing else here, Jenkins."

Jenkins leaned forward across the table, examining the heap of scattered documents. "Where are those stills from the clip? The ones with the digital enhancements."

"I've got them." Barrientos shuffled through the stack of manila folders she held, pulling one out. In bright orange lettering, the cover read *Video Evidence, Homicide, A.*

Castro Rodriguez, 419 Chester Ave #223. She handed the folder to Jenkins. "They're here."

Jenkins accepted the folder without acknowledging his partner. His long fingers went to work, flipping through the still shots, examining each with the keen eye of a raptor. The victim in stride as she rummaged through her purse, and then the silhouette of the figure in black emerging from the shadows. Whoever he was, he held something in his left hand, long and metallic. It glistened under the faint light. The detective pulled the latter image from the stack, spinning and releasing it with a gentle snap of his wrist. It spun in a circle before landing face up on the table.

Silence descended upon the room. Everyone's gaze landed on the glossy eight-by-ten photo.

"What do you see?" The inquiry didn't target anyone in particular. It was a collective prompt for the others to share their professional thoughts.

"It's the perp, Jenkins," Anzilotti piped up, not giving the others a chance. "That piece of shit who burned the girl. He's dressed in black. Probably denim pants, black shoes, and a sweatshirt."

Jenkins's glare drifted to the man, taking in his muscular frame. "We can all see that. That's clear as day. But what else do we see?" His sight swept the room, testing the others.

Detective Cooper Johnson, the baby-faced detective with less than a year in the position, leaned forward from across the table. His eyes narrowed like two black pearls, studying the photo, scrutinizing every square inch. Like a pupil in the classroom, he raised a hand, patiently waiting for acknowledgement from his instructor.

"What do you have, Johnson?" Jenkins asked, watching the twenty-six-year-old.

Johnson cleared his throat. "We know that's our guy, the perp, right?"

Nods and subtle yeses followed.

Johnson continued. "Well, in this shot and the others, his head always faces to the right, away from the parking lot. Like he's staring away from his target."

"What makes you think that?" Anzilotti interjected.

"Go on, kid," Jenkins encouraged, shutting Anzilotti down with a leer. "We're listening."

"If you look close enough, you can see the white stitching on his sweatshirt's hood. It's faint, but it's there." Johnson picked up the photo and pointed at the figure's head, showing it to the room. "Look here. The broken vertical line runs up the back of his head. We can see it, but we shouldn't be able to if he's facing forward, facing the woman."

"Enlighten us, Johnson," Barrientos chimed in, interested in the young detective's theory. "What are you getting at?"

"He's hiding his face." Johnson paused, letting the words sink in.

"He's about to abduct a young woman. Of course he's going to hide his fuckin' face," Anzilotti stated the obvious.

"Who's he hiding his face from? The victim?" Barrientos asked. It was a germane question.

Johnson chewed on his cheek for a moment. "No, not the victim. He's hiding his face from something else. I think he's hiding his face from the camera. That's why he's turning his head away."

"So he knows there's a camera in the lot," Anzilotti said, all eyes drifting his way. "If I were about to attack someone, I would be camera shy as well. Besides, most places have CCTV these days. You can't take a piss without a lens zooming in on your junk."

"Yeah, that's true," Barrientos started, a smirk crossing her lips, "but they'd have to use a really powerful lens for you, my friend." She held up her thumb and forefinger about an inch apart.

Snickers rang out among the group.

"Very funny," Anzilotti snarked.

Seeing the heat rise on his partner's face, Johnson continued. "It also tells us more about this guy. He knows the area. He's done his homework, knows the ins and outs."

"Which could mean he knew her," Jenkins offered. "Maybe this wasn't a random act of violence? Maybe there's a deeper connection between the perp and the victim that we haven't unearthed yet."

"We've talked to her neighbors, her family here in the city," Barrientos said. "Hell, we even spent a morning at the physical therapy office she worked at, grilling the manager, several of her peers, and a few clients. According to our reports, there's no one in her life who would want to hurt her. She was fun, charismatic, full of life."

Jenkins's stare shot back to the photo, the eight-by-ten glossy that now consumed his mind. His fiery gray eyes honed in on the killer, the ominous figure in black stalking from the dark. He envisioned being there that night, witnessing this pernicious machine, this shadowy monster, emerge from the pitch black. Like a bad dream, he watched it slink forward, ready to claim its prize.

Who is this guy?

A telephone rang on a desk nearby, startling the group. Shaking off the vision, Jenkins collected his bearings. "Where haven't we looked? If we've covered her apartment, her family, and her work, what options are still on the table? What are we missing?"

Johnson repeated his action from before, raising his hand. "I have an idea, sir."

"Go ahead, Johnson," Jenkins stated.

"What if the victim had another life? One where she wore the skin of someone else? A digital facade."

"As in . . . ?"

"Have we checked her social media accounts, sir? Facebook?"

2

Three hours later, the detectives reconvened around the conference table, piecing together the jigsaw puzzle surrounding the murder. They had broken up into pairs, each set of partners following the bread crumbs that might lead them out of the forest and into the realm of solving this violent crime. Johnson and Anzilotti traveled to the IT wing, using the technicians and their digital skills and expertise to comb through Amelie's social media profiles.

Jenkins and Barrientos exited the precinct's doors and embarked on a field trip. Their destination was St. Francis Church. Jenkins had already visited the clergy on two occasions, collecting information on interpreting the Bible verse left at the crime scene, but he needed to follow up once more. Father Morgan amiably opened his doors and passed on what wisdom he knew about the King James Bible and Leviticus 18:22.

Jenkins, sitting and lighting a cigarette, opened the dialogue with the group. "So, what did you two dig up about the victim?"

"All right, I'm guessing you're not an expert on this shit," Anzilotti drawled, the words thick with sarcasm. "But most people use these avenues to share pictures and news with friends and family." He flipped open his pocket-sized notepad, re-examining his chicken scratch from the time with the IT techs.

"I get the gist," Jenkins said, annoyance stacked on each word. "Here's my baby, here's my lunch, here's me on vacation. I might be a dinosaur, but I'm not in the ground yet, smart-ass."

The sly smirk Anzilotti wore gave way to a toothy grin. "Time's ticking, sir." He checked his watch. "Tick, tick, tick."

"Cut the shit. What did you two discover?"

"Sorry, sir. Sorry." That playful grin never left his lips; a child caught with his hand in the cookie jar. "Like I said, most people use these sites to engage with friends and family, but that's not always the case. These social media sites are like a mask some users wear. You can be anyone you want to be as long as you follow the platform's rules. Fake name, fake marital status, photoshopped images . . ."

"Are you saying the victim wore one of these masks?" It was Barrientos. "Was she pretending to be someone else?"

Anzilotti cocked his brow. "Yes, and no."

"Yes, and no? The fuck does that mean?" Jenkins asked.

"She used her real name in her profile: Amelie C. She listed her occupation as physical therapist. And she shared countless photos of herself. Nothing too intimate, just images of her daily life and interests: nature hikes and selfies in clubs, restaurants, etcetera."

"So where's the mystery?" Jenkins asked. "The facade?"

"Well, there's much more to Amelie Castro Rodriguez than we originally knew. And it's not so much an alternate *life*, created and self-embellished, as it is an interesting *lifestyle*. When we spoke to her family, her neighbors, even her employer, not one individual mentioned this."

"Mentioned what? Spit it out," Jenkins ordered.

"Her sexual orientation." The sentence dropped from Anzilotti's lips like a curse in church.

The other three members of the quartet shot a look at each other, a mix of bafflement and interest swirled together.

Barrientos was the first to speak, "Her sexual orientation? What the hell are you talking about, man? She's straight, right? What was the name of the schoolteacher?" She paused, searching her mind.

"David Miller," Jenkins responded, chiseling at the barrier in her memory.

"Miller, that's right. The guy she was supposed to meet up with. They had a date scheduled the night she was killed."

"Yeah, according to the schoolteacher's story." Anzilotti continued. "But we found nothing to support this on her Facebook or Instagram feeds. He's not mentioned anywhere."

Interesting, Jenkins thought.

"So what does this have to do with her sexual orientation?" Barrientos asked.

"Well, as the techs scoured her feed, her likes, her comments, and the groups she'd joined, they collected several posts related to gay pride, LGBTQ support, and others. This was a big part of her social networking life. None of this is present in her professional life, though. Her co-workers knew nothing of it. Her family knew nothing about these interests either. This opens up a mass of new leads, new theories about what happened that night. If we can pinpoint a follower, a friend in these groups, someone that has a criminal record, or a list of accusations, maybe we'll find our guy."

"There's one more thing, sir," the detective with the bright blue eyes and peach fuzz said. "Castro had received a series of messages from other users. Overall, it was very tame flirting by both parties, but as we deep-dived into who these users were, we found many of them were other women. We believe the victim was bisexual, sir."

"A flood of understanding swept over Jenkins. The metaphorical wave bubbled with clarity and truth. "I get it now," he mumbled, barely audible in the room. "That's good detective work, gentlemen," he commended, with a faint trickle of pride burrowing up from the cavern.

The three detectives stilled, watching Jenkins meticulously piece together this new information, his brow furrowed in concentration.

"What is it?" Anzilotti asked, ending the sudden coat of silence painting the space.

Jenkins's eyes volleyed around the room, accompanied by a series of nods. "I know why he targeted her."

3

"Listen up." Jenkins's voice carried with quiet authority. "We need to discuss what Barrientos and I discovered at the church today. This could be significant." The three detectives settled into chairs around the conference table, the atmosphere tense but focused. "You need to hear this."

He recounted their visit.

***

The church grounds felt unnaturally quiet for a Friday afternoon. Maybe half a dozen cars scattered across the vast parking lot. Jenkins and Barrientos approached along the stone pathway. As they walked, he caught her studying the Gothic architecture.

Her first time here? he wondered.

Heavy mahogany doors with tarnished brass handles welcomed them. As they entered, incense hung thick and warm in the air, and their eyes slowly adjusted to the gentle dimness. A couple knelt in a pew near the altar, heads bowed in prayer. Candles flickered beside them, casting dancing shadows on the walls.

To their left, a neon green *OFFICE* sign buzzed softly in a recessed alcove. Jenkins led his partner to it and knocked. After hearing a warm "Come in," he pushed through.

Father Morgan looked up from his desk as they entered, his face brightening with recognition. The wood-paneled office felt cozy rather than cramped, bookshelves filled with theological texts and community photos creating a scholarly atmosphere. Soft light from desk lamps supplemented the overhead fluorescents.

"Detective Jenkins." The priest's smile was genuine, tinged with concern. "Back again so soon? I hope everything's all right." His handshake was firm and welcoming. "And you've brought backup."

Jenkins gestured. "Father, this is my partner, Detective Angela Barrientos. I was hoping we could continue our conversation from last week."

Barrientos nodded respectfully. "Father Morgan, thank you for taking the time to see us."

The priest was smaller than Jenkins remembered, maybe five feet six, and in his late sixties. The man's wire-rimmed glasses perched on a kind face beneath a receding hairline. His eyes held the warmth of someone who genuinely cared about his community.

"Two visits in as many weeks. This must be quite serious." His tone carried concern rather than suspicion.

"I'm afraid it is," Jenkins said, pulling out his notepad. "Dead serious. Last week we discussed Leviticus 18:22. I'd like to explore that conversation a bit more, if you don't mind."

The priest's expression grew thoughtful. "Of course. Though I should mention, my views on that passage have ... evolved considerably over the years." He leaned back in his chair, the leather creaking softly. "Scripture interpretation is never as simple as it appears on the surface."

"How so?" Barrientos asked, her voice respectful but probing.

Father Morgan removed his glasses, cleaning them with careful deliberation. "Twenty years ago, I would have given you a very different answer. Black and white. Clear-cut." He paused, replacing his glasses. "But ministry teaches you that real life is lived in the gray areas. My congregation includes people from all walks of life, and I've seen firsthand how rigid interpretations can cause immense pain."

Jenkins leaned forward slightly. "So your position has changed?"

"I've learned to lead with love rather than judgment," the priest said quietly. "But not everyone in the clergy shares this perspective. Some of the older generation, particularly those in more traditional parishes, still hold to . . . stricter interpretations."

"What kind of 'stricter interpretations,' Father?" Barrientos asked.

The priest's expression darkened. "There are those who still view homosexuality as something that needs to be 'corrected.' They espouse prayer retreats and conversion therapy programs—approaches that most mainstream denominations have moved away from."

"And beyond that?" Jenkins pressed.

A long silence stretched between them. Father Morgan stared at his hands before answering, "I pray this isn't the case, Detective, but there are extremists in every faith. People who take Scripture and twist it into something God never intended."

"Could that include violence?"

The priest's face paled. "The thought sickens me, but . . . yes. There are those who might believe they're acting as instruments of divine justice."

Jenkins consulted his notes. "This killer left that verse for a reason. In your opinion, what message do you think he's trying to send?"

Father Morgan was quiet for a long moment, clearly wrestling with his response. "I believe—and this breaks my heart to say—that this person thinks he's doing God's work. That he sees himself as some kind of righteous warrior."

"So you think religious motivation is driving these murders?" Barrientos asked, her voice steady but concerned.

The priest nodded slowly, his shoulders sagging with the weight of the admission. "Everything you've described points in that direction. This isn't random violence. It's targeted, ritualistic. Someone has taken sacred text and perverted it into a justification, in my opinion."

Jenkins absorbed this, running a hand through his silver hair. "That's what we were afraid you'd say."

"I wish I could tell you otherwise, Detective." Father Morgan's voice carried genuine anguish. "No matter what one believes about Scripture, murder is never justified. Never." He paused, crossing himself—head, chest, left shoulder, right shoulder—head bowed. "I'll pray for the victims, for their families, and yes, even for this troubled soul who thinks he's serving God by taking lives."

Jenkins released a sigh. "Thank you, Father."

XVI

512 Height Street
2007

"In duh beginning, God cweated duh heavens and duh—" The boy paused, his mouth held in a quivering O, trying to wrap around the next sound. He swallowed and tried again. "Eawf." He attempted once more. "Duh eawf."

"Good. That's good, Kenny." Mother sat next to him on the couch, her stare glued to the open Bible in his hands. "Your speech is improving. But I still think you can do better, son. I want you to try harder."

The twelve-year-old took in the woman sitting on his right. Her scent was heavy today, and he could feel her raspy breath flooding the area. A few greasy strands of hair clinging damply to her temples streaked the sides of her plump face. The smile she wore was contagious.

"Dank you, Momma. I will."

"Go on, boy." She urged him with a nod, the rolls below her chin wobbling. "Keep reading."

His attention drew back to the Bible lying in his lap. It was heavy, nearly the size of a cookie sheet. A leather-bound tome from a generation before. He asked her once where the book came from, but she changed the subject by saying, *It's not important where this Good Book came from, Kenny. What's important are the lessons you learn from its teachings. You must learn it inside and out.*

After clearing his throat and sitting up (Mother always corrected his posture), he continued reading aloud, "Duh eawf was a fowmwess void, and dawkness covuhd duh face of duh deep."

He looked up from the page, taking her in for a split second. The smile she so proudly wore waned.

I think you can do better, son. The sentence looped in his mind.

He continued, the need to please propelling his effort. "While a wind fwom Gawd swept ovuh duh face of duh watuhs."

"Stop."

The command wasn't loud, but it brought the lesson to a screeching halt. It was the tone. That tone seeped into his bones, coating his marrow.

His knees began to shake; movement he had no control over. The Bible sitting in his lap jostled with each motion. She noticed. Her beady stare watched the book's subtle bounces.

"Now, Kenny." The tone from seconds before lived in each syllable. "Do you really think that was your best effort?"

He could feel her glare, a look that singed his flesh. Her fiery eyes swept over him, smoldering layers of skin and consuming each in a wisp of smoke. He couldn't face the burn she cast his way.

"Are you actually listening to yourself when you read?" Mother asked. "Well, are you?"

He couldn't respond. His eyes were downturned, locked on the book. The Good Book. The one he had read every day for the past three years. The past three years with her. A promise he'd made.

"No," Mother answered for him, knowing he had retreated to his burrow. The dark cavern he nestled in when life got tough, when challenged. The one place he could hide from his responsibilities, his commitments. "No, that wasn't your best effort. Try again."

Seconds passed. Time slowly ruptured like an infected boil.

"Now!"

His shaky stare found her, seeing the contempt aimed his way. "M-M-Momma."

She leaned in, her pimpled nose brushed his cheek while the heat from her breath scathed his skin. "Try.

Again." She held her proximity, her dagger stare puncturing him over and over again.

His mind wandered, thinking about the mouse in his bedroom wall. The tawny thing that crept out of its hole each evening, scurrying about and gathering crumbs. He thought about its pin-sized pink nose, the white whiskers adorning its tiny face, and beady little eyes that always greeted him as he sat cross-legged on the floor. But most of all, he thought about how this insignificant creature, this bite-sized morsel with the appetite of a bear, shunned its animosity and crept from the darkness. He wondered if he could do the same.

After another "Try again," his chin wavered with the sour aroma of defeat, and he collapsed to her demand. "Okay, M-M-Momma."

She inched away from his face, still scorching him with heat. She watched as his shaking stilled, and life bloomed once more in his pale flesh. "I'm waiting, boy. Try again. From the beginning."

He released a breath, one that showered him with hope, then started over, ensuring his posture met her standards, "In duh beginning, God cweated duh heavens and duh eawf."

"Again," she commanded, the fire in her eyes unwilling to extinguish. "Say it again, and listen to your words, Kenny. You can do better."

He tried again.

XVII

Thursday Evening, May 28, 2015

The forecast called for a heat wave. One for which the precinct was not prepared. The patched-up AC units on the roof strained and wheezed under the scorching conditions, pumping stifling warm air into the building.

A fresh layer of sheen clung to Jenkins's brow, slick and shining under the fluorescent bulbs above. It matched the dark stains under his armpits. He sat at his desk, a handset pinned to his ear, taking notes. On the other end was Sgt. William Lackey from Turlock, California. Sporadic okays and mm-hmms sounded from his lips. He thanked the man once the call ended.

A day prior, the detective had reached out to the small-town police department, inquiring about Ms. Heather Stoneheuer—David Miller's "mistake." The young woman fled the Bakersfield area shortly after the infidelity went public. She now lived with her aging father and worked in the local school district. Nothing incriminating to report. She hadn't answered the door when the sergeant made a house call, but overall, the relocation seemed squeaky clean. She hadn't traveled or made a peep that would turn heads since she arrived. A model member of society.

"That only leaves the ex-wife," he said to himself, glancing over his notes. "Is she in danger, or is she involved in some other way?"

A commotion across the room stole his attention. His partner held the latest edition of *The Bakersfield Californian*.

"I don't fucking believe it!" Barrientos stood from the comfort of the chair she sat in. "Jenkins, you're not going to like this."

She shuffled away from her desk, crossed the room, and tossed the newspaper down on the conference table. "The press knows everything. Come look at this shit."

Jenkins watched his partner's animation, the incredulity dripping from her gestures. "What do you mean, 'The press knows everything'? What do they know?"

"Just come look, okay," Barrientos repeated, her eyes like daggers. "It's right here on the front page."

Detective Jenkins abandoned his seat, slow strides advancing him toward the table in the room's center. The newspaper called to him, an inaudible voice that pulled him like a tether, and it was a damning sight.

"Shit" was the only word to escape the man's clenched jaw.

He reached over the table and grasped it, bringing the paper closer. "How? How, how, how?" He spun around, eyeing the others in the room. All stopped their activities and work, their nervous twitchy stares aimed his way. "How in the hell did they get a hold of this? That alley was locked down. No one in, no one out."

Barrientos knew the question was rhetorical, but she answered, trying to urge the man away from the edge. The stress and the day's stifling heat didn't help the situation. "Those cockroaches always find a way, Jenkins. They always do. Hiring freelance photographers to do the dirty work. Prying for information from anyone willing to answer a few questions. I'm honestly surprised we kept it under wraps this long."

"Well, it's out there now." Jenkins released the newspaper to collapse back onto the table. "What are the masses going to think about this? It's one thing to know a murder occurred in the city. Violence happens everywhere. It's an entirely different matter when the intricate details are shared with everyone who receives this goddamned paper. And there's not a chance in hell that it's not the major story on the news tonight. An uproar is on its way."

Detectives Anzilotti and Johnson, ties loosened and clothes disheveled, approached the conference table. The same dark, damp stains marred the armpits of their dress shirts. Wary glances leapt from Jenkins to the newspaper. In bold black letters, the headline on the front page read:

The Hand of God Strikes

Below the headline, accompanied by a photo of the alley and the Bible verse etched on the scorched brick, was the inquiry:

A messenger of the divine, or a sociopath raging war on our city?

A detailed and falsely cited article followed.

As the four stared in disbelief, Anzilotti and Johnson each muttered, "Oh shit."

"Barrientos," Jenkins said before smoothing out his feathers, running his fingers through his silver hair and slicking it back in place. "Turn on the news. Let's see how much these fucks actually know.

2

Minutes later, the foursome crowded around the television cart, anticipation rising from them like steam off the asphalt. Right on the hour, the six o'clock news jingle invaded their ears before fading and pointing the spotlight on a man in a three-piece suit named Gavin Lopez. His perfectly groomed dark hair looked like something he'd strapped on as opposed to something he needed to maintain. Impeccable, not a strand out of place. His beyond-white smile vanished as he opened the airing and spoke to the camera.

The investigators listened to the anchorman, hearing the news they feared. Indeed, the press knew more about the murders than the department had announced. Amelie's name had gone public the morning of, but other than that, the case was designated confidential, including a gag order. Obviously, that was now moot.

The news anchor, with his plastic smile, sent the live feed to a reporter on-site at the alley Jenkins never wanted to see again. He expected to see Maggie Miller in the live shot, but a young, petite brunette named Aubrey Madison appeared at the beginning of the segment.

"Thank you, Gavin," she started, her voice smooth and rehearsed with a hint of solemnity to set the scene. "I'm here in the downtown area where earlier this month, a heinous crime shook our beloved city. The following report contains graphic information that may be difficult for some viewers to hear."

The cameraman panned out, showcasing the gaping mouth between the two brick buildings behind the reporter. A web of crime scene tape still clung to the entrance, but much had loosened and hung limply just above the ground. Graffiti and debris littered the shot.

The image of the victim, the same one shown on the morning of the murder, appeared on the screen: piercing blue eyes, supermodel smile, and long, jet-black hair. Below the picture was her full name. The frame transitioned back to the live scene seconds later.

"Officials and cooperating investigators have informed us that on the morning of May 9th, the body of Amelie Castro Rodriguez, a local physical therapist, was discovered in the alley located directly behind me."

"Bullshit," Jenkins mumbled under his breath, arms crossed over his chest as he watched. "Cooperating, my ass."

"An unknown assailant abducted the twenty-nine-year-old woman from a nearby parking lot the night before and later abandoned her body."

The reporter paused, the camera steadying on the grim look she showcased. Her voice altered, tense and grave as she continued.

"We've also learned that after abandoning the body, the assailant burned the woman's remains, a detail that adds another tragic element to this already devastating case. Was she burned to hide any traces of evidence, or is there a darker motive? As sickening as the crime was, another mystery has unfolded here at the scene."

The cameraman zoomed in as she spoke, tension building with each passing second.

"A biblical message remained, scratched into the brick wall here behind me. An action that has baffled both law enforcement and the press alike. Why was the Bible verse left? What meaning does it hold?"

"Here it comes," Jenkins whispered to himself, a tide of anger rising in his core.

"Was this a crime of passion? A singular event that will haunt the city's history, or does the assailant believe the actions are divine? Do they believe they're a messenger cleansing the city? The Hand of God?"

The quartet all looked at one another, shock strangling their expressions.

"Anyone with information about the murder is urged to contact the Bakersfield Police Department immediately. An anonymous tip line has been set up as well. As the investigation unfolds, please hold the victim and her family in your thoughts and prayers, and know that Bakersfield's finest is hard at work on this case. I'm Aubrey Madison reporting live from downtown. Back to you, Gavin."

The shot transitioned back to the newsroom and the man with the painted-on smile. He swiftly moved on to the next segment without batting an eye.

"Barrientos, turn that shit off," Jenkins ordered, grinding his teeth.

3

"They've named the prick? A fucking moniker. Are you fucking kidding me?" Jenkins paced the conference room, stress and agitation radiating from the man. Everyone in the room could see it, feel it.

"That's what they do, Jenkins." Barrientos had backed away from the table, giving her partner space. "As soon as the press gets wind of a case, they dive in and make it their own. Put their stamp on it. They're fuckin' vultures. We knew this was coming."

Jenkins's jaw tightened, and he slowed to a stop, ignoring the comments. "Do you know what this means?" His stare looped through the room, locking eyes with every detective. "Do you?"

A heavy silence descended upon the room, the air thick with tension. The three held their wary glares and remained mute.

Jenkins seethed. "This means every citizen in the damn city now knows how she was killed—the burning, the Bible verse. The heat just got cranked up on all our asses to find this son of a bitch. And we've got jack shit to show. Zero progress. And now, the press is filling folks' heads with the idea that he might do it again."

An exasperated breath blew from his lips as he stood there, trying to manage the battering wave of news. In a relentless rush, it pummeled him. A humbling reminder of how far they still had to climb.

"Well then, we need to get ahead of this." It was Anzilotti. He rubbed his shaved head as he stepped closer to the others. Days-old stubble on his square chin. "The information is out there already, so what's the point of worrying and fretting? It'll change nothing."

Heads turned in his direction.

"But maybe we can use this to our advantage." Anzilotti glanced around the room. "The press has used some details from the crime—the Bible verse and the burning—to create this persona, this boogeyman. The Hand of God. Right?"

"Yeah, okay. What are you getting at, man?" Barrientos asked, a hint of annoyance and sarcasm dripped from each word.

Anzilotti continued. "Maybe this is what the bastard wants ... The attention."

"Go on." Jenkins and the others drew closer, piqued minds sifting through the ashes. "We're listening."

"Maybe that's why we've struck out on every lead, lost every inch we've gained." Anzilotti gestured at the heap of documents and photos scattered on the conference table. "He's a ghost hiding in the shadows for a reason. No one's calling him, tempting him to come back out and play."

"These psychopaths don't work that way," Barrientos stated. "They strike and then wait for the heat to die down before the urge fires up again. Sometimes years pass before they act out again."

"Slow down, you two." Jenkins's glare crossed the room, collecting everyone's attention. "We don't know if this guy is going to do it again. Don't let those assholes from the press influence you. And I better not hear anyone in this room use the word 'serial.' Evidence and facts steer our investigations, people, not the local paper or news anchors. Other than a hunch about the victim's sex life, we still don't know who this guy is or what motives drove him to prey on the victim. And we sure as hell will not call him that shitty name."

Anzilotti rubbed his head again. "I'm just saying if we embrace this, use it, maybe it'll force his hand. Perhaps it will give him a little push to show us something. Something that we've missed or haven't discovered yet. It's worth a shot."

Jenkins stood there, arms crossed over his chest, contemplating the man's idea. As much as he hated the thought, maybe Anzilotti had a point. "All right. But if this backfires, all our asses are on the line. What do you have in mind?"

4

An impromptu press conference occurred on the precinct steps an hour later. Jenkins led the charge, standing at the podium and addressing the band of reporters.

Cameras whirred and clicked as he claimed the spotlight, quieting the wave of questions firing his way. "Ladies and gentlemen. Settle down, please. I know patience in this matter has grown stale, and it is in the department's best interest to remain transparent about the investigation regarding Amelie Castro Rodriguez. We owe it to her family and our great city."

"What news do you have, Detective?" asked a reporter to his left.

"Do you have a suspect, a lead in the case?" One on his right wanted to know.

Jenkins ignored the questions. His stare hovered over the flock. "During the past few weeks, the department has conducted a substantial investigation into the murder case regarding Ms. Rodriguez. We have diligently combed through the evidence and completed a myriad of interviews with witnesses and suspects. And I am proud to announce that we are close to solving this case. A suspect has been named and is in our crosshairs."

A white lie, but they'll never know. Especially if this works, he thought.

Murmurs coursed through the crowd.

"Given your continued patience and understanding, the amazing work of this department has discovered a new piece of evidence that has linked us to the man responsible for this heinous crime."

Jenkins paused the rehearsed speech, his stare aimed directly at the horde of cameras. The murmurs instantly died.

"This is a message to the man out there who has stolen the heartbeat of our city. The man who has brought forth chaos and fear. Your days of hiding in the shadows are over. We know who you are, and we're coming for you. Justice will be served to the so-called Hand of God."

When he spoke the name, it stirred an uproar followed by a bombardment of inquiries. Each flung his way before the last was complete.

"I'm sorry. I'm sorry, everyone. That is all I have for you at this time. Trust in the process and know that the resolution is nigh. Ms. Rodriguez will have her justice. We're very close."

With that, Jenkin strolled away from the podium, rejecting the continuous probes and jabs. His slim frame vanished through the precinct's doors seconds later.

5

As the ten o'clock hour approached, Jenkins walked through the precinct's deserted parking lot. The overhead lights hummed, canceling out his tired footfalls. The day had been taxing, mind-numbing, and he needed to pull the plug for a few hours. Recharge the batteries. He prayed they hadn't made a mistake with the press conference. Before he could unlock his car door, a vibration stirred within his front pocket. He reached in and removed the cell phone. It was an incoming call from Barrientos.

"Jenkins here."

As the voice on the other line spoke, the blood drained from his face. Panic and shock immediately took root, strangling his thoughts.

"En route" was all he could muster.

Another body had been discovered.

XVIII

512 Height Street
2009

"For the last time, you're not going outside to play!" Mother snapped. "The streets are full of sinners. Godless delinquents looking to prey on the innocent. And don't even get me started on the germs and diseases out there plaguing the city. Besides, I'll never be able to help you if you get hurt. My back is too bad. You know that. Do not ask me again."

A tomato-red hue spread across his face, and a tremor pulsed through his core. "This isn't fay-uh. It's not fay-uh," he growled.

"I'll tell you what's not fair, boy." She took a stride forward through his doorway, her nostrils flaring. "For years now, I have cared for you, fed you, bathed you, taught you the word of God. And what do I have to show for it? Disrespect and defiance!"

Flinching at her words, he backed away, releasing his clenched fists. These tantrums stirred up more frequently now that he was a teenager, but a swift tongue-lashing or slap to the face always tipped him off the pedestal. He listened as her venomous rant continued, watching the heat rise and the fire burn in her dull eyes.

"I have had it up to here with you!" She took another step into the bedroom, jabbing a beefy index finger at him. The rolls on her arms and neck jiggled with each thrust. "When are you going to learn? Huh? When?"

Layer upon layer peeled away, stripping the thirteen-year-old down. He had stretched out over the years and now looked her in the eyes without straining his neck, but the spell she cast still carried weight. A trickle of urine spotted his underwear.

"And I can tell you're not practicing your speech." She seethed, her one good eye piercing through him. "Newsflash, Kenny! It's not fay-uh. The word is fair! Fair!" She reached out and grasped a handful of his greasy hair, yanking him to her bosom. "Say it, Kenny! Say it! Fair! Fair!"

He squealed in her clutch, days-old sweat and cigarette smoke striking him. "I'm sowwy! I'm sowwy!" he cried, his hands pawing at her death grip.

She pulled harder, strands of his dirty locks protruding between her knuckles. "You're still not saying it the right way! Why won't you learn? Why, why, why? It's not sowwy!"

In her grasp, he squirmed and thrashed about, desperately searching for purchase. His heels lifted off the matted carpet as she tugged, while the tendons in his thin neck stretched taut like a clothesline. Sobs joined the clash, blending in with the primal rage.

"Say it the right way, Kenny! The right way. Sorry! The word is sorry!"

A scorching, tireless torrent of pain battered him, searing his scalp with a white-hot intensity. It magnified with each passing second, the stress so high he hadn't noticed the river of piss leaking down his pants.

With a series of snaps, her grip loosened, and he could feel his feet gain stability. He collapsed to the ground a moment later, reaching for the burning pain on his scalp. His tear-filled glare shot upward, taking in the monster, the beast. Mother. She hovered over him, her fiery glare pinning him to the floor. Labored, ragged breaths heaved from her, expanding and contracting like the bellows of a blacksmith.

As he lowered his hand, he noticed the bloody tips of his fingers. But she ignored the wounds. Her attention was drawn to the mess he had made, the dark stain that ran down his pant leg.

"You filthy little—" The snarl seized mid-sentence, and she rocked backward. Her eyes sprang open, casting aside the blaze. An ashen hue painted her complexion. Clutching at her chest, she took another stride backward.

"Momma?" he called out, drool and snot clinging to his quivering lips.

A breath later, she fell backward, her heavy frame smashing into the doorjamb. Vibrations reverberated through the room, and a spiderweb of cracks blistered the drywall. She sat there, back against the wall.

"Momma!" He lifted himself from the floor and crawled to her, fear strangling his thoughts. "Momma, what happened? What's wong?"

He wedged himself between her side and the wall, taking in her round face. But something had changed. Greasy hair hid her features on the left side, but his eyes swung to the right. That whole side drooped: the eyes, the mouth, her pimply double chin. This wasn't his mother. This was a stranger. Shaking like a leaf, he brushed the thin strands from her face.

"Momma!"

Her eyes fluttered with panic before she gasped, "I can't . . . feel . . . my face. What's wrong . . . with my . . . face?" Each word slurred and distorted. "Kenny, what's . . . happening?"

He watched as fear consumed her. He tried to help, tried to speak, but the words lodged in his throat. The sounds were stolen. That was the last time he uttered a word. He became mute.

XIX

Different Alley, Different Woman

Rotating red and blue strobes painted the scene as Jenkins parked his car. Through the dusty windshield, his partner's frame materialized. Barrientos stood under an awning in front of the building with a sign that read *SMITH'S*, a family-owned bakery with deep roots within the community. She spoke to a pair of uniformed officers, delivering explicit instructions.

Jenkins eased out of the vehicle, hearing snippets of several conversations. A floodlight bathed the area behind the building where forensic technicians worked. He approached his partner, taking mental notes as he advanced. His heart fluttered with each stride, praying this wasn't what he suspected it to be. But deep within his consciousness, he knew better. He knew what awaited him behind the building.

Barrientos eyed him once he was within earshot, distress plaguing the woman's shadowed features. She didn't speak, just stood shaking her head.

"Tell me what you have so far." Jenkins's gravelly voice chipped away at the woman's reserve.

"It's . . . similar," Barrientos started. "The victim's a woman. Burned. Been here for about two hours."

"And the verse?" Jenkins paused, watching as Barrientos dropped her eyes to the pavement. "Is it there?"

Slowly, her chin lifted, but she couldn't form the words.

"Barrientos?" Jenkins leaned in, placing a hand on her shoulder. "Is the verse there?"

She gave a series of weak nods before she answered, "There's *a* verse."

"What do you mean, '*a* verse'?"

Barrientos forced a swallow. "It's not the same. It's different. A different name, different number. Different book, I'm guessing."

Shock swept in, battering away at the metaphorical dam Jenkins had built. He felt his breath hitch, and the angst that hid in the depths slowly rose to the surface, rupturing the levee. His stare drifted from his partner, landing on the building's exterior. He traced it until it ended. There, beyond the stuccoed corner where the front and side walls met, the floodlight waited. She waited. The second victim.

Releasing his grip on his partner's shoulder, Jenkins started toward the building's backside, rounding the corner seconds later. An orchestrated commotion appeared. Uniformed officers covering their noses with clasped hands gathered in clusters, their voices hushed by the drumming within his ears. Around the unis, technicians clad in disposable coveralls and face masks surveyed documents attached to clipboards. They exchanged glances as he approached.

The floodlight's intensity magnified the scene as his strides slowed to a stop. And the haunting nightmare from weeks ago reintroduced itself.

The new victim sat there, propped against the wall. Her charred and fire-licked legs jutted outward on the unforgiving, cracked asphalt. There was a slight lean to her torso, her blackened neck angled a few degrees more to the right. Blisters blanketed her scalp, where only a few strands of singed hair remained.

His eyes welled at the sight, but he forced the flood of emotions back. This wasn't a time for empathy. Shit had just hit the fan.

Mirroring the techs and officers working the scene, he shielded his mouth and nose with a kerchief before closing the distance. The sickening smell churned his guts, but he had to see her, see it.

Clumps of melded cartilage and flesh streaked her head, her face. They spread down her neck, slumped shoulder, and arm. The scorched remains of a T-shirt and bra clung to her blackened and crisp chest.

Déjà vu.

A sooty ring encircled her, and with the same ominous crawl as before, the flames climbed the wall, kissing the stucco. Jenkins's stare drifted above the woman, and the message that waited for him sank its teeth in.

As Barrientos had described, a Bible verse was there, etched into the inky grime. Like a mule, the message kicked him in the chest, and he felt a wave of nausea rush in from the blow.

Deuteronomy 5:18

2

As the witching hour approached, the clamorous energy of the crime scene came to a halt. The techs on site scoured the ground, the wall, and collected trace evidence from the victim: scraps of fabric, fingernail clippings, and a few strands of hair. They later bagged her and transported her away on a gurney. She'd spend the next few days in the morgue, where a thorough autopsy would take place.

The two detectives huddled near the bakery's front, nestled under the awning. Jenkins lit a cigarette, red ember glowing in the darkness. The air still held the sickening scent of burnt flesh, but the welcoming smell of tobacco cleansed his mind of the rot.

A grave tension drowned their words, neither knowing how to progress, but Jenkins sliced through the torrent.

"This is our fault. We did this." Guilt leaked from every word. "We called that fucker out on the news, and this is how he responded. Another dead woman. Another alley." He took a deep drag, plumes of smoke exiting his nostrils. "Another fucking verse."

Barrientos looked at her partner, but the words never came. Shock still held her in an icy grip.

Jenkins continued. "Whoever this woman is, she's dead because of our actions, Barrientos. Her blood is on our hands." He stomped out the cigarette with his heel.

"You . . . you don't know that," Barrientos choked out, chipping away at the frost. "This type of shit takes planning, logistics. We both know this prick isn't spontaneous. He's cerebral, cunning, and thoughtfully chooses his victims. Just like he did in the Rodriguez murder."

Jenkins ran his hand through his silver hair, chewing on her words.

"And a new verse is back there waiting for us. It's different from the Rodriguez scene," Barrientos said, her words flowing like a stream now. "Our actions didn't kill this poor woman. That piece of shit selected her, stalked her, and murdered her because of who she was or her lifestyle. Can't you see that? Deuteronomy 5:18. It condemns adultery, Jenkins. It fits."

"No, we taunted him, Barrientos!" Jenkins growled, the veins in his neck protruding like tree roots. "We played a hand we knew we couldn't win. And here are the results: more bloodshed, more pain, more terror for this damn city. And we still don't have a fuckin' clue who this guy is."

"Then we need to think harder, work harder. And we can start by figuring out who this new victim is. How is she connected?" Barrientos paused, her mind digging through the calamities.

"We'll know that in a day or two. Dental records will announce to the city who she is. The press is going to have a field day with it too. New murder, same calling card. The fuckin' Hand of God strikes again. I can already see the headline." Jenkins seethed, shaking his head.

Silence took hold, only the distant chirps from a police radio echoed in the open air. Both stood there, arms crossing their chests, their minds wilting with decay.

After a few moments, Barrientos shattered the stillness. "There has to be a connection between the two victims. My gut's enforcing the thought. Somewhere along the tangled web, these two have something in common. I know it."

Jenkins released a sigh, defeat setting in. "There's no connection. She's just another plaything he discarded once he'd had his fun. He's screwing with us."

"I think you're wrong, Jenkins. I really do," Barrientos said, her words gaining some strength. "Something's here. We just need to pry it loose."

"Listen. Two dead broads, two locations, two Bible verses. There's your connection, Barrientos. That's it."

The detective shook her head, defiance and determination swimming in her eyes. "No. I'm not accepting that. I have a different theory we need to revisit." She stepped closer to her partner, demanding the man's attention. "Let's go over the facts about the English teacher. The guy who received the strange text messages."

"What? I've combed through that. It's a dead end."

It was Barrientos's turn to force the hand. She reached out and gripped Jenkins's forearm, leaning into him. "Just . . . just tell me again. Let's walk through it once more together. Please."

Jenkins locked eyes with her. After a long sigh, he gave in to the plea. "We don't know what the pictures are, but the second one looks like a face. Maybe a woman's face, with blonde hair."

"That's it?"

"No. There was a name attached to the second picture. A woman's name. His adulteress."

"And where is this woman now?" Barrientos asked.

"She moved up north. She's out of the picture. Like I said, it's a dead end."

Barrientos's mind limped along, and she chewed on her lower lip before asking, "What about the picture? Are there other features besides the hair?"

"The boys down in IT tried to enhance the first one but struck out."

"Okay. Do you think our guy sent them?"

"I honestly don't know. But I've warned the kid to keep his head on a swivel just in case. I've got an unmarked car following him from work and home. Someone's fucking with him. Someone who knew about the Rodriguez murder. Could be our guy, but it's probably just some sick prank. Someone with a vendetta."

Barrientos collected that information, neatly filing it away in the forefront of her mind. "Okay. How about this? What color was the woman's hair? The one who moved up north."

"Why do you ask?"

"Because I want to know if she was a blonde."

"I already covered that base. She's not the woman in the picture."

"How do you know?"

"Because according to the English teacher, David Miller, she's a ginger. You know, like Nicole Kidman. She's a redhead. Her local police department confirmed this when I spoke to them earlier this week."

Barrientos stilled, her memory drifting back a few hours. Before Jenkins arrived, she was the first detective on the scene, and she claimed a front-row seat for the initial viewing. It chilled her to the bone. The victim's body was a disaster, charred and burnt beyond recognition, but a few clues survived the fire. Near her right temple, a clutch of locks remained unscorched, and under the blinding floodlight, she could see the color. It was a stark contrast against the blackened flesh.

"What color hair does our new victim have, Jenkins?" The question was rhetorical. She knew her partner had the answer.

Detective Jenkins paled, the blood draining from his face. "Son of a bitch."

"Do you think it's her, the redhead? The one who moved up north?"

"We're going to find out real fucking quick," Jenkins answered. "And if it is, I think we need to pay a visit to the English teacher. Either he's in grave danger or his ex-wife is."

Part Three

XX

Saturday Morning, May 30, 2015

Despite the intense temperatures of the previous days, the morning was tepid. Sparse clouds dotted the sky, and a cool breeze swept toward the northeast. It was the perfect way to start a summer vacation.

After parking the Volvo, David and Jenna walked toward a trailhead. Hiking was on the itinerary. Her idea, of course. She planned the outing, knowing the troubles and worries fretting her friend's mind. A day at Hart Park was the perfect remedy to cleanse the ills that lingered, she hoped.

They passed a few visitors during the quarter-mile trek to the trail: a family of four hosting a picnic and a group of teens trying to be as discreet as possible about the joint they passed back and forth. They even paused for a few moments to appreciate the sight of a father and daughter flying a kite. Hello Kitty winked at them from high above, fluttering in the midmorning sky.

A wooden sign nailed to a post came into view as they scaled down a mild ridge, stomping through the long and unkempt grass. Field crickets and cicadas scattered at their approach, ending the sweet sounds of nature's symphony. A sign signaled the start of the Kern River Trail—a three-mile loop that flanked the breathtaking waterway. Cut and etched into the landscape, the path was a highlight for many outdoor enthusiasts and hobbyists alike. And today, it marked the start of their adventure.

"Hey, be careful here, Jenna," David called out as he stepped over a fallen tree branch. "The river's just beyond this bend." He wore a light blue tank top and gray cargo shorts; his shoulders were already turning pink despite the mild weather.

Hot in pursuit, Jenna stepped over the same branch, noting its rotting and crumbling bark. "Right behind you." She knew this trail well and frequented it at least twice a month. It was a great place to escape. Loamy scents filled the air with each sure-footed stride.

The canopy opened up as they meandered down the trail, sandy footing replacing the hard-packed earth. Nearby, the trickling of running water sang to them, the sound both refreshing and inviting. A crow circled high above, its caws melding with the rhythmic tones.

"Wow, what a view!" David exclaimed as he rounded a cluster of saplings. The river, a ribbon of silver winding between smooth stones and moss-covered boulders, stole his attention. The sight was invigorating, and he hardly noticed Jenna sidling up next to him.

"Damn right, what a view," she said, her glare fixed on the swift flow of snowmelt. "I love this place, man. Whenever I come out here, freedom steals the show. All the built-up stress, the worry, the angst that scratches at your nerves . . . it all just rinses away. You know what I mean?"

He knew, and he didn't need to answer. That exact feeling currently flooded his body.

"The responsibilities of family, of work, they don't exist out here."

The mention of family tugged at his thoughts. Of his ex-wife, Maggie. But he wasn't here to wallow in a pit of self-loathing. He was here to take his mind off life. It was the first day of summer break, and he intended it to be a peaceful one.

"Where are your kids, by the way?" he asked. "I thought maybe I'd see them today. I love playing with those two."

That carefree look she always sported soured. "That deadbeat Pete has them this weekend. Picked them up at the butt crack of dawn and swept them off to Magic

Mountain for the day. He'll probably receive Father of the Year accolades for his troubles."

David didn't want to pry. He knew about the tension between her and the boys' father. It wasn't his place to stir the pot. "Hope they have fun. And I'm sure they'll tell you how much they missed you when they get home."

She shook off the compliment without a word, staring out across the expanse of flowing water. With her hand shielding her eyes from the sun, her gaze fell on a brood of mallards.

He joined her, reveling in the magic of nature, the ease it effortlessly injected. A drug he could get used to.

After a few breaths, he glanced her way. It was a subtle look, and he was pretty sure she didn't notice, but as he took her in, something unexplainable took root. A feeling, really. He'd always known Jenna was attractive. Most of the time he had to save her from the bands of drunken suitors she attracted, but right now, at this moment, he wasn't viewing her as his best friend. No, something deeper was forming, and he couldn't explain it.

The odd feeling percolating in his core died seconds later. A vibrating hum took him by surprise, originating from deep within his front pocket.

Who could that be? he wondered as he reached for his phone, a smidge of panic rising with each movement.

Jenna hadn't noticed, too preoccupied with the ducklings circling their mother.

The phone opened with his stare, then a bucket of ice, colder than the running water rushing in front of him, doused him. It was another message from Amelie. And this one wasn't a picture. It was a single phrase that flung him into the depths:

> *Her pain will be yours.*

2

Without a thought, he texted back:

> *Who is this? What do you want?*

He waited, anticipating seeing the three dots signaling a response. It never came.

He hammered away again, his thumbs a runaway train, and sent:

> *What do you want? What do you want?*

Still no response.

Jenna broke away from her moment with nature, glancing her friend's way and seeing the panic dripping off him. "What the hell, man? What's wrong, David?"

The world seemed to still, and a dark cloud consumed the warmth the day once held. He couldn't pull his stare from the phone screen, couldn't answer her. But a tremor ran through his whole body, and she knew she had to see what the cause was.

Pushing forward, she leaned into him and glanced at the screen. And his terror became her reality.

"When did that come through?" Shock and fear coated every word.

"Right . . . right now." He trembled. "I just got it."

"Who fuckin' sent it, David?" she demanded, grabbing the phone from his hand. Her green eyes pierced the screen's glass before drilling back on him. "Who?"

The message's icy grip strangled his response. He shook his head, unable to form the words.

Her thumbs went to work, trying to send the same message he had, but before she completed the inquiry, those three little dots appeared, and her core filled with dread at the incoming text:

> *She will suffer.*

The warmth usually evident on her face cooled to a frost. She slowly turned the phone his way, her hand shaking with each inch traveled.

The new message seared itself into his mind, burning away the traces of hope that still lived at the bottom of his soul. He knew the meaning. He knew who it referenced.

Maggie.

Breaking through the paralysis that held him in place, he reclaimed his phone and texted back:

> *Leave her alone! Leave my wife alone!'*

Seconds passed, the time slowly eroding his will, his need. Darkness crept in from every angle, smothering him in a world of black. The only sound he could hear was the thumping of blood through his ears as he stared aimlessly at the screen, praying for acknowledgment. And it came:

> *Her pain is yours now.*

The first text hit him like a right cross, staggering him to the ground. The second was just as potent:

> *You will feel it soon.*

"No, no, no, no, no!" he mumbled while typing his response:

> *Leave her alone, asshole! Stay away from my wife!*

David watched as the three little bubbles animated again, followed by:

> *Enjoy your hike. I'll see you tonight.*

3

David couldn't believe his eyes. He read the messages a second time, then a third. His stare flew to the horizon. Searching. Spinning in circles.

Where are you?

Nothing. No one.

They were alone. Two friends on a leisurely stroll through the park.

Seconds later, familiarity struck again. A steady pulse vibrated through the cell phone David held. His erratic turns and twists halted, and he froze in place.

No text waited, though.

This was a call. From Detective Bennett Jenkins.

XXI

512 Height Street
2012

As he entered the bedroom, the smell hit him like a ton of bricks: the malodorous combination of sweat, urine, and hopelessness. It coated the air in a thick layer, one that he'd grown used to. It was her scent. Mother.

Tiptoeing closer, her large, portly frame came into view. She lay there, splayed out on a sagging mattress against the far wall, one thick leg protruding from a tangle of sheet and blanket. A maze of varicose veins and bruises painted the exposed flesh.

He watched as her chest rose and fell. A wheeze from the back of her throat punctuated each labored breath. The soft whir of a table fan accompanied the distinct sounds of her sleep. Thin strands of her hair danced and tugged at her scalp with each pass of the fan's blades.

After the stroke, she spent most of her time here now, sleeping, sometimes stirring and crying out in pain. It was a constant that he accepted. Just part of life. And it was an opportunity to explore the world outside of Mother's grip.

The treasure he sought sat on the nightstand next to the fan. A relic hidden in plain sight, teasing and urging him. He had only taken the phone on three other occasions, but the desire for another taste of guilty pleasures was too tempting. Besides, if she woke up, she wouldn't be able to hurt him in her condition. Most days, she could barely get out of bed. Those moments of fear and pain no longer existed, even though the scars still bled.

His droopy glare followed the flutters of her eyelids, praying she wouldn't wake as he reached for it. And his petition was answered without a stir. The casing was cool in his palm, metallic edges sharp and gleaming under the room's dim lighting. It was the only thing she cared about during her waking hours (that and the pain meds) but now, at this moment, it was his ticket. A one-way trip.

He retraced his approach as he left the room, tiptoeing away with his borrowed toy. He didn't have long to play, but he'd delve into the media that tickled his fancy. Explore the net, dabbling in a few of the apps she'd downloaded. Pretend he was real.

As he hunkered down on the floor in his room, he opened the phone up, staring at the myriad of applications: Safari, YouTube, Snapchat, etc.

He opted for the video streaming giant, knowing an onslaught of cat videos and cartoon clips were on deck, an infinite supply of muffled laughter at his fingertips. He watched YouTube for a period, suppressing his chuckles. His stare always drifted to the open doorway after each payoff. Though the device he held delivered a sense of freedom and a childhood he never knew, the threat of Mother still weighed on his thoughts.

He left the phone sitting on the carpet as he inched toward the doorway, his ears on high alert. An abundance of caution and periodic patrols were part of the game.

Leaning through the doorway, he craned his neck down the hall. Her lair was mere feet away, across the expanse of crumbling drywall and creaky floorboards. But silence remained, entombing his persistent worry.

As he lowered himself onto the matted and stained carpet, he grasped the phone once again. His deft thumb reached for the blue and white Facebook icon—his second favorite—and it whirled him into a realm where he could watch the masses like a fly on the wall. Strangers from all walks of life argued, shared their political views, and lobbied for attention. Lobbied to be loved. It was a world where fear was dormant, and he could loiter without others noticing. Without them laughing and judging him. A digital haven.

A death scroll held him in its grip as he sat there, sifting through the posts and the profiles his mother followed. Actors, scantily clad models, and celebrities zipped by with each flip of his thumb. There they went without a care in the world. Erased and forgotten. But the numbing, endless loop ceased minutes later.

A woman he had never laid eyes on was shown on the screen. A three-quarter-sleeve white cardigan, made from a material like cotton candy, covered her torso, and a red pencil skirt hugged her figure. She was tall, but not imposing, as she stood next to a news van, her hands resting on her hips. A bright, beaming smile beneath a mop of thick blonde hair called to him, pulling him closer to the screen. But the physical traits only steered his vessel; it was her name that forced him to dock.

She shared a first name with the only other woman in his life—Maggie. Mother. A woman he loved and loathed and feared. The banner that ran along the bottom of the image read *Maggie Miller, Channel 23*.

XXII

Saturday Morning, May 30, 2015

"Mr. Miller! Are you there? It's urgent that I speak with you," Detective Bennett Jenkins barked into the phone, his gruff voice like a chisel.

David, his mind splintering into shards, held the handset to his ear, still shaking from the series of texts. "Wh-what?"

"I need you to listen to me. Are you there?" Jenkins asked.

"Yeah, yeah. I-I'm here," David stammered, trying to calm the brewing chaos. "Detective, it . . . it happened again. I just received another—"

"We know. We know," Jenkins stated, cutting him off. His tone was dire. "The victim's cell phone just pinged a tower on the outskirts of town. Out by the park. Units are en route. Are you safe?"

David scanned the area, dread pumping through his veins. "Yes, we are at the park. We're alone."

"Who is 'we'? Who are you with, Mr. Miller?"

Jenna came into his view as he made another scan of the area. "I'm with my friend. Her name's Jenna. You've met her."

"Okay. Again, units are en route, son. Hang in there. We're going to catch this son of a bitch."

David stayed on the line listening to the detective, hearing the assurance and authoritative tone in the man's voice. In the distance, a band of sirens wailed, getting closer with each damning swing of the pendulum. Yet, comfort never presented itself.

2

Fifteen grueling minutes later, heavily armed officers and department personnel were on-scene, sweeping through the rural area: up and down the trail, and expanding out in all directions. A helicopter supported their efforts from above—the eye in the sky. A BPD K-9 unit arrived with them. A Belgian Malinois trained in tracking burrowed through the thick brush beyond the trail, responding to her handler's commands. But with each pressing pass, she returned without a scent.

After the initial wave, the technicians on-site pinpointed an approximate area where the text originated using the coordinates from the victim's cell phone. And to their surprise, they discovered it came from across the river. Only a single dirt road accessed that side, and it was privately owned. Following a tense discussion, the landowner, an aged farmer not very keen on the idea of law enforcement poking around his property, granted the department access. Once the thorough search concluded, the investigation yielded only a single piece of evidence: a pair of footprints discovered on the dusty road, oriented toward David and Jenna. Whoever this subject was, they were watching from a distance before they fled.

Jenkins and Barrientos arrived amidst the organized chaos, and they quickly located the two friends. Both sat on the tailgate of a department vehicle while a paramedic took their vitals. Shock and worry swelled to a storm in their features.

Advancing toward the two, Jenkins called out, his voice carrying the weight of concern, "Mr. Miller, are you okay?" Dust clouds billowed under his footfalls with each stride.

David's stare flickered away from the paramedic, and a look of relief surfaced. "Thank God you're here. Yeah, we're fine. Pretty shook up, but we're doing okay." He glanced at Jenna, knowing that was not the case for either of them.

"Good. Good. That's good." Jenkins paused, the silence pummeling. His stare shot to the heavens, shielding his eyes with a hand before continuing. "Listen. We have little to work with as of now, but we're going to catch this guy. I promise. He's made a big mistake by reaching out again. The digital footprint will lead us right to his doorstep. We're close. I can sense it."

David agreed, delivering a nod. "I know. I know." But doubt hung in his words.

"And you, miss? Are you okay?" It was the first time Jenkins had truly acknowledged Jenna. Their few previous encounters had been short and abrupt. And this was more than that.

She leaned forward on the tailgate, her stare flowing past David's slouched shoulder. "I don't . . . I don't really know," she stammered, feeling a flood of emotions tugging at her heart. "This is all so crazy. I still don't know what the fuck is happening, man."

A wan smile formed on the detective's lips. "That's understandable. It is. Just know that we are here for you, and we'll sort this out. I've got the department's best working overtime to put an end to this. You can trust us."

A tear threatened to fall as she eyed the man. She mouthed, 'Thank you,' as she turned away, burying the avalanche of emotions cresting her thoughts.

"Hey, now that we know you're safe," Jenkins started, his view drifting back to David, "I have something else to discuss with you. Something that won't bring any comfort, but news I know you need to hear."

David dipped his chin, answering without a word. The noose that hung from his neck slowly tightened as he listened.

"This is going to be tough, but I want you to hear it from me first." Jenkins's posture stiffened, knowing he was about to drop the guillotine.

"Wh-what is it?" David stuttered as he slid off the tailgate, his hiking boots planted on the dusty trail. "What the hell do you have to tell me?"

Jenkins eyed him with empathy, but stretching this ordeal out was fruitless. He had to yank off the Band-Aid. "There's no easy way to say this . . . There's been another victim."

A ripple of panic worked its way up from David's gut, accompanying the veil of dread that smothered him. "Wh-what?"

"We found another body, Mr. Miller. Late Thursday night. Another woman. She was behind Smith's, the bakery on Union Avenue. Striking similarities from the crime scene suggest this is the same perp. After the woman was strangled, her body was dumped and then burned, just like Ms. Rodriguez."

That sudden drizzle quickly morphed into a torrential downpour, and David felt like he was drowning. "Who? Who was she?"

Silence cut like a dagger as Jenkins stood in front of the schoolteacher, forcing the words to come. "You may want to sit back down, son. This won't be easy to hear."

"Detective! Who is she?" Heads turned in their direction at the outburst, but they went unnoticed.

"Okay. Okay." Jenkins stepped forward. "After the autopsy, the dental records confirmed that the victim from Thursday night was Ms. Heather Stoneheuer."

David's eyes widened, and his heart skipped a beat. He felt like he couldn't breathe. "How is this possible?" he mumbled after reclaiming his seat.

Jenna reached over, wrapping an arm around his shoulders. Tears fell now, streaking her reddened cheeks. She was speechless.

"I wish I had the answer to that question," Jenkins replied. "He must have traveled up north and grabbed her, or he coerced her back down here somehow. I really don't know. And I need to get you out of here ASAP, son. My gut is telling me that your ex-wife's life is in dire straits."

David's eyes glazed over. "Then we need to go. We need to go now."

"My car's right over there. I'll drive." Jenkins gestured toward the dirt lot beyond the path's bend.

David could feel Jenna's touch slip away as she removed her arm from around his shoulders. He turned in her direction, seeing the strangled fear and torment flowing through her. "We have to go. I need to know that Maggie is safe, that she isn't in danger."

With a fresh batch of tears cascading down her cheeks, she said, "I know. Be safe."

"You're not coming with us?"

"I can't." Her voice cracked on the last word. "I can't deal with this, David. It's too much." She turned away, wiping her eyes with the back of her hand. "I just . . . I just need to get away from this. And I need to be home before Pete drops off the boys."

"Yeah, okay. I understand." David didn't want to pry. He could see how this event had affected her. "Call me when you get home, all right?"

"I will. I will."

Jenkins then led David toward his cruiser, leaving Jenna to collect her bearings. With any luck, they'd reach Maggie's house within the hour.

XXIII

2013

Shielding his eyes with a hand, he crept down the alleyway, stepping over the windblown collections of debris and litter. To his left and right, graffiti marred the walls; a tapestry of spray paint left by neighborhood gangs and delinquents. He wondered what the messages meant. Nicknames? It looked nothing like his bedroom walls: the calligraphy he wrote, the Psalms.

The narrow passage, barely a car width wide, funneled him to his destination. Where the alley ended, it branched off in opposite directions. But he wasn't concerned with what lay beyond. He'd explore them at a later date. The treasure he coveted waited straight ahead. It was a series of dumpsters lining the brick wall where the alley forked. Old, rusty, and on a few occasions, teeming with new toys.

This was a haven. A place where he could play without the constant worry of her. Mother.

Not that he had to worry about her much nowadays. Her bedridden state presented something he never thought was possible: freedom. He could come and go as he pleased, listening to the city, bathing in the sun's warmth. A rebirth.

He glanced around, his droopy stare searching for warnings. With no imposing threats, he opened the first lid. The acrid, sweet scent of rotting food punched at him, but he accepted the blow without complaint. Although the odor differed, it reminded him of home. Of her.

A fresh smell permeated her bedroom, originating in the past few days. Pungent yet comforting. It began as a tickling itch to his nose, but with each passing day, the potency multiplied. It seeped from her doorway, strangling the home in a fetid coat. To keep it at bay, he kept her door closed and stuffed rags into the gaps. Once or twice a day, he checked on her, but always found her asleep in the same position. She was a deep sleeper, after all.

After closing up the dumpster, he shuffled to his right. As soon as he lifted the second lid, he caught motion out of the corner of his eye. A lightning-fast flash of black, white, and gray scurried under the heap of trash bags. Hisses rang out, a primal threat filling his ears.

His lips curled up into an arch at the sound.

One by one, he tossed the trash bags onto the ground, slowly uncovering the hidden gem. It was smaller than the few he had played with before, and bared a set of sharp teeth below two masked eyes. Its puffed-up body and raised ringed tail sent a message he ignored.

Without another thought, he hopped inside and pulled out the kitchen knife hidden within his hoodie pocket.

2

He returned home an hour later, his sleeves and knees soiled in a brownish-red hue. Tufts of fur clung to his stained fingers. As he approached Mother's doorway, that familiar scent, that new scent, wafted toward him. It reminded him to check on her. He hadn't seen her since that morning when he had stolen her phone.

Her bedroom door groaned as he opened it, sliding inside with haste. He spun around and closed it, praying she wouldn't stir. She didn't.

He sidestepped toward the mattress she lay on, adjusting his eyes to the room's dimness. She was still there on her back, eyes shut, in the same position as the past three or four days. He wondered if he should wake her, help her to her feet. Maybe she needed a little sunshine, some fresh air. But he discarded the thought. He didn't want to disturb her. He knew how distraught she could be when she woke.

As he peered down at her, he noticed some subtle changes in her physical appearance: blanched complexion, sunken eye sockets, and the plumpness of her cheeks and chin had withered. He reached down and gently grazed her cheek, finding her pale flesh cold and stiff.

Was she sick? he wondered.

He backed away from her bed and left the room, ensuring the door shut noiselessly as he departed. Mother needed her rest.

Seconds later, he entered his bedroom. His view drifted along the four walls, admiring the collage of Scripture that painted the surfaces. From floor to ceiling in permanent black marker, the Lord's word called to him, ushering him along the path of righteousness. The message was clear, but it wasn't his time yet. Patience was a virtue of the divine.

With a smile strapped on his face, he sat down in the room's center, crossing his legs. He lifted the cell phone to his face and opened the Facebook app. Disappointment struck him. She still hadn't answered his DM, but he knew she would soon enough. Maggie Miller worked for the people.

XXIV

Saturday Afternoon, May 30, 2015

"David?" Maggie Miller demanded, staring at her ex-husband through the front door, slightly ajar. The security chain drew taut as she peeped through the opening. Her disheveled hair was up in a bun, a mop of blonde tendrils falling into her eyes. She wore a lavender bathrobe cinched around her thin waist. "What are you doing here?"

"Listen, Maggie," David replied, an avalanche of ill pulling him along. He hadn't seen her in months, besides when she appeared nightly on the six o'clock news. "I'm really sorry for showing up unannounced like this, but we need to come inside."

Her awkward stare drifted past David to the two detectives standing behind him. She eyed the tall, slender man with the silver hair first, then landed on the no-nonsense sneer of the woman beside him. "Who are they?"

Jenkins stepped forward, sliding past David. He opened his sports coat, flashing his badge. "My name is Detective Bennett Jenkins. This is my partner"—he glanced over his shoulder for a split second—"Detective Angela Barrientos. We need to come inside. It's imperative that we inform you about a situation."

Maggie eyed the two, then swung her gaze back to her ex-husband. "David! What is this?"

"I'll tell you everything, Mags. Everything," David assured. "You'd better put on a pot of coffee, though."

2

Maggie paced the living room an hour later, trying to digest the macabre news thrown on her plate. As a reporter, shocking, scandalous, and violent stories were a constant, but this hit too close to home. The murders, the Bible verses, and the fact that a killer was out there stalking David and possibly stalking her, sent her mind reeling.

"That woman?" Maggie whimpered, facing her ex-husband. "She's dead?"

David sat on the couch in the living room. The one they shared as a happy couple for many years, watching television while snuggling under the afghan his great aunt crocheted. The two detectives stood to his left.

He gave her some space, knowing the scaffold could come crashing down at any second. "I'm really sorry, Mags. They found her body on Thursday night."

"What does this mean?" Her voice shook with each syllable. "Why did he kill her? Because of us? Because of what you did?"

Rising from the couch, he moved toward her in the center of the room, the familiar scent of her perfume filling his nostrils and triggering a cascade of memories from their shared past. He stared down at her, seeing the tears well within her light brown eyes. The sight crushed him. He reached out and pulled her into an embrace, feeling tremors quaking through her core. Cupping the back of her head with his hand, he knew this was his fault.

"I don't know what to say, Mags. I really don't," he whispered into her ear. "I'm so sorry."

After a few moments, she pulled her face away from his chest, tears running down her cheeks. "What are we going to do?"

From the couch, Jenkins answered the question, "You two are staying here."

Both David and Maggie shot him a look.

The detective continued. "We don't know what this guy has planned, but we know he has a vendetta to settle. And it all wraps around the both of you."

Alarm replaced worry on Maggie's features. "What if he comes here?" The thought was terrifying, and it smothered her.

Jenkins eased off the couch and joined them in the room's center. "I don't think he'll be that bold, Maggie. He's already made a mistake by following David out to the park. That was sloppy. He won't make another one this soon. Doesn't fit his pattern."

"But what if he does?" David asked, releasing his embrace of Maggie. "What are we going to do if he comes here? If he tries to hurt her? Or me?"

"You won't have to—" Jenkins started.

"That will never happen!" Barrientos interrupted. She strode toward the others, self-confidence oozing from her pores. "Not on our watch. And if he's stupid enough to try, we'll nab his ass before he knows what happened."

Jenkins glanced at his partner. "She's right. If this sicko's desperate, if he needs to feed his sick desires and he arrives here, we'll be ready. A swarm will be on him before he steps foot on the property. But again, I don't see that happening."

The assurance should have brought relief, but it only confirmed reality. They were trapped, and a killer was out there. Somewhere.

3

Unmarked cars sprinkled the neighborhood, parked in strategic locations to keep a keen watch on the two-story house as the safety and warmth of the sun slowly dipped to dusk. The undercover officers inside, communicating with two-way radios, watched as vehicles and pedestrians came and went. Neighbors returning from a day of errands, rambunctious teens and kids riding skateboards and bikes, couples out for an early evening stroll with dogs in tow.

Inside the home, Jenkins parked in the living room. He sat in a foldable chair near the front room's large pane of glass. Peering out from the left side, he pulled the drawn curtain away from the window just enough to see the front porch, lawn, and a sliver of the street where Anzilotti and Johnson's car sat. The vehicle's tint hid any motion. A row of cypresses bordered the property's front yard, obstructing his view farther down the street.

Barrientos claimed the second floor. A banister overlooking the lower level showcased most of the home below. She paced the landing at regular intervals, entering each of the three bedrooms and scanning the back and side yards. Motion sensors were aimed at these areas, a win for her. If anyone or anything tripped the lights, she'd know where and when. She communicated with her partner and both detectives positioned on the street via handheld radio.

The two ex-spouses sat at the kitchen table, trying to shake the fear that continuously looped in their thoughts. Half-empty mugs of room-temperature coffee sat in front of them.

"I'm scared, David," Maggie whispered, her eyes fidgety, darting around the room.

"I know you are. So am I, Mags," David said. His voice carried a nervous quality that he attempted to hide. "But we're safe. Nothing is going to happen as long as they're here. You heard the detectives."

"I still don't understand what the hell is happening," she said, struggling to rein in the chaotic storm of feelings raging within. "Why is he doing this? Why is he after us?"

"I still haven't pieced that together," he said, staring at his coffee mug. Imprinted across the ceramic cylinder was a single word adorned with a gold, bejeweled crown: *KING*. He had forgotten all about it. "The police haven't either, but we need to trust them. They'll figure this out, and maybe someday, we can go back to living our normal lives."

The phrase "normal lives" didn't sit well as he said it. What is normal these days? Living alone, eating alone, knowing his life fell apart because of his mistake—the one thing he wished had never happened. And because of that mistake, people were now dead. Innocent people. Amelie. Heather.

Was he next? Maggie?

"Don't leave me!" She looked at him, her light brown eyes glimmering under the lights.

He returned the look. "I won't. I promise."

Minutes passed in silence as they sat there, the only constant being the ticking of the grandfather clock in the living room. It echoed throughout the house, an omnipresent reminder that this wasn't a dream.

A few minutes after eight p.m., a radio's chirp joined the clock's ticks. Muffled voices came through the speaker immediately after. David and Maggie could hear Barrientos's footsteps above as she approached the banister, wood creaking with each stride. They looked up at her, seeing an index finger pressed to her lips. The detective held the radio to her ear with her free hand.

From the living room, Jenkins's gravelly whisper cut through the silence, "I can't see him." His fiery gray eyes narrowed on the street, watching a dark silhouette in the distance.

"Wh-what is it, Detective?" David asked as he tiptoed closer, peering into the room.

"*Shhh*," Jenkins responded, never diverting his focus from his target. His voice held the conviction of a judge. "Stay where you are and be absolutely quiet."

David could feel Maggie's breath on his nape. He glanced over his shoulder, watching the color drain from her face. Neither could speak.

"Who has eyes?" Jenkins asked, radio to his lips.

A static crackle came through the speaker seconds later. "The subject just rounded the block's corner. On the other side of the street. Four houses down."

Jenkins's gaze drifted to his partner on the second floor. She'd replaced the radio with the Glock she had strapped to her belt.

"What do you see?" Jenkins demanded, returning his focus to the front yard once more. "I repeat, what do you see?"

The crackling returned after a brief stint of quiet. "Possible male, tall build, broad shoulders."

"Go on," Jenkins urged.

"Subject just crossed the street. Dark features, dark clothes."

Jenkins tried to stare down the street, pulling the curtain open wider, but it was fruitless. With the dying sun and the dark green hues of the shrubs blocking his view, he couldn't see shit.

"Where is he? I repeat, where is the target?"

"Subject just passed the neighbor's front yard. He's within range. Are we a green light, Jenkins?"

"No, do not engage. Hold. Don't act yet. Everyone hold."

As the last word slid off his tongue, a dark silhouette came into sight. It crept past the towering row of cypresses, coming up the sidewalk just outside. Jenkins took in the sight, watching the figure pace along. The image instantly stoked the fire of his memories, and the synapses burned with brilliance as the darkness rushed in.

With a series of blinks, he was no longer in the two-story home of Maggie Miller. He looked around the scene, allowing the light to adjust. Slowly, clarity took root. The conference table from the precinct, the cluster of papers and scattered documents, his desk and telephone, all came into view. The vividness oozed with realism. After another scan around the room, an object stole his focus. The television cart. A centerpiece demanding an audience. A video played on the rectangular screen, one that haunted his mind every night.

A young woman walked through a parking lot late at night. Behind her, a figure emerged, dressed in black pants and a black hoodie.

As he shook off the memory, the same figure—black pants, black hoodie pulled over his head—now paused right outside Maggie Miller's home.

Jenkins's pulse hammered against his throat. "Target is right outside. All units, we have movement right outside the home."

The figure stood there on the sidewalk. In the dim light, Jenkins watched as the suspect raised something to their face. A phone. The glow illuminated features that didn't sit well.

The radio crackled. "Hold on. Subject is on a phone call. Appears to be . . . wait . . ."

The figure suddenly picked up pace, not toward the house, but along the sidewalk. A rhythmic bounce was incorporated into their stride. Jenkins squinted harder, trying to make sense of the movement.

"False alarm," said the relieved voice through the crackling. "Subject is jogging. I repeat, the subject is a jogger. White male, approximately thirty years old, wearing headphones. Just stopped to take a call."

Jenkins watched as the jogger disappeared around the corner, his reflective running shoes catching the glimmer from the streetlight. The tension in his shoulders began to ease, but only slightly.

"Stand down, but maintain positions," Jenkins whispered into his radio. He glanced toward David and Maggie, both of whom had been holding their breath. "False alarm. Just someone out for a run."

David let out a shaky exhale. "Jesus, Detective, I thought—"

Jenkins cut him off, "Don't think. Stay alert. That wasn't him, so he's still out there."

Barrientos's voice sounded from upstairs, "All quiet on the north and east sides. Sensor lights haven't triggered."

Jenkins settled back into his chair, but kept his grip tight on the radio. The grandfather clock resumed its dominance over the house's soundtrack.

Twenty minutes passed. The neighborhood settled into its evening rhythm—porch lights flickering on, the distant sounds of televisions through open windows, the occasional car engine starting up.

Then the radio crackled again. "Jenkins, we've got another one. Southeast corner, moving slow this time."

Jenkins straightened, his blood running cold. Through the cypress trees, another shadow emerged. This one moved with purpose, no bounce in the step, no phone pressed to an ear. The figure paused at the edge of the property line, scanning the house with deliberate calculation.

"This is it," Jenkins whispered, his voice barely audible. "This is him. The Hand of God."

4

Ding-dong.

Maggie flinched at the sudden chime, burrowing her face into David's side. He held her, his glare glued to the front door. They receded back into the kitchen, the room's far wall stopping the retreat. All they could do now was watch.

"Green light. I repeat, green light," Jenkins whispered into the radio, then set it down on the coffee table. He approached the door, sidestepping forward with his weapon drawn.

Barrientos matched his strides, her Glock's sights aimed just below the door's peephole.

The deadly sting of silence shrouded the room. David could hear his heart hammering in his ears, and his vision slowly morphed into a haze. He couldn't feel. He couldn't move. All he could think about was Maggie.

From beyond the door, shouts rang out in a fiery blaze while beams of light danced through the drawn curtains.

"Police! BPD! Get on the ground!" The muffled shouts reverberated through the door. "Get on the ground!"

A blink later, a commotion occurred, and the door shuddered in place.

Nothing.

Time stretched out, throwing kindling on the pain and fear.

"Subject is in custody. I repeat, the subject is in custody."

Jenkins released the breath he held, then glanced his partner's way. A stream of sweat trickled down the side of his brow.

Barrientos returned the look, her natural complexion pushing aside the ghostly pallor.

They both lowered their weapons, trying to settle the adrenaline rushing through their veins.

It was over.

5

Jenkins slid through the front door first, Barrientos his shadow. They headed for the unmarked car parked up the street: Anzilotti and Johnson's cruiser. The two detectives stood on the sidewalk while four officers held the figure in black face down on the neighbor's front lawn. Hands bound behind his back with a thick white zip tie, the man in black struggled, flinging curses out into the cool night.

David watched the action from the stoop, feeling Maggie lurking right behind him. She gripped the hem of the tank top he wore, wringing it in a death grip. Safety was his only thought, but curiosity twisted his gut. He had to know who this guy was. What triggered the killings? Why?

With caution, he eased down the steps but found his momentum stopped. He looked back at Maggie, his ex-wife, and could feel the tautness in her pull. She shook her head from side to side and mouthed, "Don't."

"It's okay. It's over, Mags," he said, his voice anxious. "Everything's over now. Everything's fine." Her grip loosened, and he took a step backward, away from her. "I'll be right back. I promise. There's nothing to worry about anymore."

She stood there on the porch, her waves of golden blonde stressed by the overhead light. She remained silent, watching as he descended the last step. He left her.

Shouts and agitation carried into the air as David made his way down the walkway. The figure in black wriggled on the grass, pinned down by numerous knees and brawny arms. His attention swung to the commotion. As he inched up the sidewalk, fixated on the tumult, he heard something that wasn't possible. He heard the figure's distraught voice. And it sent chills up his spine.

He knew that voice.

XXV

2014

Derek: Hey beautiful, how was your day?

Maggie: Hi Derek! Long day at work, but I'm finally home. How was the construction site?

Derek: Rough. The boss had us working overtime again. My back is killing me. Sometimes I wonder if this job is worth it.

Maggie: You should take better care of yourself. Maybe a hot bath? That always helps me unwind.

Derek: You always know what to say to make me feel better. You're like . . . I don't know, like the mother I never had.

Maggie: That's sweet, Derek. But I'm only 35! I'm more like a big sister, don't you think?

Derek: Right, sorry. I just meant you're so caring. My mom would have liked you.

Maggie: You mentioned she passed away recently. I'm sorry for your loss.

Derek: Two years ago. Cancer. I still miss her every day. She used to make these amazing chocolate chip cookies.

Maggie: I love baking! Maybe I could make some for you sometime? When we finally meet in person?

Derek: Really? You'd do that for me?

Maggie: Of course! Friends look out for each other.

Derek: We're more than friends though, right? I feel like we have this connection.

Maggie: Derek, you're very sweet, but I'm married. You know that.

Derek: I understand. I can wait. I'd wait forever for you, Maggie.

Maggie: That's . . . intense. Are you okay?

Derek: Yeah, I'm fine. Just tired. The guys at work were giving me grief today about still living with my roommate.

Maggie: Roommate troubles?

Derek: He's younger than me and sometimes acts like it. Leaves messes everywhere. Typical college kid stuff.

Maggie: Wait, I thought you said your roommate was your age?

Derek: Did I? Must have meant he acts young for his age. Sorry, I'm exhausted. Not thinking straight.

Maggie: Maybe you should get some rest?

Derek: Can we talk a little longer? I love hearing from you. It's the best part of my day.

Maggie: Just for a few more minutes. I have an early meeting tomorrow.

Derek: Thank you. You have no idea how much you mean to me, Maggie. How much I need you.

Maggie: Derek, that's concerning. We don't really know each other. You shouldn't need anyone that much. Maybe you should talk to someone? A counselor?

Derek: I don't need a counselor. I need you. You're the only one who understands me.

Maggie: I think we should take a break from texting for a while. This is getting too intense.

Derek: No, please! I'm sorry. I'll be normal. I promise. Don't leave me too.

Maggie: Too? Who else left you?

Derek: Nobody. Just . . . my mom. When she died. Please don't abandon me like she did.

Maggie: Derek, your mother didn't abandon you. She passed away from cancer. That's very different.

Derek: I know. I'm sorry. I'm not making sense. I just can't lose you. You're all I have.

Maggie: I'm worried about you. This level of attachment isn't healthy. I think you should speak to a professional.

Derek: I'll do whatever you want. Just don't stop talking to me. Please, Maggie. I'll be better. I'll be the man you need me to be.

Maggie: Goodnight, Derek. We'll talk tomorrow when you're feeling clearer.

Derek: Wait! Maggie!

Derek: Maggie, please answer me.

Derek: I need you.

Read 9:23 PM

Derek: I know you read that. Why won't you answer?

Derek: Fine. I understand. You need time. But I'll prove to you that I'm worthy of your love. Whatever it takes. Mother.

XXVI

512 Height Street
December 2014

He had never learned the concept of Christmas—the gifts, the carols, the decorations—except that it was Jesus's birthday. She always reminded him of that. He didn't understand any holidays, really. Any celebrations either. They were all just abstract ideas that were never truly explained during his eighteen years on this planet. The only societal norms that took root were devotion and the Lord. And both came in heaping spoonfuls from his mother.

But she was gone.

It took ten days to acknowledge the truth. Ten painful days of confusion and torment. He'd enter her room every morning, every evening, hoping she would wake. Praying to the Lord that she would be upright, longing to embrace him in a bearish hug. But she never did. He felt alone, abandoned.

The clues were there, but he'd buried them. Spadeful after spadeful of denial. This was his mother—his strength, his reason for breath. The woman he hated with every fiber of his being, but also loved.

It started with her position in bed: how she lay there on her back, one beefy leg jutting out of a tangled sheet, day after day. His stare drifted to that leg, studying the thick, round segments and the purplish maze of veins just below the skin. But she never moved, and that peachy hue of the coarse coat of hair covering her thighs and calves slowly faded to a ghostly gray.

Another clue was in her breathing. He grew accustomed to hearing the deep purrs emitting from her throat while she slept, whether it was in bed or on that sagging couch that reeked of sweat and piss. When she first took him in, her snores bored into his skull, breaking him away from the few hours that he was allowed to rest each night and not expected to read and learn the Lord's word. But over the years, he grew used to them, and they brought a level of comfort.

After a couple of days, he noticed there were no snores sounding through her bedroom, and her thick, portly chest didn't rise and fall. It was odd. Was she playing a game?

Then came the smell. From the first day he came to live with her, she carried a signature scent: cigarette smoke, stale perspiration, and other body odors which tickled his nose. A dinginess that painted the home's interior and exterior. It clung to his clothes, his skin. He could even taste it.

Around the fourth day, he noticed something sweet and sickly had joined the putrid scents he knew so well. It was a corrosive smell, like meat rotting on a summer day. He tried his best to bat it away, keep it contained within her room, but the potency defied his efforts. Eventually, it overtook the entire house, and the truth forced his hand. Her purpose having been served, the loving and nurturing spirit that had always looked after him and imparted all knowledge ultimately left the body that housed it.

His thoughts drifted to the miracle of resurrection once he accepted the truth. Like Christ himself, would she rise after three days, come back and lead him, and finish her teachings? The idea filled him with solace, but after the seventh day, the thought died and dissipated like ash after a fire.

He now faced the inevitable: what to do with her? Mother.

Four-hundred-plus pounds of decaying flesh couldn't be moved on his own, and he had no means to reach out and ask for help. She had taught him from an early age never to trust the police, so that avenue was a no-go. Maybe Facebook? But the collection of friends he had made on the social platform didn't know him. Not really. The profile he created years ago was a facade: his name, the pictures he downloaded and used as his own, the conversations he carried on with strangers dubbed friends (Amelie and Heather) . . . none of it was real. They knew only Derek. They didn't know Kenny.

Even the short but sweet DMs from Maggie Miller, the beautiful news reporter—the only other woman his heart ever thumped for—weren't authentic. After several attempts to contact her and befriend her, she finally accepted his advances. No strings attached, of course. Just friends. The two carried on a playful banter for close to a year using only their thumbs. It was the closest thing he had to a relationship.

The choice he made wasn't easy; it was revolting, but it was necessary. He had to honor his mother, and also rid the home of the stench he could taste. The putrid odor wasn't localized any longer; it was now wafting toward the homes that flanked them. He didn't need authorities or neighbors poking their noses around.

After sifting through the crumbling shed in the side yard, he found a shovel. The handle was thick and strong. Orange blotches of rust corroded the metal, but it would work. It would dig the hole he needed. But this wasn't the only tool he found. He also found a hacksaw.

2

On the night of Christmas Eve, they came. He had only heard the sound a few times before—the knocking on the front door. It was an oddity that invoked confusion and fascination. He'd seen the action through video clips on the internet and reruns of old sitcoms, but he'd never experienced it in real life. Any time it happened, Mother always dealt with it after she ordered him to hide in his room. He was lost, lacking the logic of how to respond.

He crept from the comfort of his room, black Sharpie in his hand. Before the interruption, he was diligently working on the ceiling. Scripture covered half of the drywall. As he crept closer to the front door, he could hear muffled voices beyond. Foreign voices. Strangers.

A second series of knocks came. He watched the door reverberate from the firm blows. Small flakes of peeling paint fluttered in the air, dancing with the dust motes. He held his ground, listening, watching, his primal fight-or-flight instincts firing.

There wasn't a third knock, but silence didn't coddle him. A shuffling sound joined the muffled voices beyond the door. It was brief, and it gave way to footsteps leaving the stoop. Whoever the guests were, they left moments after arriving.

An hour passed before he mustered the courage to open the front door. And when he did, he found the porch and the yard empty. The chain-link fence at the property's edge allayed his reservations. He was alone, protected from the dangers that trespassed upon him. The event was over.

But something wasn't right. A feeling rippled through his core, and he found he couldn't breathe. Taped to the front of the door was a piece of pink paper. With a trembling hand, he reached for it and brought it to his eyes.

It was an eviction notice. The city had deemed the property *CONDEMNED*.

3

After Google explained what was to come, he ran, leaving the dilapidated structure behind. The idea of authorities and strangers entering his home, forcing him to leave, speaking to him when he couldn't reply, leveled him harder than the loss of his mother. And what he had to do with her body. But with her absence, there was no reason to stay. He grabbed her car keys and her cell phone and left.

He had never driven before, but his trusty friends on YouTube helped him to smash through that barrier. Within minutes, he was swerving down the road, leaving his childhood home in a wake of black exhaust. It wasn't easy to say goodbye, but the inevitable stoked the coals, giving him little choice.

Taking to the streets, he sought refuge in shopping centers, resorting to rummaging through dumpsters for food (and for rats and the occasional opossum to suppress his urges). But after a few days, the business owners shooed him away; they couldn't have a homeless mute and his battered old car scaring away customers and their dollars.

The pattern continued for close to a month: new alley or parking lot, always the same result. Society didn't want him; he was an outcast, lost and without a path to follow. The only refuge he found as he lay down at night in the car's back seat, huddled under a dingy, oil-slicked blanket? The memories he had of his mother and the other Maggie he loved: Maggie Miller. But even those slowly faded. After a week, his mother's cell phone stopped working and the fumes the car had run on dried up. He was stuck, alone, without guidance. Another victim of societal loss.

But as grim as life looked, a new outlook presented itself one Saturday morning. He found a new avenue of communication with Maggie Miller: a new cell phone. It was just sitting on top of a gas pump one day as he sifted through a trash can. Clearly a burner phone someone didn't care about. Some deadbeat lowlife, he figured. He charged it periodically while docked outside a convenience store, using their electricity. It was the only means of continuing the online life he had grown to enjoy so much. The life of Derek.

Days later, after learning to beg for change from the hordes of consumers coming and going at a nearby Fastrip, a new haven presented itself when he stumbled through the opening of a chained and padlocked gate. Once a prosperous agricultural shipping facility, the appearance now was that of a deserted, haunted attraction.

A series of abandoned buildings peppered the land, poking up through the parched ground like a battalion of lonely sentinels. On approach, he stepped over patches of yellowed grass that broke through the cracked and weathered asphalt. Broken shards of windows littered the floor, crushing under his boot soles as he entered the largest of the set.

Shelter. Warmth. Home, he thought, staring around the open space.

XXVII

August 2014

His eyes widened at the sight, and a flame of shock ignited as he stared at the phone. The blue light cast shadows across his dull face, making his hollow cheeks appear even more sunken. His fingers trembled as they gripped the device, knuckles white from the strain.

It wasn't possible. It must have been a mistake. No one could act with such carelessness, such disregard for her feelings. Her heart. His breath came in short, ragged gasps as he scrolled through the evidence: the photos, messages, timestamps that painted a picture so vile it made his stomach lurch. The betrayal was carnal and unforgiving.

How could he? The thought sliced through his mind like a blade.

He knew about the husband, the other man in her life; the one she rarely talked about in their harmless texts. (Texts with Derek.) When Maggie mentioned the husband at all, it was with a distant politeness, the way one might reference the weather.

David's grading papers again.

The man was a pawn, though. An afterthought, barely acknowledged by the queen he knew so well. In his mind, David existed as a shadow figure, present but irrelevant, occupying space in Maggie's world without truly inhabiting it. He never viewed him as a threat, considering him incapable of tearing out her heart and tossing it into a raging bonfire.

But he should have known better. He should have seen the signs. The way Maggie's messages had grown shorter lately, distant. The forced curtness that couldn't quite mask the hollow sadness beneath. Then, how she'd stopped responding to his messages. He chalked up her absenteeism to work stress, to the burdens of her daily life as a news anchor. He never fathomed that the husband would hurt her.

She trusted him, he thought, his jaw clenching until it ached. *She gave him everything. Her youth, her loyalty, her pure heart, and he threw it away?!!*

He stalked her feed for the rest of the day, refreshing every few minutes, reading the outpouring of messages from family and friends. The words felt small; pathetic attempts to bandage a wound that required surgery. It crushed him to see her so vulnerable and betrayed.

The worst part of the silence was that she had posted nothing in three days. No updates, no responses to the flood of sympathy. He could picture her: his beautiful, broken mother figure, curled up somewhere in the dark, crying tears that should never have fallen. The image made his hands shake with rage.

And slowly, inevitably, the shock that had stolen his focus morphed into something else entirely. The disbelief crystallized into a raging fire, one of hate and anger that consumed every other thought. David's face, pulled from his social media presence, became the target of his waking hours and sleeping nightmares. That dimpled chin, those hazel eyes, that smug smile in photos where he stood beside Maggie like he owned her.

He doesn't deserve to draw breath. He realized with startling clarity. *Not after what he's done to her. Not after breaking something so precious.*

The husband had to pay, had to feel her pain, her suffering, magnified and returned tenfold. It was just and deserved. It was what any loving son would do for his mother.

He wrote the verse he had memorized in his youth on his bedroom wall.

If a man commits adultery with his neighbor's wife, both the adulterer and the adulteress shall be put to death.

—

Leviticus 20:10

Kenny stood back and admired his work, feeling something close to peace for the first time in days. The words looked official there, like a message from a higher power speaking through his hands.

It will be done, he thought, his eyes burning with conviction. *It will be done for you, Maggie. Mother.*

XXVIII

Saturday Evening, May 30, 2015

"Get the fuck off me!" The subject's rage-filled demand echoed through the night. Every tendon in his body grew taut, rippling through his flesh. "Get your hands off me!"

David crept forward on the sidewalk, seeing the scuffle on the neighbor's lawn. The streetlight above highlighted the event. Four police officers in street clothes held the man face down, knees piercing his shoulders and the backs of his legs. They pinned him, overpowering his relentless struggle.

"If you don't stop struggling, asshole, I'll spray you with this shit."

The threat came from a man hovering over the melee. Thick muscles ripped through his T-shirt, matching the attitude of his cleanly shaven head. He aimed a can of pepper spray at the man in custody. A leaner, younger man stood at his side, mirroring the pose.

Others surrounded the commotion, holding flashlights and hands on their sidearms, prepared to protect their own and kill if needed. Leers of relief and indifference aimed the subject's way.

A growl, animalistic and enraged, flew from the man's mouth, spittle dripping from his lower lip. He heaved and pulled for freedom. As his neck strained, trying to break an arm free, his eyes landed on the man standing on the sidewalk. On David.

"Tanner?"

Suddenly the man stilled, his tense frame relaxing. His eyes widened to dinner plates, the streetlight above highlighting their light brown color. "Dave? Is that you?"

A tense wave of nausea struck the second he heard his name called. It lined his gut, forcing its way up into his throat. He froze, tasting the bile, a statue of flesh and bone shaking in the night.

"Dave?" Tanner called out again. "What the fuck is going on, man?" Tanner craned his neck, glancing at the two officers pinning his shoulders to the grass. "Who are these guys?"

David stood there, unable to speak, unable to move. A barrage of emotions battered him in an endless cycle: confusion, anger, fear, betrayal, guilt. They built a towering precipice he couldn't face.

Detective Jenkins stepped forward, obstructing the tense moment, Barrientos in tow. He aimed his glare at David, but it wasn't the face of a victor. Nor was it the smug look of a man lobbying to boast his accomplishments. It wasn't relief.

The lean, silver-haired detective wore a mask of solemnity. Beaten down and tired from the hunt. He looked like shit.

"Mr. Miller, are you okay?" he asked, wiping his brow free of a thick layer of sweat.

David shoveled away the paralysis, heavy blinks bringing him back. "No. No, not really. I don't understand this." He leaned to the left, taking in the man in custody sprawled out on the lawn. "How the fuck is this possible?"

"Do you know this man?" Jenkins asked. The inquiry sounded like a mix of indictment and surprise.

"Yeah," David said, never dropping his intense gaze. The disbelief in his features slowly took a back seat. "Yeah, I know that bastard." A boiling fury burgeoned as he clenched his fists, his posture stiffening. "How could you?" he spat.

Believing the threat neutralized, the officers pinning Tanner to the earth yanked him to his feet. They added a pair of handcuffs to go along with the zip tie. Tanner's stare magnified, wincing at the tightness of his new jewelry.

"How could you do this?" Stepping past Jenkins, David's and Tanner's shoulders collided like a bullet and a brick wall. "You fuckin' killed them! Amelie! Heather!"

Bodies funneled between the two, ending the chance of a violent outbreak. Anzilotti and Johnson held their ground, hands up, stopping David's strides.

"You killed them!" David roared, lunging forward. Arms grasped his intentions, holding him back. "Why, you piece of shit? Why?" he wailed through the throng.

Tanner's face cooled to ice, the blood draining and leaving a pallid mask. "What the hell are you talking about, Dave? What the fuck is this shit?" He shook his head, incredulity swimming in his eyes. "'Killed them'?"

David was ready to lunge again, ready to force himself through the cluster of badges and bulletproof vests. Bite and claw and maim if necessary, but a voice from behind held him to the concrete.

"David."

It was soft. A trembling voice he missed. One that he knew intimately. One from another life. One he would protect no matter what.

He pivoted on the sidewalk. Maggie stood there feet away, the streetlight shining down on her. It cast an orange glow that clung to the beauty of her blonde locks. She looked angelic.

"Maggie," David called out. He waved her off with a gesture. "Go back inside. You don't need to see this." He could feel the loathing that pulsed through his core come to a simmer. She could always pull him away from the edge.

Her eyes took him in. Soft, loving, blue eyes. Those eyes that he fell in love with so long ago. Those same eyes he betrayed. But something else lingered there just below the surface. She looked hurt. Pained.

"Everything's okay, Mags. It's ov—"

As the last word fell from his tongue, she interrupted him, "There's something I have to tell you, David. About tonight." She peered over his shoulder at the officers holding Tanner upright. "About him."

David followed her line of sight, and that scathing itch to batter the murdering son of a bitch came crashing back in. But he suppressed it, shoveling it away. He returned his stare to her. "Mags? What are you talking about?"

Her eyes welled. "He's . . . he's here because I invited him, David."

"What do you mean you invited him? I don't understand. Why would you . . ." David trailed off, seeing the armor she wore fall away. Tears broke free and meandered down her cheeks.

"We were supposed to—" The words caught in her throat. "We were supposed to go out tonight. A date."

David volleyed between the two, craning his neck back and forth. *A date?*

"What do you mean, 'a date,' Mags?" David took a step toward her. "You're dating him? Tanner?" A flood of insecurity washed in, pulling him from the shore and out to sea.

She was speechless, trembling under the dim light above.

He took another step. "How did this happen? He's a killer, Mags. He came here to kill you tonight."

"What are you talking about, man? Quit saying that shit," Tanner demanded, his teeth grinding together like a vise. "I didn't kill anyone! I don't know what the fuck you're talking about. I was here to take her out. Just like she said."

The eruption stopped David in his tracks. He turned around. The blockade of bodies thinned, and a direct line of sight opened up, showcasing the man in handcuffs. He stood there, labored breaths heaving from his core. He shook his head from side to side.

Tense silence filled the space, corroding the air as the two leered at one another.

Until Detective Jenkins broke the lull. His gravelly voice rang out, slicing through the night as he read Tanner his Miranda rights and shoved him toward a cruiser.

2

With Tanner Brown secured in the back of a police car, his silhouette barely visible through the tinted glass, Jenkins approached David and Maggie. His steps were slow, deliberate, cautious. Each footfall seemed to echo in the suffocating silence that had descended over the neighborhood where curious folks peered through curtains and whispered behind barely cracked doors.

David acknowledged him, his posture stiffening at the man's presence. The adrenaline that had carried him through the confrontation was beginning to ebb, leaving behind a hollow ache in his chest and tremors in his hands he couldn't quite control. "So, what do we do now, Detective? I mean, with him? With all this shit?" His voice cracked, betraying the fragile composure he was fighting to maintain.

Jenkins let out a sigh that seemed to carry the weight of a thousand similar nights, his head swiveling from left to right as he surveyed the scene. "Step one is questioning. We'll take him down to the precinct. Sweat him for about twelve hours, maybe longer if his lawyer doesn't show." He paused, watching David's face carefully. "Find the truth behind this mess: why he was here dressed in all black, if he had anything to do with the murders, what kind of sick game he's been playing with you."

The detective's eyes hardened, and when he spoke again, his voice carried the conviction of a man who'd seen too much darkness, "My instinct tells me this is our guy, Mr. Miller. It does. Every fiber in my body is screaming it. So now we just have to let the system work, let justice run its course."

"He sounded convincing, though." David's words tumbled out before he could stop them, doubt creeping into his voice like poison through his veins. He thought about it again, Tanner's words hitting him like physical blows over and over, each repetition making his certainty crumble a little more. "You know, about the killings. He denied it all. Said he knew nothing about it. There was something in his eyes . . . I don't know, Detective."

Jenkins studied him. A veil of empathy settled over his weathered features, softening the hard lines around his eyes. "They always do, son. They always do. You'd be amazed how convincing a sociopath can be when his life depends on it." He stepped closer, his voice dropping to barely above a whisper. "But you and I both know why he was here tonight. And it wasn't to go out on a date with your ex-wife."

He paused, letting the words sink in, watching as David's face cycled through confusion, fear, and finally a terrible understanding. "That man was here for one reason, and I won't bring it up here in front of her." His stare drifted meaningfully to Maggie, taking in how she stood there, her arms wrapped around herself as if she could hold the pieces together through sheer will. "But we both know what that reason was."

David's gaze followed the detective's, and what he saw made his heart clench painfully in his chest. Maggie stood feet away from them, her face pale as moonlight, her blonde hair hanging in disheveled strands that cast shadows across her hollow cheeks.

Without another thought, he moved to her and pulled her close to him, cradling her lean frame in his arms. She felt so small against him, so breakable, and he wondered how she'd managed to survive everything that had been thrown at her.

That sweet scent of lavender filled his nose as he breathed her in—the same perfume she'd worn on their wedding day, the same one that used to linger on his pillows long after she'd left for work. It was a ghost of simpler times, of mornings when their biggest worry was whether they'd remembered to set the coffee timer. As she wept against his chest, her tears soaking through his shirt and warming his skin, he whispered into her ear with all the conviction he could muster, "Everything's okay, Mags. Everything's okay." The words felt like lies even as he spoke them, but he forced strength that he didn't feel into his voice. "We'll get through this. We'll figure this out together, just like we always did. I'm here, and I'm never leaving you again. I promise you that. No matter what happens, no matter how dark this gets, I won't leave you again."

She pressed closer to him, muffling her sobs. For these precious seconds, they weren't a divorced couple navigating the wreckage of their failed marriage. They were just David and Maggie, holding each other against the storm, finding strength in their shared fear.

Minutes passed as he held her, the time excavating the buried memories of their happiness. And then the spell was broken. Not because the moment ended, but because a haunting vibration emerged from his pants.

As he pulled away from her, he reached inside his front pocket with fingers that had suddenly gone numb. The cell phone felt cold against his palm, foreign and malevolent, like holding a snake that might strike at any moment. He didn't want to look at it, didn't want to discover what fresh nightmare waited there for him on the glowing screen. But his need for the truth, that terrible, compulsive hunger that had driven him since this all began, steered his actions.

A new message awaited him. A message from Amelie. A message from the dead. His blood turned to ice water as he stared at the name, at the impossibility of it.

It was a picture, actually, one that was crystal clear in its horrifying detail. No pixilation, nothing obscure or blurry that might allow him to pretend it was something else. He was staring at the woman with the blonde hair, the phantom they'd been chasing, the specter that had haunted every conversation about the murders.

He nearly dropped the phone, his fingers almost betraying him as he took an involuntary step backward. The blood drained from his face so quickly that black spots danced in his vision, and for a moment, he thought he might collapse right there on Maggie's front lawn.

It wasn't a picture of his ex-wife, as he and the detective had suspected all along. It wasn't even a stranger, or some random victim chosen for reasons they couldn't fathom.

It was a picture of a woman smiling. One with a subtle gap in her front teeth. His best friend, his confidant, his sister in all but blood, who had held his hand through the divorce and never once judged him for the mistake that had torn his life apart.

Jenna.

In the photo, she stood radiant and carefree, wearing a red bikini that complemented her sun-kissed skin, smiling that brilliant smile he'd seen a thousand times before. Her newly bleached blonde hair, the same shade as in the two pictures he had received earlier, shone like a nugget of gold.

Spring Break, Pismo Beach, 2013.

And beneath the picture of this woman he loved like a sister, this innocent soul who'd hurt no one in her entire life, was a single caption that made his world tilt off its axis:

Say goodbye.

The phone finally slipped from his trembling fingers, clattering onto the sidewalk. Behind him, he could hear Jenkins asking what was wrong, could hear Maggie calling his name with a growing alarm, but their voices seemed to come from far away, as if he were hearing them from the bottom of a cavern.

Because now he understood. This was about him, about making him suffer for what he did to his ex-wife—the infidelity. This psychopath, the Hand of God, would inject the pain Maggie felt tenfold and then some. And there was nothing he could do about it but sit back and watch from the sidelines.

And Jenna, sweet Jenna with her infectious smile and her terrible habits, was next on the chopping block.

XXIX

Saturday Night, May 30, 2015

David's fingers trembled as he snatched the phone from the sidewalk. He scrolled frantically through his contacts, his vision blurring as panic set in. Jenna's name appeared, and he jabbed at it with desperate urgency.

Ring.

Ring.

Ring.

"Come on, Jenna. Pick up the phone. Pick up the fuckin' phone."

The mechanical voice of her greeting cut through him like a blade. "Hey, you've reached Jenna! I'm probably out having more fun than you are, so leave a message and I'll get back to you when I'm done being awesome!" Her cheerful tone, recorded months ago in happier times, now sounded like a ghost's whisper from beyond the grave.

David ended the call and immediately dialed again, his breath coming in short, sharp gasps.

Ring.

Ring.

Ring.

Voicemail again.

"Fuck!" The word exploded from his lips, causing several nearby officers to turn in his direction. He tried once more, praying to hear her voice. Same result.

His fingers flew across the screen, typing a text message with shaking hands:

> WHERE ARE YOU? CALL ME RIGHT NOW. THIS IS AN EMERGENCY!

He hit send and stared at the screen, willing those three dots to appear that would show she was typing back. Nothing. The message showed as delivered, but unread.

"Mr. Miller?" Detective Jenkins's voice cut through his mounting hysteria. "What the hell is going on? You look like you've seen a ghost."

David spun around, his eyes wild and unfocused. "We got the wrong guy, Detective. Tanner's innocent. The killer… he's still out there, and he's got my friend. Jenna."

Jenkins stepped closer, his weathered face creased with concern and skepticism. "Slow down, son. What are you talking about? What makes you think—"

"This!" David thrust the phone toward the detective, the screen displaying the photograph of Jenna in her red bikini. "He just sent me this. The same bastard who's been tormenting me. Look at the timestamp! One minute ago!"

Jenkins took the phone, squinting at the image in the dim streetlight. His face went ashen as the implications hit him. "Jesus Christ," he muttered. "This is your friend and the same woman from the other photos."

"That's what I'm saying, Detective. That's Jenna. She bleached her hair blonde a couple years back before spring break." David's voice rose in pitch, hysteria creeping in at the edges. "He's going to kill her. Just like he killed Amelie and Heather. And it's my fault. All of this is my fuckin' fault."

Behind them, Maggie had moved closer, drawn by the commotion. "David? What's wrong? What's happening?"

David stared at his ex-wife with wide, panic-stricken eyes. Before he could answer, a young man clutching a laptop approached the group. Not an officer, an IT tech.

"Detective Jenkins," the tech said, slightly out of breath. "Sir, I need to speak with you immediately. It's about the cell phone we've been tracking, the one sending the messages."

Jenkins looked up from David's phone, his gray eyes sharp and alert. "What about it?"

"We just got a ping, sir. For the first time since this whole thing started, the killer didn't turn off the Rodriguez phone after sending a message. We're tracking an active signal right now." He opened the laptop, the screen illuminating his face in a sea of blue light. "And sir . . . it's moving. Fast. Like he's in a vehicle."

The words hit David like a sucker punch to the jaw. He grabbed the tech by the shoulders, probably harder than he should have. "Where is he? Where is the son of a bitch?"

The tech, startled by the physical contact, pulled up a real-time GPS tracking display on the laptop. A red dot pulsed steadily across a street map of the city. "He's currently heading east on the Crosstown Freeway. Just left the old warehouse district. Speed shows he's doing about eighty miles per hour. He's flying."

"Where's he going?" David asked, his voice hollow with dread. He turned to Jenkins, desperation etched on every line of his face. "Where's he going, Detective?"

"I don't know, but we're going to meet his ass there." Jenkins already had his radio pulled out, his instincts kicking in despite the shock of the revelation. "This is Detective Jenkins," he said into the microphone. "Requesting immediate backup and patrol units. We have a potential homicide in progress. Suspect is armed and dangerous."

Static crackled back. "Copy that, Detective. Location?"

"East side of town. I repeat, east side of town. Stand by for more specifics."

"Copy that. Patrols en route. Estimated twelve minutes out."

"Twelve minutes might as well be twelve hours," David said, starting toward the police cars parked along the street. "He'll be done with her by then. We have to go now!"

"Hold on there, son." Jenkins grabbed David's arm, stopping him in his tracks. "This is police business. You're a civilian, and you're emotionally compromised. You'll stay here with your ex-wife while we—"

"Like hell I will." David wrenched his arm free, his face flushed with anger and fear. "That psychopath has my friend because of something I did. Because of my mistake. Jenna's going to die because of my fuckup, and you want me to stay here and wait?"

Maggie moved closer, her voice soft but urgent. "David, please. Let the police handle this. You could get hurt. Or worse."

"Jenna's going to get hurt, Mags!" David shouted, then immediately regretted raising his voice at her. He lowered his tone, but the intensity remained. "I'm sorry. But I can't just stand here and do nothing while someone I care about dies. I won't lose another person to this madness."

The tech looked up from his laptop, his face tense with concentration. "Detective, the signal just stopped moving. It's stationary now at . . . let me check the exact address." He hammered at the keyboard, then stated, "512 Height Street."

Jenkins's stare sharpened, his gray eyes cranking up to a dangerous level. "Did you say 512 Height Street? Are you sure?"

"Yeah. Look for yourself." The tech handed the detective his laptop.

"Son of a bitch," Jenkins mouthed as he stared at the screen. An ashen veil spread across his flesh.

"What is it?" David asked, noticing the shift. "Do you know the address, Detective?"

Jenkins looked at David, then at the laptop screen, then back at David before nodding. "Yeah. Yeah, I do. Margarette Kowalski used to live there."

The name meant nothing to David, but Jenkins's look sent a wave of dread flooding through his veins. He glanced at his ex-wife, thinking about the name. "Who's . . . who's Margarette Kowalski?"

"I'll tell you on the way," Jenkins replied, thinking back to the conference room and his conversation with Barrientos about the one Grand Prix and owner unaccounted for—the three-hundred-pound recluse they ignored. "But you follow my lead, you do exactly what I tell you, and if I say run, you run. Understood?"

David nodded, relief fusing with the worry. "Understood."

Jenkins was already moving, barking orders into his radio as he went. "Barrientos! We're rolling. Now!" he shouted toward his partner.

She didn't ask questions. Just nodded and pulled her keys from her pocket, heading for the unmarked cruiser parked at the curb. David was right behind them, his heart hammering so hard he could feel it in his throat.

Jenkins yanked open the passenger door and turned to David. "Miller, get in the back. And remember what I said: you follow orders, you stay out of the way, and you don't do anything stupid."

David opened the door and slid into the back seat without a word as Barrientos dropped behind the wheel. The engine roared to life, a throaty growl that seemed to shake the entire vehicle. Through the window, David caught sight of Maggie standing on the sidewalk, her arms wrapped around herself, her face pale and uncertain in the harsh glow of the streetlights.

"Wait," David said, before the car moved.

Jenkins twisted in her seat. "What is it? What now?"

"Maggie." David pointed through the window. "Should . . . should she come with us?"

"She shouldn't," Barrientos said, her hands already on the steering wheel, ready to punch the accelerator. "We don't need any more liabili—"

"She's a part of this, Barrientos," Jenkins interrupted, his gravelly voice cutting through the tension. He was looking at Maggie now, studying her through the window with those sharp eyes that missed nothing. "She's been in it since the beginning."

David's stomach twisted. "Detective, I can't put her in danger. Not again. Not after everything—"

"Listen up, Miller." Jenkins turned fully in his seat, his weathered face deadly serious. "Something tells me this psychopath knows who she is. He knows where she lives. He's been watching you, which means he's been watching her too. Right now, the safest place for your ex-wife is with us, so we can keep an eye on her. You understand what I'm saying?"

David's mouth went dry. The detective was right. The killer had been three steps ahead of them the entire time.

"Shit," David muttered.

"Damn right, shit!" Jenkins pushed open his door and stepped out, motioning to the woman. "Maggie! Get over here!"

Maggie looked startled, but she moved quickly, jogging over to the cruiser. Her face was a mask of confusion and fear. "What's going on?"

"Get in," Jenkins said, his tone leaving no room for argument. "You're coming with us."

"I . . . what? Why?"

"Because we need to stay together," Jenkins said, opening the rear door on the other side. "And because we need to face this threat as one."

Maggie's eyes widened. She looked at David, and he saw the unsaid question written across her face. He gave her a small nod. It wasn't much, but it was enough.

She slid into the back seat beside him.

As they pulled away from the curb, tires squealing against the asphalt, David closed his eyes and tried to push away the image of Jenna's smiling face from the photograph. Tried to forget the caption underneath it.

Say goodbye.

But he couldn't shake it. He wondered if they were already too late.

Jenkins said into the radio, "512 Height Street. I repeat, 512 Height Street. All units converge on that location. Consider the suspect armed, dangerous, and possibly holding a hostage. Approach with extreme caution."

Static crackled back. "Copy that. ETA nine minutes."

"Nine minutes," David muttered. "Jesus Christ."

"We'll be there in five," Barrientos said, her voice confident and focused. The speedometer climbed past seventy as they hit a straightaway. Streetlights blurred past the windows in streaks of orange and white.

And in the back seat, David and Maggie sat in the darkness, watching and waiting, as the seconds ticked by like hours.

"David," Maggie whispered.

"Yeah?"

"If something happens . . . if we don't—"

"Don't," he interrupted, squeezing her hand tighter. "Don't do that. We're going to be fine. Jenna's going to be fine. We're going to end this."

But even as he said the words, he didn't believe them.

2

The cruiser's tires screeched as Barrientos whipped the vehicle to a stop in front of 512 Height Street. A single streetlight flickered at the street's corner, casting a weak light across the cracked driveway and overgrown lawn. The '78 Grand Prix sat in the driveway at an angle with the trunk popped open.

From the back seat, David pressed his face against the window, his breath fogging the glass. The house loomed before him like a still beast, its windows black and lifeless. But it was the front door that made his stomach clench. It was ajar. Not wide, just cracked. Maybe six inches.

"Oh no," Barrientos muttered, killing the engine. The sudden silence was deafening.

Jenkins already had his service weapon drawn in his leathery hands. He turned in his seat, his gray eyes hard and uncompromising. "Both of you stay in this car. You don't move. You don't get out. You don't even breathe. Am I clear?"

"Detective, please—" David started.

"Am I clear?" Jenkins repeated.

David swallowed hard and nodded. Beside him, Maggie's hand found his in the darkness. Her palm was clammy.

"Good." Jenkins pushed open his door, the interior light flooding the cab for a moment before he shut it again, plunging them back into shadow. Barrientos was already out, her own weapon drawn and held low; her movements practiced and efficient.

David watched as the two detectives moved toward the house, their silhouettes barely visible against the darker bulk of the home. Jenkins took the lead, his weapon raised and his body coiled like a spring. Barrientos flanked him, covering his blind spots. They moved like shadows, synchronized and silent.

Weeds pushed through the fissures of the cracked concrete walkway leading to the house. Jenkins stepped carefully, avoiding the patches where his footfalls might make noise. Barrientos did the same, her eyes constantly scanning the windows, the roofline, the dark spaces between the house and the neighboring properties.

They reached the porch steps—three of them, wooden and warped with age. Jenkins tested the first one with his weight before committing. It held without a sound. The second step creaked slightly, a low groan that seemed to echo in the stillness. Both detectives froze, weapons trained on the open door.

Nothing. No movement. No sound. Just that narrow slice of darkness between the door and the frame, like an old scar on the house's face.

In the car, David's heart hammered against his ribs so hard he thought it might crack them. He leaned forward, his hands gripping the back of the front seat. "Come on," he whispered. "Come on."

Maggie's grip on his other hand tightened. "David, I'm scared."

"Me, too," he admitted.

David watched as the detectives reached the door. Jenkins stood to one side, his weapon held in a two-handed grip at chest level. Barrientos took a position on the other side, mirroring his stance. They exchanged a look, some silent communication that only partners who'd worked together for years could understand.

Jenkins reached out with his left hand, keeping his right on the weapon, and pushed the door open slowly. The rusty hinges groaned, a long squeal that cut through the night like a scream.

The door swung inward, revealing nothing but darkness.

"Police!" Jenkins called out, his voice strong and commanding. "This is the BPD. We're coming in. If anyone's in this house, make yourself known now!"

Silence answered him. The kind of silence that felt heavy, oppressive. The kind that pressed against your eardrums and made you strain to hear something, anything, that would break it.

Without another word, they turned on their flashlights and disappeared into the blackness.

3

In the car, David couldn't take it anymore. He reached for the door handle.

"David, no." Maggie grabbed his arm. "He said to stay in the car."

"I can't just sit here," David hissed. "What if they need help? What if—"

"What if you get them killed by getting in the way?" Maggie shot back, her voice sharp with fear. "You're not a cop, David. You don't have a gun. You'll just make things worse."

She was right. He knew she was right. But every fiber of his being screamed at him to move, to act, to do something other than sit in this goddamn car while Jenna was somewhere inside that house, possibly dying, possibly already dead.

He released the door handle and slumped back against the seat, feeling her tight grip loosen. But after a few heavy breaths, he opened the cruiser's door and stepped outside.

"David! Get back—"

"No, Mags. I can't." David whipped around, staring at his ex-wife through the car door opening. "I have to do something. Jenna's inside, and if she's still alive, she needs me."

He watched as Maggie's expression mirrored a mask of empathy, but she remained still and quiet.

"Listen, all of this is my fault. I can never forgive myself for the act, for the betrayal, for the pain I caused you, but I have to do something to end this. And if that means I face that son of a bitch inside, then I will."

Her nervous eyes stilled, gaining a clarity he hadn't seen all night. "Okay," she finally whispered. "But I'm coming with you. You're not leaving me alone."

"Mags," David started, shaking his head, "I don't think that's a—"

Maggie cut him off, her voice firm despite the tremor running through it, "I'm not staying in this car. You think I want to be out here alone in the dark?"

David opened his mouth to argue, then closed it. She had a point. A terrible, logical point that he couldn't refute.

"Okay. Stay behind me," he finally said. "And if I tell you to run, you run. No questions."

Maggie nodded and slipped out of the cruiser, easing the door shut with a soft *click*. They stood together on the sidewalk for a moment, staring at the house. The open door was like a mouth waiting to swallow them.

David's legs felt like lead as he forced them forward. Each step across the cracked walkway seemed to take an eternity. Behind him, he could hear Maggie's breathing, quick and shallow.

As he reached the porch steps, feeling Maggie's hand clutch the hem of his shirt, he took in the home. The house looked even worse up close: peeling paint, rotted wood siding, a broken window covered with cardboard and duct tape. And that gaping mouth of a door. It beckoned him like an invitation.

Despite his reserve, he whispered into the darkness, "Jenkins? Detective Barrientos? Where are you?"

Silence pressed back against him.

Maggie's fingernails dug into the cloth of his shirt. "Oh God," she breathed. "Oh God, David, we need to go back to the car. We need to—"

Light exploded from the hallway ahead, a flashlight beam, brilliant and blinding. David threw up his hand, squinting against the glare.

"Miller?" Jenkins's voice, rough and strained. "Jesus Christ. I told you to stay in the car!"

The relief that flooded through David nearly made his knees buckle. "Detective, thank God. I thought I could—"

"Could what? Get your ass back to the car," Jenkins demanded. "Take Maggie and—"

A sound pulsed from somewhere in the home. A door opening. Footsteps.

Jenkins swung his flashlight toward the sound, landing on a hallway, and his other hand came up with his service weapon. "Barrientos!" he shouted. "Barrientos, you copy?"

No answer.

The detective steadied and aimed the beam at an open doorway where a ribbon of light danced from within the room.

"Barrientos?" he called again.

This time she answered, her voice muffled but dripping with concern, "Yeah, I'm here. You need to see this, Jenkins. You need to see what the son of a bitch did to the walls and ceiling."

With the tension ratcheting up like a tightening noose, he turned back to David. "Get back to the car, Miller. Now!"

Not waiting for a response, Jenkins disappeared back into the home, he and his flashlight making a beeline toward the room with the open door.

After watching the darkness swallow the detective, David stepped backward off the porch, feeling Maggie still hovering as close as she possibly could. But he stopped mid-stride, his body clenching. The stinging stench of gasoline hit his nose.

"What is—" Maggie started, but her words died as they both turned around.

There, positioned directly in front of the unmarked cruiser, stood a young man in a black hoodie. The fabric hung low over his face, casting his features in shadow, but David could feel the weight of his stare: cold, patient, predatory. The man's stillness was worse than any sudden movement could have been. He wasn't hiding. He was waiting.

Maggie's scream tore through the silence.

David's eyes dropped to the man's boots, and his heart seized. Crumpled on the sidewalk in front of the hooded figure was Jenna. She lay motionless, her body twisted at an unnatural angle, hands wrenched behind her back and bound. The faint amber glow from the streetlight above illuminated her face—too pale, too still—and her hair.

It was soaked. So were her clothes.

Wet tawny strands clung to her cheeks and neck. Liquid dripped onto the pavement. The smell intensified, and David's stomach lurched as understanding crashed over him.

Gasoline.

"Jenna!" The name exploded from his throat, raw and desperate. His body moved before his mind could catch up, legs propelling him forward in a blind sprint toward his friend. Everything else fell away: Jenkins's order, Maggie's presence behind him, the danger screaming at him to stop.

All he could see was Jenna lying there, drenched and defenseless.

He made it three steps before the man moved.

One hand emerged from the hoodie pocket, and David heard the sharp *click-click-click* of metal striking flint. A small flame burst to life, impossibly bright in the darkness. The man held the lighter out at arm's length, perfectly still, the tiny fire dancing between his fingers.

David skidded to a halt so abruptly he nearly fell, his shoes scraping against the pavement. His chest heaved as he stared at that single flame, mesmerized and horrified. Such a small thing to hold so much power.

One flick of those fingers, and Jenna would—

"Don't." The word came out strangled, barely more than a whisper. David raised both hands slowly, palms out, trying to project a calm he didn't have. "Don't. Please."

The man in the hoodie said nothing. The flame flickered in the silence, casting wavering shadows across Jenna's gasoline-soaked hair.

"It's me you want." David's voice cracked, desperation bleeding through every syllable. "Not her."

The hooded figure remained motionless, that terrible flame still dancing between his fingers.

"Please." David took half a step forward, his hands trembling in the air. "I know what I did. And she has nothing to do with this." His vision blurred with tears he didn't bother to hide. "Please, just . . . just let her go."

Still nothing. No words, no movement. Just that steady, invisible stare from beneath his sweatshirt's hood and the lighter held out like an executioner's blade.

David's legs nearly gave out. He could see Jenna's chest rising and falling, shallow breaths, but breathing. She was right there, and he couldn't reach her. Couldn't save her.

"I'm begging you." The words tore from somewhere deep inside him. "Please don't hurt her. It's me you want. I'm the one who should be hurt. Kill me if you want, but let her go. She's—" His voice broke completely. "She's everything. Please."

The man's head began to move.

Slowly, almost mechanically, he started shaking it from side to side. The gesture was deliberate, final, devoid of any emotion or mercy. An unmistakable "No."

The flame continued its macabre dance, indifferent to David's pleas.

David felt something die inside his chest. "No, no, no, please—"

"FREEZE! BPD!"

The shout exploded through the night like a gunshot. David's head whipped around to see two figures sprinting toward them, weapons drawn and extended, badges glinting under the streetlight.

Jenkins and Barrientos.

"PUT THE LIGHTER DOWN!" Jenkins's voice was pure command. "DO IT NOW, ASSHOLE!"

Barrientos fanned out to the left, her gun steady, her voice cutting through the chaos. "Step away from the victim! Hands where we can see them!"

The hooded man finally moved. His head turned toward the approaching detectives with eerie slowness, but the hand holding the lighter remained perfectly still. Ever so close to Jenna's gasoline-soaked body.

David stood frozen between them all, his heart hammering so hard he thought it might explode. One wrong move. One flick of those fingers.

"Don't do it!" David screamed, his voice hoarse. "Don't make them shoot! Just put it down!"

The hooded figure's arm began to move. A subtle shift, barely perceptible. The lighter lowered, flame reaching toward Jenna.

From David's left, a gunshot cracked through the night air.

The man in the hoodie jerked backward, his body convulsing from the impact. The lighter tumbled from his fingers, clattering across the pavement away from Jenna, its flame extinguishing as it skittered into the darkness. His hand flew to his chest, where a dark shape began blooming across the fabric, spreading like spilled ink. He swayed for a moment, that faceless hood still turned toward David, then collapsed onto the asphalt with a heavy, final *thud*.

David didn't think. Couldn't think. His legs were already moving, carrying him toward Jenna in a desperate sprint. He dropped to his knees beside her, his hands hovering over her gasoline-soaked clothes, afraid to touch her but unable not to.

"Jenna! Jenna, wake up!" His voice was raw, frantic. He carefully cradled her face, his thumbs brushing her cheeks. Her skin was too cold, too pale. "Come on, Jenna, please. Open your eyes. Please!"

Her eyelids fluttered but didn't open. A soft moan escaped her lips.

"That's it, that's it. I'm here. You're safe now." Tears streamed down his face. The chemical stench of gasoline burned his nostrils, but he buried the sensation. "Stay with me. Help is coming. Just stay with me, Jenna."

Behind him, he heard the detectives shuffle past, their footsteps quick and purposeful. Jenkins's voice cut through the ringing in David's ears. "Suspect is down. I repeat, suspect is down. We need an ambulance now! Hurry!"

David barely registered the words. His entire world had narrowed to Jenna's face, to the shallow rise and fall of her chest, to the hope that she would open her eyes and look at him. That she would be okay. That this nightmare would finally end.

But as he stared at her, an emotion he didn't recognize came burrowing out of his heart. Something he couldn't explain. He wasn't staring at his best friend. He was staring at something much more meaningful and precious. He was staring at the woman he loved.

Somewhere close, sirens blared into the night, and they were getting closer. Barrientos's voice joined the symphony, tense and controlled. "Got a pulse. Weak but steady. We're losing him, though."

David's stare shot to the two detectives kneeling alongside the man in the hoodie. Knowing there was nothing more he could do for Jenna, he lowered her head onto the cold pavement. His hands trembled as he stood, every instinct screaming at him to stay. But he needed to know. He needed to see the face of the person who had tossed his life upside down.

The hooded man lay sprawled on the concrete, Jenkins and Barrientos crouched over him. The dark stain across his chest had grown larger. As David approached, his footsteps felt heavy.

"Miller, you shouldn't—" Jenkins started, but the words died when he saw the schoolteacher's face.

David knelt beside the body, his breath catching in his throat. With shaky hands, he reached for the hood, hesitating for just a moment before pulling it back.

His stomach dropped.

It wasn't a man. It was a kid.

Maybe seventeen. Eighteen at most. Baby-faced beneath the blood and sweat, acne scars dotting his jawline. His features were soft, unfinished, like he hadn't fully grown into himself yet.

"Jesus Christ," David whispered. "He's just a kid."

The boy's eyes were wide open, darting frantically between the faces hovering over him, wet with tears and terror. The kind of fear that came from knowing you were dying and there was nothing anyone could do to stop it.

"Easy, easy," Barrientos murmured, pressing her hands against the wound. "We've got help coming. Just hold on."

Light footfalls approached from behind—hesitant, reserved. Maggie appeared at David's shoulder, her face pale under the streetlight. "Who is he?"

The boy's head turned at the sound of her voice. His gaze locked onto her face, and something shifted in his expression. The panic intensified, but beneath it was something else. Something that looked almost like recognition. Like relief.

"Who are you?" she asked.

His mouth moved, forming words without sound at first. Then, barely audible over the approaching sirens, a whisper escaped his blood-flecked lips, "Maggie, I'm"—he coughed—"K...K..." He paused, a pool of blood leaked from his mouth's corner. "I'm D...D...Derek."

"Derek?" Maggie's face went white. "No. No, that's not—"

"I wuv you, Momma," he croaked. The words were childlike, slurred and broken. Spoken the way a toddler might say them, not a teenager. But the emotion behind them was raw and unmistakable. "I wuv you."

Then, without notice, his hand fell and his chest stopped moving. The light in his eyes faded, leaving them fixed and glassy, still staring at Maggie's face. At his new mother's face.

David remained frozen on his knees, staring at the boy's face. That young, terrified face. His mind couldn't process it. Couldn't reconcile the monster who'd killed those women, the monster who almost killed Jenna. The young man who'd tormented and terrorized the city of Bakersfield for weeks. He broke his gaze and looked up at Maggie, but something was missing as he eyed her. He would always care about the woman he married all those years ago, and he'd never forgive himself for the betrayal, but at this moment, as emotions and confusion flooded his core, he knew he could never go back to her. Someone else gripped his heart now. And he had to go to her.

The sirens were deafening, red and blue lights washing over the scene in waves. An ambulance screeched to a halt in the middle of the road, paramedics already jumping out.

David forced himself to turn away from the body, away from Maggie's awestruck face. His legs carried him back to Jenna, back to where she lay still and pale on the gasoline-soaked pavement.

He was so confused, but right now, only one thing mattered.

He knelt beside her again, taking her cold hand in his. "I'm here, Jenna. I'm right here."

The paramedics flanked the couple, their voices professional and urgent, but David didn't let go. He couldn't.

Amidst the chaos, Jenna's eyes slowly fluttered open, landing on David, and after a tense few seconds, she whispered, "Hey, you."

The End

Did you enjoy the story?

I'd love to read a review on Goodreads and Amazon.

Acknowledgements

Writing a thriller is never a solitary endeavor, and *The Hand of God* would not exist without the incredible people who supported me through every twist, turn, and sleepless night.

To my wife, Tara—you are my foundation, my first reader, and my greatest champion. Thank you for believing in this story even when I doubted it, and for giving me the time and space to disappear into dark places so I could bring this book to life.

To my daughters, Emma, Aubrey, and Aria, and my son, Luke—you are my inspiration and my reason for everything. I hope this book makes you proud, and I hope you always chase your own dreams as fearlessly as you've encouraged me to chase mine.

To Matt Seff Barnes, whose stunning cover art captured the essence of this story in ways words never could—thank you for making *The Hand of God* impossible to ignore on the shelf.

To my editor, Dani Yeager—your sharp eye, thoughtful questions, and unwavering commitment to the story elevated this book beyond what I imagined possible. Thank you for pushing me to dig deeper and for making every page stronger.

To my author friends—Chad Miller, A. G. Mock, Mark Jenkins, and Rachel Graham—thank you for the late-night conversations, the honest feedback, and for reminding me that I wasn't alone in this journey. Your friendship means the world to me.

To my Beta team—your early feedback shaped this story in crucial ways. Thank you for your honesty, your enthusiasm, and for catching the details that would have otherwise slipped through the cracks.

And finally, to my ARC readers—thank you for taking a chance on this book before anyone else. Your support and early buzz gave this story wings. I am forever grateful.

This thriller belongs to all of you.

About the Author

J. B. Arnold is a thriller and horror writer who crafts his darkest tales under the bright California sun. He lives with his beautiful wife, their four children, and his most dedicated writing companion—Max, a gray tabby with impeccable taste in plot twists. When he's not exploring the shadows of the human psyche on the page, he can be found navigating the cheerful chaos of family life, proving that the best horror writers know how to balance the macabre with the mundane.

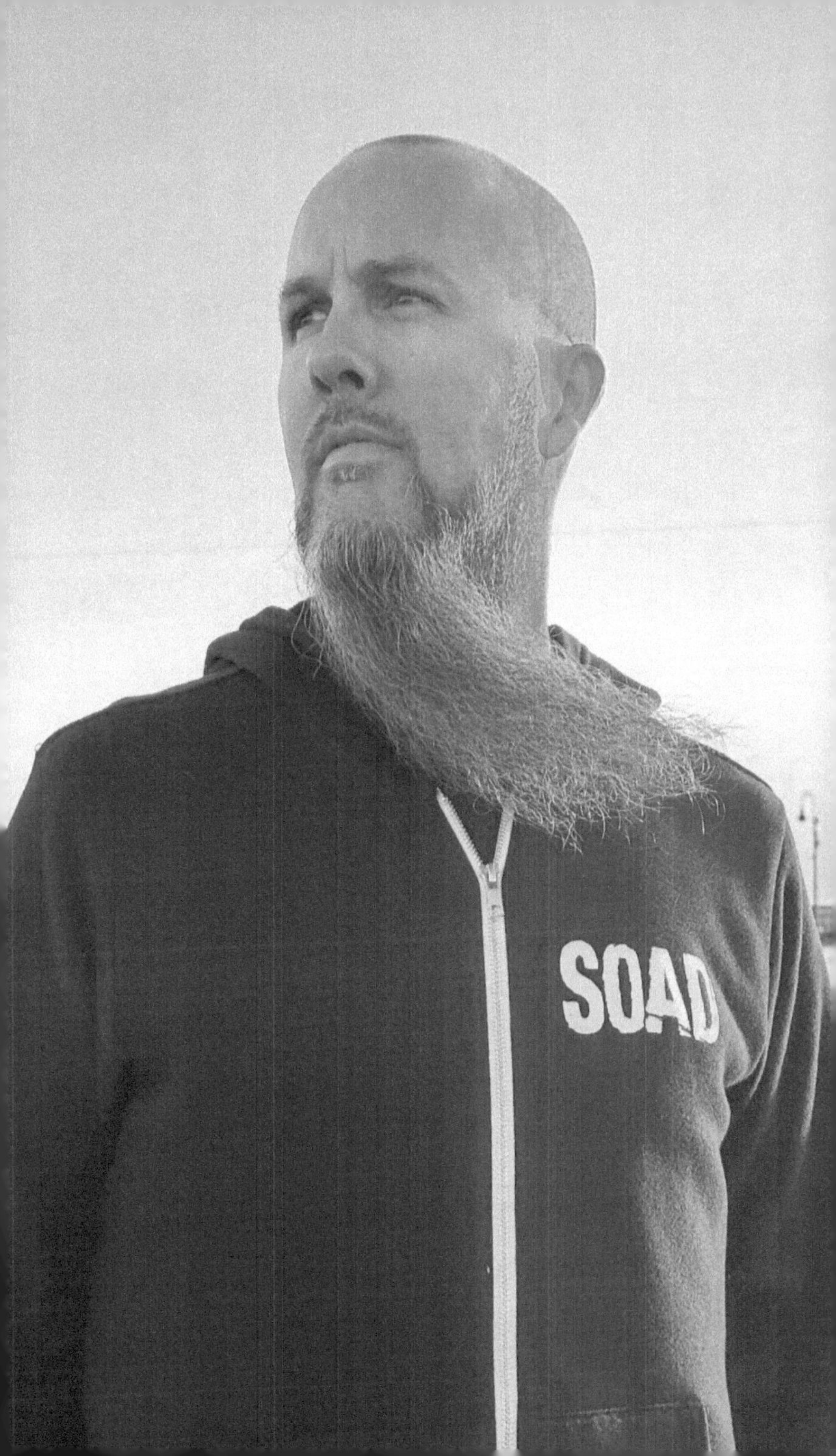
SOAD

Jenkins and Barrientos' story doesn't end here.
Keep reading for a sneak peek at their next case.

Container 4417

Thursday night, September 8, 2016

Bakersfield, California

"Are we going to play this game all night, asshole?" Detective Bennet Jenkins barked, his palms resting on the interrogation room's table. His fiery gray eyes burned into the man cuffed across from him. "Or are you going to tell us what we already know?"

"I ain't telling you shit, cop." The man returned the blazing stare, his blood-shot eyes piercing the detective under loose strands of greasy hair.

"Hardball, huh?" Jenkins abandoned his lean on the table. His thin build cast the man in a shadow. "Last chance, Josif. After this, all deals are off."

"Where's my fuckin' lawyer?" Josif spat, the chrome chain of his cuffs pulled tight.

"He's on his way." Jenkins ran a hand through his silver mane. A grin formed across his face as he took the man in—not in admiration but judgement. The tacky gold chains, the coarse patches of chest hair, the bands of rings adorning his fingers, the thin mustache riding his upper lip like a parasite. "I'll go find out how much longer he'll be. Maybe while I'm gone, you'll come to your wits and remember where the fentanyl you were peddling came from?"

The man in handcuffs remained defiantly silent, his eyes boring holes like a drill. Jenkins ignored the wrathful look and pivoted, making his way to the door, leaving Josif to sweat under the harsh fluorescent lights.

Seconds later, he joined his partner, Angela Barrientos, along the one-way mirror flanking the room. "Tight-lipped and sealed."

Her gaze never wavered as he saddled up next to her. She stood there, arms crossed across her chest. "They always are." A tinge of frustration and resentment lathered her words. She knew this type vividly. "He's just another pawn on the chessboard, man; a peg in the spokes. He'll crack."

"Yeah, he will." Doubt stirred in the back of Jenkins's mind. Over the past few months, they'd hit this group with a vengeance, confiscating drops and taking down street dealers. But a subtle change was growing—the intimidation and clout the detectives once held over these small-timers slowly eroded away. The perps stopped talking, especially once the lawyer arrived.

Minutes passed in silence, the only constant being the ticking of the wall clock behind them. Each tick shoveled another spadeful of dirt onto the case.

"Want me to take a crack?" Barrientos broke the tension, finally breaking her gaze to glance at Jenkins. Wisps of her long dark hair had broken free from the tight braid she always wore, and her eyes looked drained after the long night. "I'll sling some words around, get him to think we know a bit more than we actually do."

"Hammer away." Jenkins's stare drifted to the exit door behind them; the door that would open any moment now with the lawyer in stride. "You only have a few minutes, though. That piece of shit lawyer is already en route."

"Minutes?" She scoffed. "Low lives like him don't last minutes with me, partner. They pop in seconds, man. I'm that good." A teasing grin formed on her lips as she strolled away toward the interrogation room's entrance.

Jenkins mimicked her look. Through the glass, he watched Josif like a raptor, waiting for his partner to make her appearance. And with the precision of an actress hitting her mark on stage, she entered the room with authority.

"Josif Popović." She rounded the table and pinned him with her amber eyes. "Been a while, hasn't it?"

"Save it, pig." Josif leaned back in his chair, the legs screaming against the worn linoleum. "I already told that old piece of shit buddy of yours I'm not talking. Now do your job and get my lawyer—bitch."

She ignored the insult, swiveling the folding-chair opposite him around. With the deftness of a ballet-dancer, she straddled it, her forearms resting on the backrest. "Let's cut the shit, man. Say his name and we can all get some rest."

Josif held his glower, but also his tongue.

"Alright. Here's how this is going to happen." Her voice was calm yet seeping with absolutism. "I know where the dope came from, my partner out there, he knows where it came from, and you know where it came from, motherfucker. So let's end the bullshit and get down to business."

Josif's mouth twisted into a wicked smirk as he listened, but a response never came.

"This is your last chance."

"Piss off!"

Jenkins watched through the glass as Barrientos leaned back, letting the silence stretch like a rubber band. Josif's defiant look never wavered, though.

"You know what, Josif?" Her voice dropped to a conversational tone that somehow felt more dangerous than her earlier threats. "I've been thinking about your situation."

"What fuckin' situation?" He sneered, but his voice lacked the venom from before.

"The one where we've been watching your bank accounts." She leaned forward slightly, her amber eyes never leaving his face. "All those little wire transfers. The offshore accounts. That construction company in Fresno that somehow never builds a thing but moves a quarter million a quarter through its books."

Josif's indignant look died completely. His hands, still cuffed to the table, clenched into fists.

"Oh yeah." Barrientos noted the reaction. "We know about the extortion too. All the restaurant owners and their monthly insurance payments. It's amazing how many of them suddenly found the courage to talk once we started asking questions."

"You're full of shit." Josif's voice cracked on the last word.

"Am I?" She stood up, moving to pace behind her chair like a predator circling wounded prey. "Because I've got about thirty hours of recorded conversations that say different, man. Your voice carries real nice on those mics we planted in your liquor store and smoke shop."

Through the glass, Jenkins saw what he'd been waiting for—the exact moment Josif's world crumbled like a sandcastle in the rising tide.

"The DA's practically salivating over this case. Money laundering, extortion, and now drug trafficking." She paused, letting the words batter him. "You're looking at twenty-five to life, minimum, amigo."

The color drained from the man's face.

"What's wrong, man? You don't look so good." She mocked. "Worried about something?"

"My family . . ." Josif whispered, the words barely audible.

"What about them?" Barrientos stopped pacing, her voice suddenly sharp. "Your wife? Your kids? What were their names again? Maria, Nikola? They're gonna have a real hard time without daddy around, huh? Without your money, your protection from the other assholes clawing for a piece of the pie. They might just be prime targets if you're no longer around to watch over them."

Sweat beaded on Josif's forehead despite the room's chill. "They're not involved in my business. They're innocent."

"Yeah, I'm sure they are. But innocent doesn't pay the rent, does it? Doesn't put food on the table or keep the lights on either, huh?" Barrientos moved closer, her voice dropping to almost a whisper. "Twenty-five years, Josif. Your kids will be adults before you even have a chance at parole."

"Stop." It came out as more of a plea than a command. His sight drifted to his cuffed hands.

"Unless . . ." Barrientos let the word dangle.

Josif looked up at her, his eyes swimming with desperation. "Unless what?"

"Unless you give me what I need. His name." She sat back down, straddling the chair again. "You help me, and maybe we can work something out. Witness protection. New identities. A chance for your family to start over somewhere safe; away from all this shit. I'm talking about a real life where you don't have to worry."

"You don't understand." His voice broke. "He's everywhere . . . If I talk, he'll kill me. And when he's done with me, he'll go after my family just to send a message to others."

"Maybe. Or maybe we get to them first. Keep them safe. But here's the thing you need to understand—" She leaned forward, her face inches from his. "With or without your help, we're bringing that motherfucker down. The only question is whether you're going down with him or starting a new life somewhere where he can't touch you."

The room fell silent except for Josif's ragged breaths. Jenkins watched the man's internal war play out across his face: loyalty warring with survival, fear battling hope.

Josif stared at his handcuffed hands. When he looked up, his eyes held the hollow look of a man who'd run out of options.

"His name . . . is Samvel Melkonian."

Jenkins felt his pulse quicken from behind the mirror. Finally, after months of chasing these street soldiers, one cracked and gave up the name they needed. The one name that would spring a leak in the international crime ring he ran.

"Tell me about the drugs, Josif. The fentanyl; the mollies? How is he getting them into the city?"

Josif closed his eyes. "It comes through the ports hidden in cargo shipments. A new one is coming tomorrow night."

"Where?"

"Long Beach. A container shipped from Thailand." He opened his eyes, looking directly at Barrientos. "The drugs are sewn into textiles. Fabric rolls. Thousands of pills in every shipment."

"How do you know this?"

"Because I'm supposed to be there tomorrow night to help coordinate the pickup." His voice was hollow.

Through the glass, Jenkins watched his partner nod. She was getting everything they needed.

"You did the right thing, Josif. This is the right thing to do for you and your family."

He slumped back in his chair, looking ten years older than when Barrientos had walked into the room. "What happens now?"

"Now we make some calls." Barrientos stood up. "And tomorrow, we end this shit."

As she headed for the door, Josif called out. "Detective?"

She turned back.

"My family. You swear they'll be safe?"

Barrientos looked at the broken man cuffed to the table, a man who'd likely just signed his own death certificate.

"I swear."

As the door closed behind her, Jenkins stepped back from the glass. His partner had done it again. In less than five minutes, she'd cracked the man in two, brought him to his knees.

Jenkins nodded in her direction as she approached. "Sounds like we have a field-trip tomorrow."

"Hopefully, the last one for a while. After we pop this bastard, I'm taking a long vacation, man."

"You and I both, Barrientos. You and I both."

2

Friday, September 9, 2016

Port of Long Beach, California

The salty air hung thick as Jenkins and Barrientos navigated through the maze of shipping containers, their flashlights cutting through the darkness. Around them,

Long Beach PD officers took positions in the shadows, weapons drawn, waiting for the signal.

"Should be row J, container 4417." Barrientos whispered into her radio, checking the manifest Josif had provided. The container yard stretched before them like a steel fortress, thousands of identical metal boxes stacked in geometric precision.

Jenkins nodded, his hand resting on his service weapon. After twenty-seven years of service, his instincts had kept him alive through countless operations. Tonight, those same instincts screamed that something wasn't right.

They found the container twenty yards ahead, its rusted surface barely distinguishable from the hundreds surrounding it. A faded shipping label bore Thai characters and the number 4417.

"This is it." Jenkins motioned for the tactical team to move into position. He approached the container doors, noting the heavy padlock securing them. "Bolt cutters."

An officer materialized beside him with the tool. The lock gave way with a metallic snap that echoed through the quiet port.

Jenkins gripped the door handle, sharing a glance with Barrientos. Her amber eyes reflected the same anticipation he felt. This was it—the break they'd been hunting for months.

He pulled.

The door swung open, metal groaning against metal.

The smell hit them first, a nauseating cocktail of human waste, sweat, and fear that made Jenkins stumble back a step. His flashlight beam swept across the container's interior, and what he saw made his blood turn to ice.

Children.

At least a dozen of them, maybe more, huddled in the darkness. Filthy. Terrified. Their hollow eyes squinted against the sudden intrusion of light.

"Jesus Christ." Barrientos's voice cracked beside him.

The children ranged in age from what looked like eight or nine to early teens. They wore tattered clothes caked with grime. Some cowered in the corners; others simply stared with vacant expressions that spoke of horrors Jenkins didn't want to imagine. Empty water bottles and food wrappers littered the container floor. The fabric rolls and textiles surrounded them.

"Get medical here now!" Jenkins barked into his radio, his training overriding the shock. "We need ambulances, child services, translators—everything!"

Barrientos was already moving forward, holstering her weapon and kneeling near the container entrance. "It's okay." She purred into the darkness, her voice trembling. "You're safe now. We're police. We're here to help."

A small girl, no more than seven, stared at her with eyes too old for her face. She didn't respond, didn't move. None of them did.

Jenkins felt rage building in his chest like a pressure cooker about to explode. Josif had given them the container number, but he'd left out the most important detail—or maybe he didn't know. Maybe that's how Melkonian kept his operation compartmentalized, feeding his soldiers only fragments of the truth.

"They've been in there for days. Maybe longer."

Jenkins pulled out his phone, fingers shaking as he dialed the Precinct. This wasn't just about drugs anymore. This was something far worse, something that made his twenty-seven years of chasing dealers and traffickers feel like chasing shadows.

"Captain." His voice was tight when the line connected. "We found the container. But we've got a situation here. A big one."

As EMTs flooded the scene and began carefully extracting the children, Jenkins watched Barrientos. She'd coaxed the small girl into her arms, holding her like she was made of glass. Tears streaked down his partner's face, cutting through the stoic detective facade she wore so well.

"How many more?" She looked up at Jenkins. "How many more containers? How many more kids has that bastard smuggled?"

That was the question that would haunt him. If this container held children, how many others did too? How long had Melkonian been running this operation right under their noses while they focused on drug busts?

Jenkins turned to the closest officer his eyes found. "I want every container with a Thai imprint searched. Tonight. I don't care if it takes until dawn."

"That's hundreds of containers, sir."

"Then you better get started, kid." Jenkins's voice left no room for argument.

Seconds later, his phone buzzed. A text from the captain: Just got wind of this, Jenkins. Josif Popović is dead. Gunned down in a back alley hours after the lawyer sprang him. No suspects at this time.

I can think of one, Captain, he thought, feeling the layers of stress bury him alive. He stared at the message, then at the children being carried out of the steel tomb.

"We need to get back to Bakersfield, Barrientos. Popović is dead."

She gently handed the little girl to a paramedic, whispering something Jenkins couldn't hear. When she turned back to him, her eyes blazed with a fury he'd rarely seen.

"He's dead?"

"Yeah. The captain just messaged me."

"Okay. Melkonian goes down." Her voice was steady despite the tears. "Whatever it takes, man. We end this piece of shit."

Jenkins nodded. They'd wanted to crack the drug ring. Now they'd stumbled onto something far more sinister—a trafficking network that treated children like cargo.

As they walked back through the container yard, Jenkins couldn't shake the image of those hollow eyes staring out from the darkness. Somewhere out there, Samvel Melkonian was sleeping peacefully, counting his blood money, completely unaware that his empire had just started crumbling.

But he would know soon enough.

Jenkins would make damn sure of that.

www.ingramcontent.com/pod-product-compliance
Lightning Source LLC
LaVergne TN
LVHW091620070526
838199LV00044B/869